Nicki sea  **ls,**
hoping she had ٦'t
fare well for hc ٦'t ____ ٦'ther in the same ten
minutes.

"What'll it be?" asked the bartender as he cleared the space in front of her.

"Margarita, rocks, no salt."

"I'll have a vodka martini. Straight up." His deep voice curled around her. "Is this seat taken?" Without waiting for her response, he sat, his knee brushing against her thigh in a sizzling flash.

Whoa. She inched away, the burn searing straight to her toes. This guy was on fire.

She held out her hand. "I'm Nicki Reading."

He took it and brought her fingers to his lips. "Dex Hanover." Green eyes with a hint of gray hooked hers, the intensity a bit overwhelming. In a good way.

She withdrew her hand, needing some space, some air. And a cold shower. Raising her glass to him, she used her silkiest voice. "Nice to meet you, Dex Hanover."

He clinked her glass with his, and his crooked smile turned into a full-blown attraction. "Nicki."

His inflection did funny things to her insides. She sipped her drink, trusting the cool liquid would douse the small fire within before it got out of control.

Praise for Maria Imbalzano

"Unchained Memories"
"Unchained Memories" was the winner of the Write Touch Readers' Award and ACRA Readers' Choice Heart of Excellence Award.

"An excellent read that catches you off guard and pulls you in until you can't put the book down... A beautiful love story."

~ *BooK Addict*

"Wow really does not describe this story....A very current and relevant story line....It kept my interest right to the last word, and leaving me wanting more. Fantastic job, highly recommend."

~ *Bea Lester*

"Dancing in the Sand"
"The pleasure of the read is as much in the carefully crafted prose as in the plot and character development....Both sexy and thoughtful; smart and funny."

~ *BJC*

"All I can think about is when will the movie be coming out....I LOVED this book!!!"

~ *Ann Laurie Fraticcioli*

Sworn to Forget
by

Maria Imbalzano

Sworn Sisters Series - Book 1

Enjoy!

Maria Imbalzano

Sworn to Forget

Cover Art by *Diana Carlile*

The Wild Rose Press, Inc.
PO Box 708
Adams Basin, NY 14410-0708
Visit us at www.thewildrosepress.com

Publishing History
First Champagne Rose Edition, 2018
Print ISBN 978-1-5092-2108-0
Digital ISBN 978-1-5092-2109-7

Sworn Sisters Series - Book 1
Published in the United States of America

Dedication

To my high school girlfriends Eileen, Paula, Diane, and Elaine who are still my wonderful, funny, and endearing friends—even after all these years.

Chapter One

"Come on, Little Joe from Kokomo." Jonathan warmed the ivory cubes in his hands before hurling them down the craps table. They bounced off the green felt and tumbled forward before coming to an abrupt stop. "Four!" he shouted, pumping his fist in the air as the other players cheered with him.

He grabbed Nicki around the waist and planted a loud kiss on her cheek. "You're my lucky charm."

Nicki gave him the smile he wanted but inwardly rolled her eyes. This cruise vacation was not turning into the getaway Jonathan had promised. Yes, there were dozens of activities to choose from—a floating hotel catering to the adventurers, the foodies, the late-night party animals, and the lounge chair potatoes. But she hadn't anticipated her vacation partner would spend every waking hour in the neon-lit casino.

A bud of uncertainty sprouted in Nicki's stomach. Had she jumped the gun in agreeing to a weeklong getaway with a guy she'd been dating for three months? And only on weekends, given both of their busy work schedules. It had seemed like a good idea when they discussed it a few short weeks ago.

But she couldn't blame their recent friendship on her hesitance. Sure, Jonathan met most of her requirements for the man of the moment; single, successful, confident—although he leaned toward egotistical—passable looks, and fun loving, at least if they were doing what he wanted.

He reminded her of past boyfriends. As long as they attended professional sporting events, viewed adventure movies, and ate at the most popular restaurants, he was exuberant. Her suggestion of an art gallery exhibit, ballet, or play met with resistance and an alternative. She had no doubt this relationship would be as short-lived as the rest.

Oh well.

He nuzzled her neck, planting tickling kisses close to her ear.

She pulled away, not wishing to go there right now. Yet he knew how to get her attention. Perhaps if she put in a little effort, he'd be the one to change her mind about relationships.

She sighed. Highly unlikely.

Nicki gave her purple chiffon frock a little swish. When she dressed for the evening, her plan had been to hit the dance floor at Venus, the penthouse nightclub.

"It's nearly midnight," she advised Jonathan. "Let's go dancing."

"I'm on a roll now, Nick. We'll go later."

Disappointment punctured her balloon, and for the first time tonight, her feet throbbed in her crystal-embellished strappy heels. She slipped one foot out of her shoe as she perused the crowd standing around the table.

A stranger's intense gaze from across the heated table action halted her review mid-scan. He stood behind a striking woman with long, dark hair and a red, clingy dress. The brash sounds around her muffled as Nicki zeroed in on him, dressed in a designer suit.

Elegant, confident. Hot. A gorgeous man making up one-half of a gorgeous couple.

Nicki pulled her attention from the too-handsome guest and continued her sight path around the table. No one else held her interest. Not like him.

Instinct demanded she avoid the area, but her eyes disobeyed, and she caught a crooked smile and a head nod. She couldn't help it. She smiled in return.

He signaled with his thumb toward the bar, then arched a brow. There could be no mistake. An invitation.

She'd been standing at this damn table for over an hour, and the only time Jonathan noticed her presence was when he had the dice and pretended to include her in his ritual before releasing the cubes. He wouldn't care if she went to get a drink. Besides, her feet were screaming, and a bar stool and an icy Margarita beckoned. As well as a very handsome stranger.

"I'm going to sit down for a bit. I'll be at the bar." Nicki's heartbeat quickened. *Ridiculous*.

"Sure, babe. I'll catch up with you soon." Jonathan's attention never wavered from the gaming table.

How could she not have known her semi-boyfriend of three months had a gambling problem? Because she only saw him on weekends when the spirit moved her.

Nicki searched the bar for two empty stools, hoping she hadn't misunderstood the signal. It wouldn't fare well for her ego to be rejected twice in the same ten minutes.

"What'll it be?" asked the bartender as he cleared the space in front of her.

"Margarita, rocks, no salt."

3

"I'll have a vodka martini. Straight up." His deep voice curled around her. "Is this seat taken?" Without waiting for her response, he sat, his knee brushing against her thigh in a sizzling flash.

Whoa. She inched away, the burn searing straight to her toes. This guy was on fire.

She held out her hand. "I'm Nicki Reading."

He took it and brought her fingers to his lips. "Dex Hanover." Green eyes with a hint of gray hooked hers, the intensity a bit overwhelming. In a good way.

She withdrew her hand, needing some space, some air. And a cold shower. Raising her glass to him, she used her silkiest voice. "Nice to meet you, Dex Hanover."

He clinked her glass with his, and his crooked smile turned into a full-blown attraction. "Nicki."

His inflection did funny things to her insides. She sipped her drink, trusting the cool liquid would douse the small fire within before it got out of control.

"Is he your husband, boyfriend, brother?" The spark in his eyes told Nicki he hoped for the latter.

"Some would call him my boyfriend. I'm still on the fence. And after this week, I'm leaning toward friend."

"You're not having a good time?"

She inhaled, not wanting to throw Jonathan under the bus to this unknown, albeit captivating creature. Until this trip, Jonathan straddled the line between a temporary possibility and a washout. Moderately handsome, with touchable brown hair, milk-chocolate eyes, and a killer job as an entertainment lawyer, he gave Nicki the space she needed. As an added bonus, he was uninterested in procreating to advance his gene pool. Yet something key was off.

So why not leave a door open for further conversation with her intriguing bar mate? "Gambling is not my thing. Apparently, it's Jonathan's." She lifted a shoulder. "Who knew?"

Dex nodded. "The high of winning is on par with sex."

Nicki raised her brow. "I only offered dancing. Maybe I should have been more carnal."

"I'm glad you weren't because I would have missed this opportunity to meet you."

Her attention zeroed in on kissable lips. She swallowed. "What about you? Aren't you with the woman in red?"

"We are here together, Lisa and I. But we're not dating."

Good answer. Surely, there was much more to the story, but now was not the time.

Dex continued. "Where are you from, Ms. Nicki Reading?"

"Philadelphia. What about you?"

"Me too. What a nice coincidence." His aura held her in a cocoon of privacy, blocking out the din of the other patrons hovering nearby.

"Here you are." Jonathan's voice broke through her haze, shaking her out of the magical dream she'd just experienced. He placed his arm around Nicki's shoulders, a transparent sign to Dex she was off limits. At least in man code.

"What made you leave the table?" Nicki blinked to return to reality, attempting to hold back a smirk, knowing full well her dog came to mark his territory.

"The dice were getting cold. It was time to move

on. Do you want to hit Venus or go back to our room?" His suggestion couldn't be camouflaged as anything other than what it was. Jonathan's attempt to make Dex jealous.

"This is Dex Hanover. He works in Philly too."

"Jonathan Walsh." He stuck out his hand, but there was no friendly smile or genuine interest. "Let's go." Jonathan tugged on her upper arm, clearly not wanting to stay and make small talk.

"It was nice meeting you, Dex." More than nice, although the heat index plummeted when Jonathan came to claim her. Nicki focused in on his eyes, loathe to break the connection. "I'm sure we'll run into you and Lisa over the next few days."

She smiled, promising something—although what, she didn't know.

Chapter Two

Dex sat in a lounge chair by the pool, his electronic tablet streaming the news of the day. But his attention had been hijacked.

Nicki laid her pool towel on the lounge chair across the way, then slid her filmy cover-up over her head, allowing him to feast on plenty of tanned skin and fantasies of what lay beneath her hot pink bikini. She slipped slender feet out of tiny-heeled sandals, before laying her long, sensual limbs on the recliner. Sunglasses covered her eyes, and her straight blonde hair was braided and pulled to the side, the end of which grazed one of her perfect breasts.

She dug into her bag and came out with sunscreen. He swallowed as she poured lotion into the palm of her hand, then rubbed it over her toned torso. His reflexes jumped to attention, urging him to go over and help lubricate those hard-to-reach places.

Dex should feel guilty for getting so hot and bothered over a woman he met at the bar last night. But he didn't. Lisa was still sleeping, and when she finally did wake up, she'd go shopping or gambling. Why he agreed to come on this cruise with her was a mystery.

But then he wouldn't have met Nicki Reading.

Bolstered with an affirmative plan instead of hiding behind his sunglasses and fantasizing, he hit the pool bar, then headed in her direction. Yes, it was before noon, but they were on vacation and it was important to hydrate.

"Where's your keeper?" He stood over her, two glasses in hand, unable to see her beautiful blue eyes behind aviator shades.

Her beaming smile eclipsed his disappointment.

"In the casino." She reached toward him with a long, willowy arm. "Is that for me?"

"Margarita, rocks, no salt. I hope you don't mind a little alcohol in the morning."

She slid her glasses on top of her head and took a sip, a dreamy look crossing her face. "Perfect. Thanks." She looked up at him. "You're blocking my sun. Why don't you have a seat?"

He obliged, doing a high five in his head.

"Where's your non-date?" Nicki pulled her shades back over her eyes. Too bad, since he couldn't see the thought process behind the question.

"Sleeping. Or something." He shrugged.

"You don't care?"

Now there was a loaded question. He needed clarification. "That she's sleeping? Or about her in general?"

"The latter, of course." Her lips twitched.

"We're not on the same page. It wasn't working. So we broke up—a month ago."

She turned her head toward him, her braid inching over the swell of her breast. "Then why are you here with her?"

Good question. "We planned this trip months ago. Paid for it. So we decided to take it despite our state of affairs."

"You're free to meet others?"

"I don't know if she would state it in those specific words, but sure, why not? Once we leave this ship, it's clear to both of us we won't be hanging out together."

Nicki's brow furrowed. Adorable. "Are you sure it's clear to her?"

A ripple of uncertainty spread through him. "Why do you ask?"

"Maybe she's hoping to win you back while you're drinking martinis on the aft deck."

He chuckled. "Sure. That's why she's here with me right now."

Nicki studied his face and the heat of her stare unnerved him. He needed to turn this around. "What about you?"

"What about me?" Her clear annoyance told him she didn't like the question.

Good. Keep her off balance. Two could play this game. "What's going on with you and your bodyguard?"

A laugh escaped. He liked when she laughed. "Not much. He's more into craps than me. I'm glad I found out before I invested too much time in the man."

A similar answer to last night's. Good. She wasn't reconsidering. "Since we've both been deserted by our companions, how'd you like to go to the art auction? It started a little while ago in Saturn Hall."

"Sounds like it could be fun." She took the last sip of her drink and placed the glass on the small table between their chairs. Rising from her lounge, she shook out the dress she removed not long before and slipped it over her bikini. The flowery material wasn't quite opaque, and he could see the outline of her bikini beneath. Very nice. Very sexy.

9

"Are you coming?" Her smile told him she appreciated his interest.

"My stuff is over there." He pointed across the pool. "I need to grab my shirt and sandals."

"I'm good with you not wearing a shirt." Her eyes roamed over his chest, searing his skin and nudging his libido. Her flirtation could get them in trouble real fast.

"Funny lady." He grabbed her hand and headed toward his previous location.

They needed to get out of here before Lisa or Jonathan—what a stuffy name—ruined their plan.

****

Saturn Hall was crowded with prospective purchasers of mediocre, mass-produced art work.

Nicki took in the scene. "Why do people think they're getting a good deal on this stuff because they're on a cruise ship? And why would anyone want to spend hundreds, maybe thousands, on art work with no significance or connection to the places they're visiting?"

Dex leaned in close to her ear, a move that sent glorious shivers down her spine and tingles to her core. "Are you an art snob?"

She turned to look in his eyes, a few inches from hers, and saw the playfulness in their depths. "Yes," she whispered, not at all sure she was answering his spoken question.

His eyes grew serious as their color darkened. Their lips were so close, getting closer, and Nicki wanted nothing more than to be kissed senseless by this gorgeous, funny, sensitive guy who found her last night.

"Excuse me. Would you like a drink?" A waiter

with a tray of white and red wine looked at them expectantly, and the moment vanished.

"No, thanks." Disappointment at the interruption vied with relief.

She shouldn't be going down this road with a virtual stranger. She was here with Jonathan, although Jonathan didn't seem to be here with her. His weakness for gambling tipped the scale against him. *C'est la vie.* One more casualty in her long list of casualties.

But considering someone to replace him before he even knew he was being replaced was mean. Although it wasn't her fault. It wasn't like she was looking.

Dex steered her toward a wall of paintings, modern in technique and subject matter. "Here are some originals for your consideration," he teased.

"That one wouldn't look bad in my office." Nicki stepped to the left, then the right, to see it from different angles. "I kind of like it." Maybe the spirit of the cruise was infiltrating her brain. Or Dex.

"The art snob has reconsidered."

She smiled and inched closer to him as they moved around the room. She didn't care about the art. It was a means to spend time with Dex, in a venue where Jonathan wouldn't venture. Hopefully, Lisa was similarly averse. She wanted to feel the heat Dex generated, the fizzy sparks that ignited within at his mere presence. An emotional overload she hoped wouldn't short circuit.

An hour passed much too quickly. "I told Jonathan I'd meet him for lunch at one thirty." Frustration over making such a date deflated her high.

Dex pulled her into a corner of the room. Facing her, he traced her cheek and jawline with his index finger, green eyes penetrating hers with a power that lunged into her soul. He leaned close, then brushed his lips over hers, so softly, so fleetingly, she wasn't quite sure she'd just been kissed. Yet her body hummed to life and heated from within. His mouth was a breath away from hers, his eyes holding her captive. Pure desire coiled in her core and her hand, seemingly of its own volition, reached up to caress his face before sliding around his head to pull him closer, her fingers getting lost in dark, soft hair. She angled her mouth to connect with his, and he complied with her silent plea. Light pressure turned insistent and demanding as he swept his tongue inside. She shamelessly pressed her body to his, reveling in the firmness of his muscles, his strength. She kissed him back with all the pent-up hunger that had built within, since she first saw him across the gaming table.

Nicki reached for her senses. This was crazy. And dangerous.

She pulled away, a delicious burn singeing swollen lips.

"I have to go." Her husky voice rasped like raw sex, the same passion she saw in his eyes.

She slipped sideways, her breasts brushing his chest, fanning the flames of their smoldering chemistry.

She had to escape this soon-to-be inferno.

Despite her yearning to ignite it.

****

"You look great, babe." Jonathan glanced at Nicki as he buttoned his Armani shirt.

She hated the term "babe," but his pointed compliment underscored his commitment to civility, which would get them through the rest of the week.

Nicki showed her appreciation by perfecting the knot on his tie. "I know our discussion at lunch wasn't easy, and we didn't anticipate this vacation would underscore our differences when we booked this trip."

"I get it. We're on parallel paths. You want to go dancing. I want to play in the casino. You want to get up early and explore whatever island we're docked at, and I want to sleep in."

She had to give Jonathan credit for his maturity in discussing their floundering relationship. The conversation turned out much better than Nicki expected. Although Jonathan resisted at first, pointing out the fun they had over the past three months, he finally acknowledged their initial connection had started to fray. With three days left to this vacation, they agreed that each would do what made them happy separately during the day, but they'd meet up at night for dinner and anything else they could agree on. Vacation days were at a premium in her fast-paced, high-stress job. No sense in ruining it completely.

Nicki stepped into sparkly silver heels, which complemented the crystal belt cinching her white silk dress. Jonathan agreed to accompany her to Venus, and she might even convince him to dance; an improvement over tossing his money away at the craps table.

"You're in a good mood tonight." Nicki took in his light-hearted demeanor as he fastened the clasp to her diamond bracelet.

"I had a good day at the tables." He slipped his arms into his suit jacket, preening in front of the mirror. "I hope you enjoyed your time at the pool."

A smile begged to insinuate itself on Nicki's lips, but she held it back. "I did." Although she hadn't seen

Dex since this morning, a thrill ran through her blood as she replayed the very hot, very erotic kiss they'd shared.

Jonathan followed Nicki out of their stateroom and walked toward the elevator. "Don't you have any lower heels?" he asked, straightening his shoulders to make himself taller.

"These go with my dress." She didn't have to care anymore if he felt insecure over her height. It was all such a relief.

They entered the nightclub to the beat of an Usher song, and as soon as the music seeped under her skin, Nicki's spirits lifted. She followed Jonathan to the bar and ordered a vodka martini, for the sole purpose of remembering her time with Dex. If Jonathan thought it odd, he didn't comment.

They found a high-top table with a view of the dance floor and sipped their drinks. Jonathan would need a few minutes to settle in before she dragged him out into the writhing mass.

Perusing the room and noting the fashion choices of the other women for future consideration, Nicki danced in place until her eyes stopped short. Across the bar was Dex. And Lisa.

Her heart galloped and a hot flush heated her face. She grasped her glass to transfer the icy cold to her fingers, then her mouth.

"I'm going to the ladies' room," she announced before slipping away in search of some privacy.

Envy coursed through her veins. Ridiculous. She'd just met Dex the previous night. And she was with Jonathan—at least until the end of the cruise. She had no right to feel anything.

Before she reached her destination, a hand branded her upper arm. She turned and Dex stood precipitously close to her personal space. Her eyes darted past him to make sure neither Lisa nor Jonathan could see them, even though the facilities were down a narrow hallway near the entrance.

"I was hoping I'd see you here tonight."

The intensity of his eyes kept her rooted to her spot. Without thought, she reached out and stroked the planes of his cheek. He held her wrist to prevent her from breaking away.

"I'm glad you're here," she breathed. "But we can't spend much time together."

"This is going to have to be enough." He lowered his head and gave her a toe-curling kiss. So deep and long and sensuous, she spun into his orbit, never wanting to leave. Strong hands roamed over her bare back and a needy groan reverberated from his chest to hers.

Parted lips travelled to her ear and he whispered, causing a delicious shiver. "When we dock in Key West tomorrow morning, get off the ship. Alone. Meet me outside the aquarium."

She nodded, knowing she'd follow him anywhere. "Till then."

Already having taken too much time for her stated destination, Nicki turned and walked in a daze through the club, buzzing with adrenaline—and need. One glorious kiss, one provocative invitation, had the power to tickle her insides and place a permanent smile on her lips. She practically sashayed to where Jonathan stood.

"It took you long enough," he grumbled. "I thought you wanted to dance."

"There was a line. You know how ladies' rooms are."

No longer wanting to be at the club, where she insisted they go tonight, Nicki searched for a reasonable explanation. "I got too much sun today. I have a headache. Do you mind if I go back to the room? You can go to the casino."

Jonathan put his hand around her waist and pulled her close, kissing the side of her head. "Good idea. It's too loud in here anyway. This noise can't be helping your headache."

What a gentleman.

They headed out of the club and back to their room where Jonathan deposited Nicki, then escaped to his obsession. Perfect. Now she could dream in peace about spending an entire day with Dex.

Nicki glided around the small stateroom, getting ready for bed before slipping under the cool sheets; thoughts of Dex spiraling through her brain. She replayed their sensuous kiss at Venus and allowed stimulating fantasies to take it further. Her illusions turned to steamy dreams, which had her twisting in the sheets.

Throughout the night, she woke once an hour, checking her cell phone for the time. The estimated time of arrival in Key West was nine a.m. and she planned to be off the boat at 9:01. At eight, Nicki crept out of bed, trying to make as little noise as possible getting ready—although Jonathan was dead to the world, having come in at five.

She chose her outfit with care, a yellow-flowered sundress and flat sandals, in anticipation of walking through town most of the day. Leaving her long, blonde hair down, she threw a covered elastic band into her over-sized purse for an emergency ponytail, and also tossed in a white cotton sweater. No outfit, in Nicki's mind, was complete without jewelry, so she inserted gold hoop earrings and placed two thin bangles on her wrist.

The thought of being with Dex for the entire day had her stomach dancing. Looking around their small room to make sure she had what she needed, she glanced at Jonathan. Thankfully, she'd had *the conversation* with him yesterday, so guilt couldn't ruin her day. Besides, he wouldn't want to traipse around Key West in the heat, shopping at local galleries or perusing touristy jewelry stores. He'd much prefer the air-conditioned temperature of a casino amongst his new-found friends.

At the last minute, she left Jonathan a scribbled note stating her whereabouts and advising she'd be back by six to get ready for dinner. This is what they'd agreed to, so there should be no problem.

As she closed the door to their suite, excitement shot through her. She shook her head. What was wrong with her?

Chapter Three

Dex stood in front of the aquarium, watching the throngs of tourists disburse in all directions. Maps and smart phones held most of their attention as they collaborated with their spouse or friends about what to do first. The driver of the Old Town Trolley waited patiently for the seats to fill before beginning his umpteenth trek around the island. The Conch Market, with its trinkets and sponges, swarmed with patrons, and Mel Fisher's Treasure Museum had a line out the door. As his eyes roved over the masses, they fell on the one person he desperately wanted to see.

Nicki looked like spring in a yellow sundress and a sunny smile, her straw bag slung over her shoulder; a model ready for her photo shoot. She knew how to stand out in a crowd of tourists sporting shorts, T-shirts, floppy hats, and sneakers. He took out his cell and snapped a picture as she approached.

Her smile widened when she saw him, and she picked up her pace to greet him. "Don't I know you?"

"I believe so. You're the woman I kissed outside the ladies' room last night. Or was that someone else? Let's see." He swooped in for a comparison but kept it short, knowing where that could lead.

He took her hand. "Let's walk for a bit to get away from these crowds."

They strolled down Duval Street, the main drag,

passing dozens of jewelry stores, T-shirt shops, and eateries, all catering to the cruise ship tourists. Gaudy signs written in orange neon marker advertised the deals of the day, no doubt the same every day. The open-front bars already had bands playing, customers drinking, and crowds laughing—a real party scene that started early in the morning and went on long past midnight.

Pretty college girls roamed the streets in packs, wearing bright mini-dresses over bikini bathing suits, their hair perfectly tousled, their make-up expertly applied, while rowdy college guys sporting rumpled shorts and loyalty team T-shirts eyed them with appreciation. Their hair hadn't seen a comb today, and their razors must have been safely stored in their carry-ons.

"I've never been here before," said Nicki, taking it all in. "What a fun town."

"I was here once with my frat brothers in college. Looking like one of them." He pointed to a male group approaching, downing light beer instead of orange juice.

"You can drink on the streets?"

"You can do anything here. It's the Conch Republic. They don't think they belong to the United States. There's a shop farther down, next to a tattoo parlor, where you can have your entire body painted. No clothes necessary. There's also a bar right across the street with a clothing optional area."

Nicki raised her brow. "You seem to know all the spots where you can find naked ladies."

He smiled. "Oh, yeah. When you're a college kid here, one of your goals is to be as raunchy as possible.

And we were. We stood in line for over an hour one night waiting to get into Cowboy Bill's. They have a mechanical bull and on Wednesday nights, there was topless riding."

"No," she said, shaking her head.

"Yes. But don't worry. I banished my party animal persona years ago. Today, I'll do anything you want. But if you decide you want to ride the mechanical bull or have your body painted, I'll cheer you on."

She pushed him playfully and he caught her wrist, pulling her closer before kissing her cheek. She smelled so good; a citrusy, flowery aroma. It was Nicki, and if he ever came into contact with that scent again, thoughts of her would swarm his brain.

"Are you hungry?" he asked.

"Starving. I skipped breakfast on the ship because I didn't want to be late." Her blue eyes sparkled, telling him she was as eager as he to meet up.

"There's a little café a few blocks over. They make their own jam and preserves and specialize in breakfast."

"Lead the way."

They turned off Duval onto Southard. The side street was lined with palm trees, and although it was warm and humid, the sun wasn't high enough yet to blast over the trees and buildings.

Nicki zeroed in on the architecture of the houses, pointing out the gingerbread below the eaves and the colors of the porch roofs. "My friend from high school, Sam—Samantha—has a time share down here. I can see why she loves it so much. A little bohemian, a little artsy. It reminds me of New Hope. But better because it's warm year long and surrounded by water."

"You're a water girl?"

"Born in late January, Aquarius." She glanced at him. "What about you?"

"Gemini. My birthday's in May."

"If I'm not mistaken, Aquarians and Geminis go well together."

He didn't need astrological signs to confirm his combustible attraction to the intriguing, independent, and beautiful Nicki. But if she needed proof, he was game.

"Extremely well," he agreed, without any knowledge of the effects the zodiac had on physical chemistry.

After breakfast, they spent the first half of the day exploring the town's eclectic shops on the way to the Butterfly Museum—not particularly a must-do on his bucket list, but Nicki's delight bubbled over as they came into contact with hundreds of species of the fluttery things in the oversized greenhouse. And frankly, he was thrilled to spend time with Nicki, wherever she wanted to be.

"I love how all museums have exits depositing their patrons right in the middle of their gift shop." Nicki stopped to study some wildlife earrings.

"Since we're here, I want to look at the books." He scanned the shelves searching for the perfect gift, before picking out a book on lizards.

"Yuk." She glanced at his choice. "Here's a pretty one with beautiful colored butterflies."

He chuckled. "No. I mentor a young boy through Big Brothers Big Sisters. He loves geckos and iguanas." He flipped through the pages and stopped at a large, green lizard. "This will be perfect."

Nicki looked over his shoulder, her arm grazing his. Her scent, all Nicki, infiltrated his head and hijacked his attention. All he wanted to do was grab her and kiss her until they were both breathless.

"How old is your little brother?" Nicki's question brought him back.

"Thirteen." He shook his head to unscramble his brain. "He's a really good kid. I've known Kenan since he was five."

Nicki arched an eyebrow. "You've been volunteering as a Big Brother for eight years?"

"Does that surprise you?"

She nodded, her brow furrowing as she processed the information. "That's a big commitment for a single guy."

"It is. Kenan deserves to have a male figure in his life. To teach him things. To answer questions. And to keep him focused on the straight and narrow." Dex wanted nothing more than to keep Kenan interested in school and away from the gangs.

Nicki smiled that gorgeous smile. "That's admirable. I'm impressed."

Dex didn't volunteer at Big Brothers to impress anyone, but any points he could rack up in Nicki's book were fine with him.

They found their way to the outside bar at Louie's Back Yard and sat at a weather-splintered table shielded by an oversized umbrella where they ordered colorful drinks. The aqua-blue water of the ocean fanned the horizon, reaching as far as the eye could see. But all Dex saw was Nicki; a masterpiece of color and light with jewel-toned eyes competing with the sea and long lashes framing their depths. He wanted to raise his fingers and thread them through her long, blonde hair, to tame the errant strands from the breeze that blew in on the salty mist. The texture would feel like pure silk warmed by the sun. But caution kept his hands still, protecting him from the electricity he'd conduct with that one small move.

Better to focus on his analytical ten-point checklist. Sure, the attraction was powerful, but what did he really know about Nicki? Other than she chose the wrong guy to vacation with.

"I know where you live, but I don't know much more about you." He took her hand and massaged her palm, wanting the connection before he dove into his interrogation, hoping the contact would help ease them into the more serious conversation he wanted to have.

"Where did you grow up?" A perfectly easy beginning question.

"Lawrenceville, New Jersey. Near Princeton. And you?"

"Long Island. Northport. It's on the Sound. My mother's still there."

"Is your father alive?" Nicki asked with hesitance.

"Yep. Lives in San Francisco. Has a new wife. New life. Left us when I was nine without ever looking back." He hadn't meant to add that last part.

"I'm sorry to hear that." Sympathy shone clearly in her eyes. "My father died when I was seventeen. My mother died five years later, but she was really gone before that—depression hit her hard after my father's death."

Dex covered her hand with his and swallowed. He had meant to get at some basic facts, not raise painful pasts. "That must have been awful. I'm sorry, Nicki."

She shrugged. "We both made it through tough times. We have something in common."

Did they? His father was still alive, although he'd abandoned Dex for his new family. His mother, on the other hand, had his number on speed dial. Nicki had no one. Time to change direction. "Have you ever been married?"

She paused with her drink halfway to her lips and connected with his eyes. "No."

Her answer seemed tentative. "Is there more to that answer?"

She laughed easily, confirming her response. "No. It's not even on my to-do list."

He turned that over in his head. "Then I guess you've never been engaged."

"Not close. What about you?"

"No, but I considered it."

"I probably don't want to know what happened or whether it was recent. So can we stop this portion of the getting-to-know-you quiz? I'd rather wait for a few more dates before we have to bare our souls."

Dex took a gulp of his drink, pondering her request. "Does that mean we're going to see each other after this cruise is over?" He had every intention of making it happen.

She took her time answering. "I don't know." The side of her mouth inched up in a half grin. "Perhaps. What do you think?"

He nodded slowly, playing her game. "Perhaps."

Blue eyes flashed in amusement. "I don't date men who have a girlfriend. It's low class."

"I already told you, we broke up last month. As soon as we walk off the ship on Saturday, we're history.

What about you and Jonathan?"

She peered out toward the ocean, obviously considering what to tell him. "We're not even together on this trip. It was fun for a while, but we'll also be parting ways before the weekend is over."

The set of her mouth and the resolve in her eyes told him she wasn't lying.

They sat in silence for a few minutes. Maybe Nicki was mourning the pending dissolution of her relationship with the guy who would rather count his chips than make love to an amazing woman. Maybe not. But Dex was celebrating. Despite the odds, he'd met a dynamic, intelligent, beautiful woman who just might be the person he was looking for.

****

Nicki arrived back at her cabin at six, wiping the smile from her face before entering.

"Where've you been?" Jonathan asked from his prone position on the bed, cell phone in hand, no doubt reading work emails. Or maybe an article on how best to beat the odds.

"I left you a note this morning." She tossed her purse on the bed and removed her sandals.

"You were gone a long time. How could you spend nine hours in Key West?"

She sat on the chair in the corner, not wanting to lie next to him lest he think her nearness was an invitation despite their cancelled relationship.

"There's a lot to see there."

And a lot to learn. Dex was an extremely handsome and confident man. But what lay underneath had her more intrigued. Although he held some animosity over his parents' divorce and his father's

25

desertion, instead of allowing it to affect his view toward relationships, he channeled it into a positive action. His mentoring of a child who didn't have a father figure in his life warmed her heart.

"What are you smiling about?" Jonathan's focus switched from his cell phone to her.

Nicki removed the smile. "Nothing. What time did you wake up?" She tried to keep the ire from her voice. There was no point in getting into an argument over sleeping the day away, when she didn't want to spend the time with him anyway.

"Noon. Maybe one."

"What did you do this afternoon?" Politeness was the only way to get through this.

He sat up and swung his legs off the bed. "I'm sorry I got in so late last night. I don't blame you for being annoyed. We're on vacation together and I should be doing things with you. Even if we are going to end it."

"It's okay. I don't mind. I like relaxing by the pool or sightseeing. I don't need company." Unless of course, it was Dex.

"Where are we docking tomorrow?"

"Nassau. In the Bahamas."

"Okay. I'll go there with you."

No, no, no. She hadn't asked him to go. And she didn't want him to. She and Dex were meeting there at noon for lunch. Her mind spun with excuses to avoid this dilemma, yet she couldn't bring herself to tell the truth. She wasn't into hurting Jonathan. "I've had my fill of walking around today. I'd rather sit by the pool and read tomorrow." So far from the truth, but it would have to do.

"Maybe you'll change your mind. We'll wait and see. Either way, we'll spend tomorrow together. Our last day before we return home." A hint of sadness crossed his face.

Maybe she should go to Nassau with Jonathan. What harm would it do? But she couldn't help the inward lament over the situation she now found herself in. It was her own fault. Despite that, she couldn't see her way to spending the day with Jonathan while fantasizing about Dex.

To avoid further discussion and hopefully come up with an alternative plan, she rose and grabbed her towel. "I'm going to take a shower."

And she stayed under the spray until her fingers pruned.

****

They had their own private table in the dining room, requested by Jonathan upon signing on for the cruise. At the time, Nicki assumed it would be romantic. Now she looked at the group tables and longed for the laughter and comradery that came with making new friends while cruising the Atlantic.

She surreptitiously searched for Dex, needing to inform him of her change of plans. Even though she'd sprained her brain in the shower, trying to come up with a valid reason to ditch Jonathan tomorrow, nothing viable came to mind without being downright cruel. Despite having told him their relationship was over, she still needed to get through the rest of their trip without rancor.

"I forgot butter. Do you need anything from the buffet table while I'm up there?" Nicki didn't even have a roll, but she intended to take her time examining the fully laden tables, in the hope Dex would see her and appear at her side.

"Sure. Bring me back another slice of tenderloin. This is delicious." Jonathan was thoroughly enjoying his meal, and her mental absence didn't affect him in the least.

Nicki took the long route around the room, scanning each table as she passed. Until a warm hand brushed her shoulder in an unmistakable caress.

"Keep going," he whispered, guiding her toward the other end of the room, behind the dessert table.

When she turned, she caught her breath. Dex's somber gaze made her knees wobble. His handsome face was all planes and shadows, defined by an unshaven jaw. Hot, sexy, and gorgeous. She wanted nothing more than to keep walking right out of the dining room and into a private suite reserved only for them. But there was no such place and there would be no such ecstasy.

"I can't meet you tomorrow," she said in a rush, needing to tell him before she forgot. Those green eyes of his were very dangerous to her memory.

"Is everything okay?" His furrowed brow showed worry.

She nodded, then reached to touch his cheek, but her fingers wandered over his lips.

He held her wrist to stop her. "That's a daring move," he murmured. "I'm reading it as an invitation and you may not be able to follow through."

Nicki closed her eyes, perilously close to leaning in and stealing a kiss. Dex pulled her farther away from the crowds descending on the chocolate lava fountain.

The moment was lost, and Nicki launched into the

reason for having to abort their date. "Jonathan is feeling guilty I spent the whole day alone in Key West, and I didn't have the heart to tell him the truth." She gave him a wry smile. Should she tell Dex she broke up with Jonathan yesterday, or would it put too much pressure on him—on them? "He said he'd go with me to Nassau tomorrow. I told him I didn't want to go, because I had tired myself out sightseeing today. I can't spend the day with him, doing the things I want to be doing with you. I'll probably go to the pool and read." The frustration grew greater as that same emotion cast a shadow over Dex's face.

"Meet me tonight on the upper deck near the Mars Jazz Lounge. Do you think you can get away?"

A glimmer of optimism set a fuse, and Nicki's brain set to work. All she had to do was beg off going to the casino with Jonathan. He'd go on his own in a heartbeat if she suggested it. "Let's try for eleven."

She wished they had exchanged cell phone numbers, but they decided to keep their friendship private on the cruise, with no evidence that could be easily found. They had nothing to gain by hurting Jonathan or Lisa, despite their terminal relationships. "If I'm not there, it's because I couldn't get away, not because I changed my mind." Nicki didn't want him to draw the wrong message from some unexpected kink in their plan.

A slow smile curved Dex's mouth. Delicious. But she couldn't risk getting lost in those lips. "Jonathan's going to wonder what happened to me. I better get back."

"I'll see you in three hours."

Nicki's adrenaline pumped at the promise of their

meeting, and she quickly searched for butter and grabbed another helping of beef.

When she arrived back at the table, Jonathan gave her an odd look, but maybe he'd been wondering where the hell she was. "These people are vultures. It was next to impossible to get close to the tenderloin. You should see the dessert table." She avoided his eyes as she picked up her fork and began eating.

"I'll go next time. You have to be more aggressive or you'll be pushed aside."

Nicki agreed, keeping her telltale smile to herself.

Three hours.

Chapter Four

Dex paced the upper deck near the appointed meeting spot, his anxiety at high-water level. Would Nicki come? Vying for his angst was the possibility of running into Lisa, albeit slim. He had accompanied her to the casino the first few evenings, but once he met Nicki, he preferred to be alone if he couldn't be with her. Lisa didn't question his plans or his solitude, also trying to make the best of a vacation with an ex-lover.

He stopped and draped his forearms on the rail, watching the sea rush by under a quarter moon and thousands of stars. Dex raised his eyes to the sky and picked out the brightest sparkle. Was there anything to wishing on a star? If so, his wish was for Nicki to join him so they could spend more time together. But tonight, he didn't want to sightsee and talk. He wanted to kiss her and hold her and… No point dreaming of what he really wanted to do. There was no place for them to go. Abstinence would make it all the more pleasurable when they finally could come together.

"Dex?"

His heart buzzed at the sound of her voice, and he turned toward her. The sleek, orange dress she'd worn earlier looked even better as he took in her stimulating curves. And what he wouldn't do to thread his fingers through those silky tresses dancing with the breeze. Her smile exploded, and she ran the last few feet and threw herself into his arms.

"It's so good to see you," she exhaled.

He covered her mouth with his, all thought of finding a private spot on the deck forgotten for the moment. He moved his hands up and down her back as he plunged his tongue into her warm, sweet mouth, doing what he'd been dying to do since he saw her in the dining room.

Her hands roamed under his suit jacket, and every place she touched sent electricity to his core. He pulled back a few inches, needing to breathe and settle down, but the angel in his arms was making it hard to do.

"Let's find a less public spot," he rasped as he unwound her from his torso and took her hand.

He had investigated the deck twenty minutes earlier, searching for a place where they could have a modicum of privacy, but there was no such cubicle. He did find a lounge chair and dragged it into a semi-dark corner. It was the best they were going to get if no one else had confiscated his oasis.

"I know it's not perfect, but maybe we can pretend we're alone." Dex escorted her to the lounge. "Are you cold?" A cool breeze kicked up, ruffling Nicki's hair.

"A little." She rubbed her bare arms to warm them.

"Take this." Dex shrugged out of his navy suit jacket and draped it over her shoulders.

He then sat and motioned for her to slip into his embrace, so he could keep her warm and close. Beautiful, long legs stretched out next to his, and he itched to stroke one, then the other, from her toes to the top of her thighs.

He grew hard at the fantasy, but talking would have to preside. "How'd you get away?" If she talked about Jonathan, that would cool him down.

"I suggested we have a drink at the bar in the casino. I knew the lure of the craps table would take his attention away in no time. I was right." Her smug smile made him chuckle.

"Good thinking. You're very shrewd. I'm going to have to keep that in mind."

She turned and looked into his eyes. "What about Lisa?"

"I told her I was going to the Lounge to see a jazz trio. She hates jazz."

"Is there a jazz trio playing there?"

"I don't know." He chuckled. "But she wouldn't check. At least I don't think she would." He pulled Nicki closer and kissed the top of her head.

"We're both such liars. That can't be a good thing." Nicki snuggled into him as she questioned their deceit.

"You're right. We should look at this as a learning experience so it doesn't happen again."

"And what have you learned?"

"To not go on vacation with someone you just broke up with. Although, I have to say, it didn't work out badly for me."

He brushed her soft cheek with his knuckles, wanting to do so much more.

She took his hand and kissed it, lingering over his fingers, her warm breath pulling at his groin.

"Maybe this wasn't such a great idea," he admitted, twisting in the lounge chair in an attempt to send blood to other body parts.

"Why?" Her brow furrowed and he massaged the lines away.

"Because I want to be naked in bed with you, not fully clothed on a public deck."

She didn't immediately respond and instead interlaced her fingers with his. "I want that too." Crystal blue eyes met his, and her suggestive smile underscored the truth of her words.

Dex groaned with the knowledge it couldn't happen. He hugged her closer, breathing in her scent, not wanting their time together to end. "So what now?"

"Are you talking about tonight now, or the future?"

"I need to know I'm going to see you on Sunday, in Philadelphia, alone. With all ties to Jonathan broken."

She nodded. "That's my plan."

He sifted his fingers through long, glossy strands. "Let's go get a drink to celebrate. If we stay here any longer, I won't be responsible for my actions."

It had taken every ounce of control not to get lost in her kisses. Not to run his hands down her neck, over her breasts, under her dress. He wanted to experience every inch of her, kiss her senseless. But most of all, he wanted to make love to her.

He had to survive two more days.

The longest two days of his life.

****

Nicki entered the restaurant on Walnut and Second, jumping beans doing a number in her stomach. Running away from one man straight into the arms of another wasn't as insane in her world view as it might be to others. Dating many and often kept her spirits up and the risk of establishing a real relationship low.

Yet free falling with Dex had her head turned and maybe not in the right direction. At least from the perspective of her ingrained philosophy. Of course, he was magnificent and could wear a suit as if in an ad in GQ, giving off that smoldering intensity punctuated by smoky green eyes. But he had something else that drew her to him, something different than the others. He wasn't self-centered or egotistical. And he had a Little Brother. A kid he'd taken under his wing for the past eight years and he clearly intended to continue the relationship. His loyalty to a child, given what his father did to him, was incredibly admirable.

But of course, things would cool down between them in a month or two. They met on a cruise under atypical circumstances, the thrill of secret liaisons ramping up the sexual tension. No matter how great a guy she thought he was, now that they were back in the real world, the thrill would simmer to an easy, calm predictability, eventually bordering on monotony. And then it would be over. Like all the rest.

Her unfortunate cynicism grew from past history. And what she wanted. Or more specifically, what she didn't want. No need to dwell on that tonight.

Strong hands wound around her waist and a sensual kiss tickled her neck, stopping all negative musings. "Dex." Her smile grew as she studied his handsome face. And to prove her insane attraction, butterflies, yes butterflies, whizzed around her stomach. "I'm so glad you're here."

"Me too." Dex's smile matched hers and those crazy butterflies swooped and somersaulted.

They followed the hostess to a table near the window on the second floor, and took their menus, but Nicki couldn't keep her focus off Dex. His dark, wavy hair was still damp from a shower, and those flashing green eyes were sinful once she fell into their depths. Which she did within seconds of being in his presence.

"Any misgivings?" Nicki asked, fairly certain he had none whatsoever.

"Nope." He took her hand in his and brought it to his lips, whispering a kiss over sensitive knuckles. That one little move sent tingles up her arm and through her veins. "What about you?" His grin told her he knew the answer.

"None for me either."

"How did Jonathan take it?"

"Good. I had told him on Wednesday things weren't working out. That we needed to end it."

"You're kidding. Right in the middle of your vacation together?"

"It wasn't fair to be thinking about you while spending time with him. It was better that way." At least in her mind. Now, she wondered if Dex believed her too heartless.

"What did he say?"

"He knew it was coming. He protested a little, but in the end, he agreed we weren't compatible."

"How long were you dating?"

Nicki counted in her head. "Three months."

"That's all? And you went on a cruise with him?" Dex's surprise caught her off guard.

"Why not? We got along well when we first met. It was an ideal time to take off from work. It sounded like a good idea when we planned it a month ago." Did Dex think their short-term relationship didn't qualify for a one-week vacation?

"I guess I should be thankful." He reached for her hand and stroked her palm in the most responsive of places, sending sensual triggers to her core.

"Why didn't you tell me you broke up with him?" His caring, caressing words followed the same path.

She looked straight into his ever-changing green eyes. "I didn't want you to feel any pressure about us. We just met. Admitting I ended things with Jonathan the day after we met might have spooked you."

He laughed. "You're not worried you're spooking me now?"

Nicki bit her lip. "No. If you are, tonight will be our last time together and we'll both move on. But I don't believe you're going to walk away. I believe this is just the beginning."

He tilted his head. "You're a candid person, Nicki."

"Is that a good thing?"

"Yes, if your directness doesn't wound."

"I'd never want to hurt you." Could she be saying these heartfelt words after knowing him for a few days?

Thankfully, the waiter showed up, and Dex ordered a bottle of Merlot after consulting with Nicki. Their orders came next. Something less personal to dwell on.

"It's back to work tomorrow," Nicki chirped. "I'm normally a little down at the end of vacation, but meeting you changed my outlook." Since the man sitting across from her held so many new possibilities, she couldn't find a negative emotion within her.

"Agreed. Although I'd rather ease back into my schedule. I took a look at my calendar for the week, and I don't have a free moment. One of the cases I'm involved in is going to trial, so I have to brush up on my testimony."

"I thought you were an accountant." She had

learned that much about his career. "Why do you have to go to court?"

"Not every accountant does tax returns. I do forensic accounting. A lot of business evaluations for shareholder disputes and divorce cases. If the disagreement ends up in court, I'm called in to testify for whatever side hired me."

"That sounds more interesting."

"You thought I was boring?" He smirked.

"Not you. Your job." She sipped her wine, looking over the rim of her glass with a new appreciation for Dex. As if she needed more. "That's why I didn't ask you much about it. I didn't want to listen to the joys of analyzing IRS regulations and finding the loopholes."

He raised an eyebrow. Even more sexy than his intense stare. "I intend to show you, Ms. Reading, that my conservatively boring job, in your estimation, does not follow me into my personal life."

Ooooohhhh. If she were reading him right, he meant the bedroom. Her thighs clenched and heat pooled between her legs.

Just then their waiter brought their food, and innuendo went by the wayside in exchange for sauces, spices, and food choices. A good thing, since the temperature in the room, or more specifically at their table, was rising to a dangerous level.

They talked more about their respective jobs, with Nicki sharing comical anecdotes about the music artists she represented as a marketing and public relations director at Snow Leopard Music, and Dex more matter-of-fact about his typical clients.

As dinner came to a close, Dex intimated at what had been on Nicki's mind the entire night. "It sounds like we both have busy weeks coming up. Is there any chance I could convince you to come back to my apartment for a drink tonight?"

Nicki wanted nothing more than to go back to Dex's place, knowing a drink never meant a drink. But something pulled her back while her inner Aphrodite practically yanked her out of her chair. She inhaled, confused over her warring desires. She didn't want this relationship, or whatever it was, to be like any of the others. She liked Dex more than she considered possible. Jumping into bed with a gorgeous, driven guy had never caused her to question the sanity of it all. No thought went into what would happen after the act. Who cared? But this was somehow different. Odd deliberations were interfering with her carnal craving. Nicki wanted Dex to see her as more than a sexual playmate. And she wanted more from him too. What in the world had gotten into her bloodstream on the cruise? Who was she tonight?

Surprised at her own recognition, she reached for his hand and gave him a wan smile.

"Can I take a rain check? It may sound silly, given our whirlwind romance on the cruise, but I don't want to ruin this by moving too fast. We met under crazy circumstances, and even though we have an amazing connection, we don't know each other well." She dug for the right words to make this come out like a rational statement. "I want to know everything about you. I want to spend as much time with you as possible, so we can get to that place where we know it's right."

Who was inhabiting her body and taking over her mouth? She'd been dying to get naked with Dex since their first kiss.

But maybe if she didn't treat Dex like all the others, it would last longer. Maybe more than three months. Maybe she'd find what two out of three of her best friends from high school had found—her Sworn Sisters as they referred to themselves. She almost choked on the thought.

"So you're taking a giant step back." He squeezed her hand, and she hoped this small gesture meant he would give her the requested space and time without walking away in frustration.

"Please know I can't stop thinking about you. I loved every minute we were together on and off the boat. It's scary." She lowered her lids to keep him from seeing the vulnerability rising to her surface.

"Thanks for that." He raised her hand and brushed his lips against it, the whole time penetrating her eyes with his powerful gaze.

She could get lost in those eyes. "Can we get together some time next weekend?" An affirmative response would go a long way in allaying the emptiness that grew within at the thought of going an entire week without seeing Dex.

His hesitance in responding had her ready to change her mind about tonight.

"I'll call you," he said, disappointment underscoring his words.

Dex motioned for the check and paid with his credit card. The night she had looked so forward to was coming to an abrupt end, and it was all her fault. What misguided notion of needing to know him better hijacked her brain and demanded she slow them down? Or was it fear over this foreign feeling?

Dex ushered Nicki out of the restaurant and hailed

a cab. Before she got in, he kissed her on the cheek, a blow to her ego as well as her allure. "I'm going to walk," he said. "Good night."

Everything had turned so formal, almost cold between them. That wasn't her wish. Nor her fantasy. She wanted Dex in every way. But she also knew herself. She jumped into relationships without much thought, which is why they lasted all of three months. That had never been a problem for her before. She cherished her independence and the control she had over her life.

Then why did her inner voice suggest she change her ways if she envisioned any hope of having a real relationship with Dex?

Nicki spoke back to that nagging voice. *You better not have blown this before it even got started.*

Chapter Five

Flowers—huge yellow lilies—arrived on Nicki's desk at work on Monday.

"These must be from Jonathan." Her assistant, Cheryl, caressed a bloom and smiled. "You are so lucky. You go on a romantic cruise for a week, then you get flowers. I wish my husband would do this once in a while."

Nicki kept the truth to herself as well as her smile. "You have a fabulous husband who adores you."

"I do, don't I?" Cheryl smiled, lingering much longer than usual in Nicki's office.

"Is everything okay? Did something happen while I was gone?"

"I wanted to talk to you before you went on vacation, but you were so busy."

Nicki froze. "You're not quitting, are you?" They made a great team and Nicki needed her.

"I'm pregnant." The words burst from her mouth followed by an overpowering grin.

Nicki took a moment to digest her words. "Congratulations," she stuttered, stumbling over the sentiment. She should have put more enthusiasm into her response, seeing the joy on Cheryl's face, but she was too shocked.

The two of them had been on the same page about relationships and kids when Cheryl first started at Snow

Leopard Music a few years ago. Neither of them wanted any interference with their climb up the corporate ladder. But then Cheryl fell in love and got married. Still, Nicki never dreamed she'd take that next step, which would surely lead to career suicide. At least that's what she told herself. And Cheryl.

"Say something," begged Cheryl.

"This won't change anything workwise, right?" Nicki held her breath.

"I'm not leaving if that's what you mean. But once the baby's born, I won't be able to put in all the late hours you require." Cheryl bit her lip and twisted her hands together.

Nicki exhaled, having dodged the bullet of losing her right arm. "Don't worry. We'll figure it out. I'm so relieved you'll be staying on." Nicki dug deep for a smile. "I can't believe you're going to be a mother."

"Me either. I can't wait. Kevin and I are over the moon."

A pang of regret washed through Nicki, but she pushed it down deep.

"Is everything set for next Monday?" Getting back to business seemed the safest option at a time like this.

"All scheduled. You'll be flying to Nashville on January twenty-eighth for four days, meeting with Perry Adams, his band mates, their agent, their publicist."

Excitement shot through Nicki. This was big. She'd be following the country band's every move to learn a little more about them personally and professionally, as well as their fans. Having worked on their marketing campaign for the past five months, Nicki would now be able to fill in the blanks before promoting the launch of their new album in May.

"Kurt called while you were away. He wants to push the launch date up for the album from the end of May to March twenty-third."

"Very funny." Nicki chuckled, but Cheryl didn't join her. "You're joking, right?" The President of Marketing for Snow Leopard could not have moved the launch up by two months while she was on vacation.

"I'm serious. He wants you to call him at eleven this morning to discuss the logistics."

Nicki took in a huge, slow breath and closed her eyes, calling on all her relaxation techniques to keep from bursting.

"If you pull this off, Nicki, you'll be in prime position to become VP of Marketing."

There was that. She exhaled. Pride and promise flowed through her system like water, easing the anxiety a tad. "Oh, I'll pull this off." Despite two months slashed from her schedule, Nicki was that confident in her ability. She'd already put in massive amounts of time gearing up for this launch, starting weeks before the project was even given to her. Okay, maybe she was a little OCD, but she'd never be caught unprepared.

Cheryl returned to her own office and Nicki plopped into her chair, warring between disappointment over Cheryl's pregnancy and her need to slip into fast forward. Everyone wasn't like Nicki, whose sole goal was to race up the corporate ladder without allowing any obstacle to get in her way. Although she'd hoped Cheryl was more like her than not, Nicki could not control how others chose to live their lives.

She opened the top drawer of her desk to get a pad and pen. A photo tucked in the corner caught her eye;

her parents with their arms around each other, a seven-year-old Nicki in front of them. The perfect family, smiling for the camera, exuding love. Would she ever have that? Probably not.

And now Cheryl was headed in that direction.

She drew in a breath to tamp down the unwelcome envy. It's not like she wanted that. Easing her shoulders back, she grabbed the envelope that came with the flowers and tore it open.

"This will be a long week. Meet me at the Barnes Museum Saturday at noon. Dex."

A delicious current ran through Nicki, and she fingered the petals of the same flowers they saw in Key West. Thoughts of that day sent her senses into overdrive.

And she loved the Barnes, a fact that didn't go unnoticed by Dex. Rooms and rooms of Impressionist and post-Impressionist paintings, but not half as overwhelming as the Philadelphia Museum of Art. What a perfect date. Unless she let her mind get in the way of her excitement. No, she wouldn't let that happen. What she felt for Dex on the cruise was amazing, and she'd only be hurting herself if she didn't act on the possibility of a relationship.

Maybe, in spending more time with him, she'd clone some of the optimism that infiltrated his attitude. He wasn't averse to relationships like she was. Despite his parents' divorce and his father's desertion, he had turned that negative experience into a positive by helping out another kid without a father. Given her own antipathy toward pint-sized humans, Dex's devotion to Kenan should be turning her off, not turning her head. Yet his selfless commitment made him all the more attractive.

Up until now, she'd done a yeoman's job of keeping men at a distance. Her *modus operandi* was to date handsome, driven guys and have fun while it lasted. So why was she considering—no, hoping for—a real relationship with Dex?

The phone rang, pulling Nicki from her self-inspection. Being extraordinarily busy at work would assure this week would race by without much time to think about her warped sense of relationships.

On the other hand, five entire days stood in the way of her date with Dex.

****

"Thanks so much for meeting me, Denise." Nicki blew into the Princeton eatery like a whirlwind, her usual pace once she was in work mode. She quickly disposed of her coat and gloves, then gave Denise—one of her Sworn Sisters—a hug before sliding into the booth across from her.

"I'm glad to see you. It's been a while." Denise smiled her bright white smile, giving Nicki the time to take a breath and relax.

"Since I was in Princeton on business, I hoped we could catch up a little." She missed her girlfriends—Denise, Sam, and Alyssa. She needed to make more of an effort to put them into her busy schedule.

They ordered promptly, so they could focus on each other. Although they only lived an hour apart, their lives were worlds apart.

"How's your family?" asked Nicki.

"A challenge, but good." Denise grinned but sadness clouded her eyes. "Since Ben's brother and his wife died, their adopted son, Bobby, has been living with us. It adds another dimension to raising the kids. He's ten years older than Jennifer, and I had to catch up fast."

The shadows under Denise's eyes, even though expertly covered with make-up, gave testament to her hardship. It couldn't be easy to have two kids under five and then add another, who had to have emotional problems due to his parents' car accident and deaths.

"Oh, Denise. I'm so sorry. When they died in September, it was such a tragedy, but I wasn't focused on how hard this must be on you."

Tears shone in Denise's eyes, but she took in a breath to ward them off. "I was really close to Sally. I miss her every day. I can't imagine how devastated Bobby feels at losing his mom. And his dad. But we try to make things as normal as possible on a day-to-day basis. And of course he sees a counselor, although he resists most of the time."

"Did he have to switch schools once he came to live with you?"

Nicki recalled her father's death during her junior year in high school. Her good friends helped her through that painful and difficult time. She wouldn't have survived if it weren't for her Sworn Sisters being there for her day and night.

"No. They lived in our school district. At least he has some stability there."

Nicki couldn't fathom taking on such a heavy responsibility, but Denise and her husband, Ben, were named as guardians under the will and didn't have a choice. Not that they wouldn't have gladly jumped in to take on the task.

"How are Jennifer and Johnny?" Nicki hoped to

lighten the conversation by turning their attention to Denise's children.

Denise's sadness lifted in an instant. "They're great. Jennifer is in preschool and loves it. She wants to be an artist when she grows up. Or a baker. Or a waitress. Depending on the day. And Johnny is a two-year-old terror. He's either climbing onto things or dissecting things. His new favorite toy is the vacuum." Denise shook her head and chuckled. "I now end up vacuuming the house three times a day, because he goes to the closet where I keep it and starts screaming that he wants to push. I have the cleanest floors in Princeton."

Nicki inwardly cringed. Kids were not her favorite people, and she couldn't understand why parents gushed over them nonstop. They were loud, messy creatures whose language was difficult to understand. And to think Denise gave up a high-powered banking job in New York City to stay home and raise the critters. It was beyond comprehension.

"I've been going on and on about my life. What's going on in yours?" Denise bit into her panini as Nicki poured dressing over her salad.

A wave of happiness spread from within. "I met someone on the cruise."

Denise's puzzled look was comical. "But you went with Jonathan."

"I did. It didn't work out so well with us. You can really get to know a person on vacation. He's a gambler, and that's all he was interested in during the trip. We pretty much did our own thing once I realized I'd have to hang out in a noisy, clanging room, lit with fluorescent lights and recirculating air if I wanted to be with him."

"Only you could meet another man on vacation when you were already with someone." Denise gave her a half grin. "Do you intend to date this new guy?"

"Oh, yes." Nicki intended to do much, much more in the not too distant future. "He lives and works in Philly. Is that fate or what?"

"Great." Denise said the right word, but her tone belied her enthusiasm.

"You disapprove?" asked Nicki, her defenses kicking in.

Denise shrugged. "I'd be wary about someone I met on vacation. It's such an idyllic setting. Once you're back home, it may not be as exciting as it was while away. Those types of romances are doomed to fail."

Nicki's stomach sank. She hadn't anticipated gloom and doom from Denise, who generally had an upbeat disposition. Now, she couldn't even tell her the whole story of how they met. If Denise learned she broke up with Jonathan the day after she met Dex, she'd think Nicki was flighty. She'd become even more cynical about the prospects of this relationship going anywhere. Perhaps it was time to change the subject.

"Have you seen any of our other Sworn Sisters?"

"I'm sorry if I seem so negative about your new guy, Nicki. Ignore me. Have fun. Maybe I'm wrong and it'll work out." Denise gave a half-hearted smile, obviously feeling bad about her less than enthusiastic response to Nicki's news.

Nicki nodded as an unfamiliar lump lodged in her throat. For some odd reason, she wanted it to work out. Dex was magic. He took into consideration how she wanted to spend their time together. It wasn't all about him. He made her feel special. Perhaps she needed to revise her acceptable date requirements. Yet given her history, she couldn't blame Denise for her skepticism.

Denise played with a french fry, probably considering whether she should stick to the current subject or pick up on the line Nicki had thrown out there.

She chose the latter. "I talked to Sam recently. She's crazy busy, as usual, with her divorce practice. She barely has time to see her husband. But of course, they still live and breathe New York City. I don't know how she can live there, but she says the same thing about me living in Princeton." Denise blew off their differences, and Nicki knew each of her Sworn Sisters' priorities would never affect their friendship. "I asked her to file adoption papers for us for Bobby. I'm so glad she has her New Jersey license to practice law in addition to New York. She said it would go through easily."

Nicki's attention was waning, which wasn't fair to Denise, especially since she had to hire a babysitter for Johnny so she could meet Nicki for lunch. She needed to get her mind off Dex and participate in this new thread.

But Denise's words had Nicki worried. Maybe it was too Pollyanna to believe the enchantment she experienced on a cruise ship could translate into something real on dry land.

Maybe she shouldn't even try.

****

"Hello, beautiful."

Nicki turned at his greeting, and her smile went straight to Dex's heart. This Nicki didn't wear a flowery sundress but sleek black pants, heeled boots, and a leather jacket. *Oh, yes.*

"Hi, yourself." Her greeting was breathy, sensual.

Did they really have to walk through the museum today? Dex leaned in for a kiss, careful to make it chaste, then took her hand and led her to the cashier. "Have you been here before?"

"I was at the Barnes when it was in Lower Merion. I've been dying to come to this new location. So glad you invited me."

He'd been eager to see it too, but now that he had Nicki by his side, his brain had other ideas. Very erotic in nature.

Convincing himself to slow down and enjoy the day took some doing, but he settled into sharing his views on his favorite artists, Matisse and Cezanne, while Nicki encouraged him to add Renoir and Van Gogh to his preferences. Their divide could not be bridged, but they had fun attempting to win each other over.

In mid-afternoon, they stopped at a café on Rittenhouse Square to rest their tired legs and have a late lunch.

"How was your week back at work?" Dex was sure this subject would keep his thoughts off exploring Nicki's body.

"Busy, but good. I'm heading to Nashville on Monday to meet a country singer we signed six months ago. The launch of his new album is soon, so I want to make sure I know everything about him."

"Him, huh?" He zeroed in on Nicki's eyes and lost his train of thought.

"Don't worry. He has a girlfriend. At least at the

moment. Besides, I don't date clients."

"What a relief. Because I sure don't want to compete with a good-looking country guy who can sing you a love song while playing a guitar."

"They all go for models or actresses anyway." She tossed her mane of blonde hair over her shoulder and posed, adding a giggle.

If she only knew she looked like a model herself.

Changing the subject, she asked, "Did Kenan like the book you got him in Key West?"

"I haven't seen him yet. I spend one Saturday a month with him. It seems like so little time, but it's hard to even find those hours. I wish I could do more."

Nicki fingered the condensation on her glass. "You are doing an incredible service to that little boy. You've been with him for eight years, and I'm sure he knows he can reach out to you at any time."

He nodded. "He can. And he does sometimes. It just doesn't seem enough."

"How did you get involved as a Big Brother? It's not something most single guys would do."

"After my parents divorced and my father moved to California, my mother believed I needed an adult male influence in my life. So she signed up to match me with a Big Brother. Harry was amazing. He stuck with me for years, taking me to baseball games, teaching me how to play different sports, helping with my homework, giving me advice when I had a rough time in high school. I wanted to pay it forward." He sighed. "But as I said, it's not enough."

"Nonprofit organizations always need money to help fund them. You can do something like putting together a race, or a golf outing, or a gala. Money would help many more children."

"I wouldn't know the first thing about doing any of those things. Besides, that sounds like a huge time commitment when I don't even have time to see Kenan more."

"It's not hard if you have a big committee and are good at delegating. I'm sure there are people from your firm who would be interested. You went to Drexel, right? There are thousands of students there, some of whom are community minded and some who may need to get involved for credit. Either way, you could populate your committee quickly with volunteers from just those two places." Nicki stared out the window, her brow furrowing as she drummed her fingers on the table.

"It sounds like you've done something like this before."

"I work on major events for my job. I've never put together an event for a nonprofit, but the basics are the same. Dedication to a cause makes it easier, and you definitely have dedication."

"If I decide to follow through on this thread, maybe you could give me a hand."

"Sure, if it's behind the scenes." Her crystal blue eyes flashed with interest. "Please know I am not volunteering to be on your committee. This is your thing. I'll brainstorm with you. Come up with potential sponsors and participants. If you decide on a run, we can create a flyer and post it in all the gyms around here. You'll need a sponsorship letter to send to accounting firms, law firms, other companies in the area." Her enthusiasm and knowledge energized him.

But the ideas flying out of Nicki had the potential

to take up the next two hours, and though Dex was intrigued and more than excited to consider a fundraiser that would make a real difference to his organization, he had other plans for this afternoon.

He leaned across the table and took Nicki's hand. "I promise I won't put you on my committee. In exchange, I'm hoping I can convince you to come back to my apartment?" The invitation was ever so clear and he inhaled, seeking to calm his raging lust. But his patience was nonexistent.

Her sensuous lips curved into a smile. "You don't have to convince me. Let's go."

His heart thumped an uneven beat. If he wasn't already stupid crazy for her, he'd be even more insane. She didn't play games and she didn't lead him on.

Within five minutes they were ascending in the elevator of his building, wild anticipation crashing around his system. It had been nine days since he'd shared space on a lounge chair with her on the deck of a cruise ship, her body pressed close to his, but not close enough. He'd wanted her then, but that night was an impossibility.

Heat emanated from every pore, and he needed to douse that heat, but not before taking slow pleasure in exploring her racy body covered in black.

Dex unlocked the door and stood aside to let Nicki in, her special scent inundating his olfactory sense as she passed. He closed the door and locked it, then peeled her leather jacket from her shoulders. A form-fitting tank top lay underneath, leaving her tanned, toned arms bare but for the thin silver bracelet he'd bought her on a whim and a promise in Key West.

"Can I get you anything?" He pulled his manners

out before slipping off his sports coat.

Her blue irises flashed with heat, and she moved into his space, running her hands up his chest and over his shoulders before she molded herself to him. Full lips brushed over his, softly at first, but he captured them in his and she increased the pressure, taking what she wanted. He groaned with pleasure as their tongues mated and danced.

Slender fingers danced at the top of his shirt, releasing the buttons as she leisurely fanned warm hands over his chest, uncovering it inch by inch. His skin was on fire. As well as every other part of his anatomy. Needing more contact, he placed his hands on her hips, then slid them around to her butt, pulling her into him, pressing her against his erection. Such exquisite pain.

Her mouth moved from his lips to his jawline, then to his neck, sending jolts of electricity to his core. Pulling her top from inside her pants, he stepped back to ease it over her head. She wore a red lace bra showing plenty of cleavage. Too bad it had been hidden all day by her jacket and tank top, but a good thing given their outing at the museum.

He couldn't take his eyes from her breasts as he fondled the perfect mounds offered before him. Nicki moaned when he rubbed his thumbs over her lace-covered nipples, and her head fell back as her body arched, giving him greater access. He eased the lace down to expose her tightened peak, then laved it with his tongue before taking it into his mouth. Nicki's fingers slid through his hair, holding his head to her as pleasurable noises escaped her lips.

They hadn't moved far from the door, and it had

not been part of Dex's plan to take her on the living room floor. With effort, he raised his head. "Let's go to the bedroom." Without waiting for her answer, he grabbed Nicki's hand and pulled her down the hall and into his lair.

The late afternoon sun bathed the room in adequate light, for he wanted to see every inch of Nicki. He reconnected with her soft, wet mouth while unclasping the top of her pants and sliding the zipper down. Kneeling before her, he removed her boots, then dragged soft wool down long, beautiful legs, and over slender feet. Tiny, red, lace bikini panties teased his heightened senses, and he hooked his index fingers onto each side and eased them down the same path as her pants.

Dex ran his palms up toned thighs, then kissed her navel, sliding his tongue into the tiny indentation. Her sharp intake of breath was all the motivation he needed to continue his assault on her silky-smooth abdomen and parts south.

His name echoed on a strangled breath. "Dex, please. I want you inside of me."

Oh, yes. He stood and quickly disposed of his clothing before ushering her into bed.

Long, golden hair fanned out over the pillow, and her hot, liquid gaze ignited a firestorm in his groin. He leaned over and imprisoned her mouth with his, as the loose control he attempted to harness slipped away. Need and want reached their highest limit, having simmered in his being for over a week. He strained to open the nightstand drawer and blindly rooted around for a condom. Dragging his mouth away from Nicki's long enough to rip open the foil, he quickly sheathed his rock-hard penis.

"I'm on the pill and I'm clean." Nicki's hands fluttered over his chest and down his torso, causing taut nerves to jump at each new sensation.

"Good to know," he said through gritted teeth.

Then she closed her hand over his shaft, and all bets he could slow this down were off. He spread her legs with his knees and positioned himself at her opening. Nicki raised her hips and he inched in, slowly at first, then plunging until his length was completely surrounded by her heated walls. They found their rhythm and each stroke was ecstasy.

Dex studied the lioness in his bed through hooded lids, watching her reach for the height. Her body tensed as she got there, then spasmed around him as her eyes closed and cascading pleasure took over. He was right behind her, pumping in and out with a fever that only Nicki could cure. He exploded with an intensity he'd never felt before, as Nicki writhed under him, pulling every last drop from his body.

He never wanted to leave this bed.

Chapter Six

Nicki awoke at dawn, wrapped in Dex's arms, her back to his front. She wanted to see him, watch him as he slept. Sliding slowly onto her back so as not to awaken him, she repositioned his arm over her torso. But his hand moved up and cupped her breast as if it had radar, and an electric current zapped straight between her legs. How could he have this effect on her? Every muscle in her body ached from their decadent night of love-making. They'd never left his apartment once they fell into each other's arms, as if on a mission to explore every inch of each other several times over before passing out from lack of energy.

She turned her head to examine the sleeping tiger next to her. Dark brows curved slightly over closed eyes and converging upper and lower lashes produced a thick feathering over high cheekbones. His day-old beard shadowed a strong jaw and highlighted an incredibly sensuous mouth—one that could give such pleasure. A blush heated her cheeks at the thought of where that mouth had been last night.

Easing out of bed, Nicki went to the bathroom and turned on the shower. Water, the sustenance of life, would revive her and massage her aching muscles. She stood under the hot deluge for a long time, getting lost in the fantasy of her and Dex the night before. When the water started cooling, she stepped out and found a large bath towel to wrap around her. Using another to squeeze the water from her hair, she then searched under the sink for a toothbrush. Although she'd had her mouth all over Dex, she didn't think it proper to use his toothbrush without asking. Chuckling at her hygienic dilemma, she opened a new box.

When she returned to the sex chamber, the bed was empty. Nicki opened his double-wide closet in search of something to wear and found a terry cloth robe in the back. She pulled it on and knotted the belt as she regarded the neatness of his shirts, jackets, and pants, color-coded and organized by type. Interesting. Her closet looked similar.

She headed for the kitchen in search of coffee, but as she got closer, the amazing aroma of bacon came wafting at her. Her stomach growled in protest, demanding to be fed.

Dex's back was to her as he stood at the stove making scrambled eggs. He had on a worn pair of jeans that hugged his hips and perfect rear. Nothing else. So, so sexy. Did he know how he affected women?

He must have heard her sigh, because he turned and regarded her with carnal interest. "Where'd you get the robe?"

"I found it in your closet. In the back. I hope you don't mind."

"Now I remember. My mother got it for me one Christmas. She obviously doesn't know men don't wear robes." He smirked. "But you look good in it."

It was way too big and hung down to mid-calf, but it was comfy and warm and perfect for Sunday morning breakfast with Dex.

"The coffee maker is over there." He pointed to the

corner of the counter. "The cups are above it."

Nicki followed his direction and made a cup—strong, black, and hot. Wonderful. "Can I make yours?"

"I don't drink coffee. I'll have juice."

Nicki noticed the table was set with plates, glasses, juice, and syrup in a small pitcher with a spoon.

"What's the syrup for?"

"Bacon."

She laughed. "Who puts syrup on bacon?"

"I do. And maybe you will too, once you taste it. It's the best."

She had her doubts, but to each his own.

Once the eggs were done, they sat before a veritable feast. In addition to the eggs and bacon, there was buttered toast, croissants, and three different jams to choose from. If they had been at Nicki's apartment, all she would have been able to offer Dex was coffee, and he didn't even drink it.

"You're amazing," Nicki murmured as she dug into her eggs. "These are delicious."

"I figured you'd be starving this morning. We missed dinner last night." A wicked gleam in his eye sent her mind right back to their feats of athleticism between the sheets, and her cheeks burned in remembrance.

No response was necessary, so she continued to enjoy breakfast, studying him as she ate. He picked up the pitcher and drizzled syrup in a straight line over one strip of bacon. His precise artistry had her grinning.

"What?" he asked.

"Nothing."

He stood up and came to stand next to her, his plate in hand. "Close your eyes."

She did as he asked, not able to wipe the grin from her mouth.

"Turn your head toward me." His voice was commanding, but soft. "Open your mouth."

She parted her lips, and warm, sticky syrup touched her top lip. Dex then moved the bacon strip like a paint brush over the rest of her lips, thinning out the syrup.

"Bite down."

She did, and the salty sweetness of the offering burst with flavor over her tongue. "Mmmm."

She kept her eyes closed and savored the taste until Dex's expert tongue licked her lips clean.

A moan escaped her mouth, and Dex took the opportunity to sweep his tongue against hers. He pulled open the top of her robe and caressed her breasts as he deepened his kiss.

Moving his mouth toward her ear, he whispered, "Keep your eyes closed."

Cool air rushed over her exposed breasts, and her nipples tightened as she ached for Dex to touch her again. The spoon dinged against the glass pitcher, then warm beads of liquid hit the top of her breast. Thick drops slid over her bared skin before a hot mouth covered her taut peak and sucked.

"Soooo good," he murmured as his tongue circled and teased.

His hand cupped her other breast, and Nicki arched her back like a cat, begging for more contact. The tie around her waist eased open, and Dex pushed the robe over her shoulders and down her back so she was completely naked in his kitchen.

Nicki raised her lids to see what Dex had in mind,

but her sight was cloudy, dazed. He dipped his finger into the syrup and covered it in the brown sweetness.

"Spread your legs," he said, his voice husky, sensual.

Whoa. But her thighs had a mind of their own, and she complied with his wish.

He massaged her nub with his sticky finger before easing into her opening.

She closed her eyes, not able to watch the erotic scene, but all other senses were heightened to the limit.

"You're so wet. And hot." He stroked her slowly at first, but when her stomach clenched he sped up his pace, continuing the outer massage with his thumb.

The power built until the firebolt struck, and she screamed his name as she came and came and came.

She laid her forehead against his, gasping for breath as she pulled together her shattered senses. He kissed her lips, then swept her up into his arms and brought her to his bedroom.

****

Nicki flew nonstop from Nashville to Philadelphia International on Thursday evening, bone tired from being "on" for four days. She'd met with Perry Adams and his band during the day and followed them to the most popular Nashville haunts at night.

Nicki loved this part of her job, getting to know the artists, listening to their music in small venues before they became "big," learning their brand so she could improve her marketing plan to sync more accurately with their style, their current followers, and hopefully engage tens of thousands of new fans.

It wasn't until she fell into bed each night, exhausted from her rat-race day, that thoughts of Dex—

beautiful, powerful, sensual Dex—bounded through her brain, refusing to let her sleep. This past weekend had been magical and shocking and addictive. She craved more.

But would this last? It never did. As soon as the excitement of a new man wore off, Nicki sought a replacement. She knew her operating procedure. Yet every time she tried to change, hang on for a few more weeks to see if she could make it work, things got worse. As if she were sabotaging the relationship to assure a continued steady stream of failures.

The reason was clear. She couldn't, wouldn't end up like her mother, falling into a deep depression when her husband, best friend, closest confidante, suddenly died. The bond her parents had in life, so special while it lasted, was savagely slashed, leaving her mother in a free fall until she too succumbed from the blow.

No, she wouldn't be having that.

Nicki stared out the window of the taxi, seeing nothing but a blur of cars and trucks racing into the city, trying to push thoughts of Dex away. Yet they persisted. What was he doing this very moment? Probably in his office working. When she spoke to him two nights ago, he was deep into preparation for his testimony as an expert witness in a divorce case. The trial had already started and he was on call.

That's when the seed of a plan took hold, despite her warning to keep things between them calm and cool.

"I've had a change of plans," she told the taxi driver. "Take me instead to Market and Seventeenth." She unbuttoned another button on her silk blouse beneath her suit jacket before alighting from the cab.

The freezing February wind attacked her face, but nothing would deter her. Tugging her small wheeled suitcase for half a block, she entered an office building, signed in, then headed for the elevator. Her stomach bunched, yet butterflies managed to flit about.

She held her breath as she rose to the twelfth floor, praying Dex would be here. It was such a crazy, misguided plan. At this time of night, the front door to the accounting firm would be locked. It was after nine. Why had she been so impetuous?

As she stepped off the elevator, a man was exiting the office. She turned on her best open, friendly smile. "Could you hold the door, please?"

He gave her the once over, must have determined she wasn't a mass murderer, and followed her request.

Pushing her luck, she asked, "Do you know if Dex Hanover is in? I need to deliver something and he said he'd be here late."

"He's still here."

She kept her sigh of relief contained. "Could you point me in the direction of his office?"

"Third office on the right." He nodded down the hall past the reception desk.

"Thanks."

Nicki strode down the hall, her goal within shouting distance. She stopped short of his door and placed her suitcase against the wall. Then she took a step and her eyes lit on Dex, sitting behind his desk, white shirt sleeves rolled up, necktie loosened, and hair rumpled. Could he look any sexier?

"Hi," she said, her voice husky from pure need.

He looked up from the document he was reading. It took a moment before a smile broke over his mouth, sending her pulse racing. He stood and came over to her, then pulled her into his office, closed the door, and gave her an electrifying kiss.

So worth the angst of the last half hour.

He pulled back without releasing her from his arms. "What are you doing here?" His eyes sparked their approval.

She toyed with giving him a joking response. She'd gotten lost. Couldn't find her key. Was starving and didn't want to eat alone. But she wasn't one to play games. Except maybe in the bedroom. Or the kitchen. Fire burned her cheeks every time she replayed their scene from Sunday morning.

"I missed you." A totally honest answer, stripped of any qualification.

He looked deep into her eyes with his trademark intensity. All traces of his smile vanished and in its place, raw desire. "I missed you too."

Nicki yanked on his tie to bring him back into her space, and she covered his mouth with hers, drinking in his deliciousness, his nectar. She didn't stop until they were both breathless.

"This may not have been such a great idea." Her breath came in gasps as she tried to rein in her raging hormones.

He pressed his forehead to hers and grasped her hands. "It was an excellent idea."

She swam in the deep pools of his green irises before lifting her lips to his again.

A knock on the door went unanswered as Nicki devoured Dex's mouth with hers.

"Excuse me, Dex." A female voice had her jumping back. "Sorry for the interruption." A smirk appeared on the woman's face. "I have a question about something in the Graycort audit report."

Dex sighed, a smile playing around his beautiful lips. "Closed doors don't mean much around here. Nicki, this is Karla. She's an intern here. Karla, Nicki."

They murmured hellos before Dex spoke. "I'll come to your office in a few minutes."

Karla backed out the door. "Okay. I'll wait."

Dex drew his attention back to Nicki. "Sorry. I can't do what I want to do to you right now." The wicked gleam in his eyes told her maybe he could have, if not for Karla. "I made her stay late to help with a report that's due tomorrow, so I can't blow her off."

Pure sadness settled in Nicki's chest. "I'll let you get back to work then."

How could he elicit such strong emotions in such a short period of time?

"I wish I could leave with you now."

She nodded. "That's okay. I understand. I have to get home and unpack. I have a full day of meetings tomorrow."

Nicki turned to go when Dex spoke up. "I know it's not an exciting proposition, but how'd you like to go with me to my sister's on Sunday? It's my nephew's birthday, and I promised I'd show up after the kids' party for a family celebration."

She'd go anywhere, do anything with Dex. Even go to a kids' party. "Sure. Will I see you before then?" Hope swirled through her. She couldn't wait until Sunday, especially knowing they wouldn't be alone.

"I'm giving a seminar Saturday morning for a bar association group on business evaluations. I should be done by one. I can come by your place if you're free, and we'll figure out what to do then."

Her spirits lifted. "Perfect. See you then." Nicki gave him a chaste kiss on the cheek. Getting them both into a lather was fruitless. And frustrating.

She turned and left his office, a mixture of melancholy and anticipation vying for preference in her analytical mind. She loved the thrill of having a new man in her life. But along with it came the angst over knowing it would end all too soon, given her issues.

"Good luck getting your report out," she called as she retraced her steps from twenty minutes earlier.

Maybe Dex would be the one to free her from herself.

Chapter Seven

Dex was the last speaker on the panel Saturday morning, and every minute seemed like an hour as he counted down toward the time he'd be able to escape. As a conservative accountant, he should take some of that cautiousness he lived by in the office and apply it to his personal life. The characteristics he loved about Nicki—her independence, career ambitions, and strength—didn't mesh well with his life plan. He spent the last ten years working hard to become a partner at his firm. Success in his career was important, but now that he achieved it, he wanted more. He wanted a wife, a family. Knowing Nicki for only a few weeks, he couldn't swear she didn't want the same, but a husband and kids didn't quite fit into her busy schedule and myopic focus on career advancement.

And she did say, when they were in Key West, that getting married was not on her to-do list. Of course, she'd never met the right guy. Perhaps he was the one who could change that.

Time would tell and he sure wanted to spend time with her.

He arrived at Nicki's door at one thirty, overdressed in his suit and tie, and overanxious to see her.

A bright smile and gleaming blue eyes greeted him. "You look very handsome although a bit formal."

Should he admit to his decision against going home to change because he didn't want to waste another minute before seeing her? "I should have brought casual clothes with me. I was in a rush this morning and wasn't thinking."

"How did the seminar go?"

"Slowly." His libido kicked up a notch as he raked his gaze over Nicki's attire—black leather pants and a red, silky halter top. He arched his brow. "What is your plan for us today?"

"I have options." She took his arm, drawing him into her living room. "There's an art show at the Third Eye Gallery. Ed Kolsky's work. He's kind of edgy, vibrant. It could be fun. Or we can go to The Philadelphia Museum of Art. There's a Picasso exhibit."

She eyed him, awaiting his choice.

"At this moment, only one option seems preferable, and it's not on your list." He didn't want some paintings to get in the way of other, more carnal possibilities.

She seized his tie and tugged him closer, giving him a sensuous kiss, proving she was game for his plan.

"Nice," he whispered.

He tenderly traced a line from her temple to her collarbone, then boldly dipped his hand beneath the fabric of her top, caressing her breast. Her breath hitched, causing pure desire to roll through him.

He covered her mouth with his, pulling her into him, embracing her curves. Nicki's hands roamed up his chest and over his shoulders, sliding his suit jacket off, then tossing it onto the couch. Next, she worked the knot of his tie until it slipped from around his neck and onto the floor in a snake-like coil.

Amusement tinged by desire flashed through Dex. "This is much more fun than analyzing art work. Although you look pretty close to a masterpiece to me." His palm skimmed her arm, sending a promise of much more.

"Perhaps we can analyze each other in my bedroom."

"Lead the way."

****

When Dex opened his eyes, the sun no longer peeked through the slats in the blinds, and long shadows lay across Nicki's bed. Her head nestled on his shoulder, and he spontaneously drew her closer.

Nicki stirred with his movement. "What time is it?" She burrowed into him, her eyes still closed.

He looked at the clock on her nightstand. "Six twenty."

"I guess we missed the art exhibit."

"I didn't." He smiled at the memory of Nicki's naked, glorious body straddling him. Nothing could compare.

"Are you hungry?" she asked, still drowsy.

"Starving. What about you?"

"Me too. The only thing I have to make are eggs and toast. No bacon. No syrup."

He chuckled. "You have some grocery shopping to do. I guess we'll have to order in. Eggs won't do it for me tonight." His stomach growled in confirmation.

"What's your preference?" she asked. "Chinese? Italian? Thai? Burgers?"

"I love Thai. Do you have a menu?"

"Of course. My favorite Thai place is right down

the street. Although unfortunately, they don't deliver. We can go pick it up and bring it back or eat there."

"I was hoping to not stray far from this bed. Other than to answer the door."

"Can you switch your craving to Chinese? They deliver."

"Done," he said, grazing her cheek with a kiss.

Dex threw on his suit pants. He'd have to be more prepared next time. Nicki donned her yoga pants and a zip-up. They moved into the living room, sat on the floor in front of the coffee table, opened a bottle of wine, and after ordering their food, drank and talked, barely pausing in their nonstop colloquy to breathe. Dex wanted to know everything about Nicki—her favorite movies, musical groups, artists, restaurants, cities, sports. The list went on and on, and they covered a big part of it while laughing, joking, eating, and drinking.

After dinner, Nicki turned the subject to less mundane things. Leave it to a woman to delve. "You told me a little about your background in the past. I take it you don't see your father. What about your mother? Is she remarried?"

He shook his head. "No. She's too busy working and keeping up with her social life. She has a lot of friends and might be seeing someone, but that's not a topic she and I talk about. Maybe she tells my sister more. I don't know."

"What does she do for work?" Nicki sat cross-legged on the floor, sipping her wine.

"Owns a women's clothing store. She loves it, loves fashion. A younger woman works in the store, who hopes someday to wrestle the business from my mom. Good luck to her, although it's a great retirement plan for my mom. I'm just not sure she intends to do that anytime soon."

"What does your dad do?"

"He's an accountant too."

"You're following in your dad's footsteps."

"No. At least I hope not. When I marry, it's going to be for life. And I would never leave my kids."

"Do you see him at all?"

"When he moved to California, we saw him one or two times a year. Now, I see him if he comes to Philadelphia and makes a point of reaching out. The last time he did that was three years ago."

"That's sad."

"Very sad for the young boy who wanted nothing more than to be with his father. Who wanted to spend some time playing ball or hanging out. But as the years went on and the disappointment quadrupled, I became numb to it." Dex inwardly squirmed at the un-truth. He wasn't numb. Angry might be a better description. And hurt. And so disillusioned that if he were ever a dad, he'd do everything completely different from the way his father handled parenthood.

"Why did they get divorced?"

"They were total opposites. Although sometimes that works out. In my parents' case, it severed their relationship. My mom's independent. She doesn't want or need anyone telling her what to do. My father, from what I could deduce from conversations with my mom, was too controlling. He believed he had all the answers when she wasn't even asking a question."

"Are you close to your mom?"

"Sure. I see her once or twice a month. She calls

every few days, although I don't always answer." He let out a guilty sigh. "Let's not talk about my parents anymore."

She ignored him. "You're lucky your mom calls. She cares about you. That's nice."

He reached for her hand and stroked her palm. "You must miss your parents a lot."

"I do. But I'm used to it. It was hard when my dad died though. I went through a difficult time. My mother was so depressed; she rarely left the house. I don't think she ever recovered. She was only forty-two when she died."

"Any siblings?"

"Nope. Just me. I know you have a sister. Any others?"

"Only Janice. She's my twin, born five minutes before me."

Nicki's eyes widened in surprise. "I didn't know you were a twin. Does she look like you?"

Dex pulled Nicki toward him and kissed her hard on the mouth. It was difficult not to touch her. "She has the same color hair and eyes. Pretty. But she's always harried these days, with two young tots under foot all the time."

Nicki looked at him in mock horror. "Why did she do that? Kids interfere with all the fun parts of life."

Dex laughed at Nicki's joke. "You'll be there someday and loving every minute of it."

"Not me." She shook her head, her eyes sparkling. "I'd rather do X-rated things with you for a long time to come without ever having to worry about the possible side effects."

All visions of playful toddlers disappeared, and

Dex drew Nicki onto his lap and kissed her thoroughly. "I'm so glad I found you." He raised her chin with his index finger to look directly into her crystal eyes. "We're very compatible."

Nicki's smile disappeared. "I agree. I hope we never find each other's fatal flaw."

Dex seconded her wish.

****

Dex left her apartment at noon the next day to change, wrap his nephew's present, and pick up his car for the drive to his sister's house in Cherry Hill.

At three thirty, he pulled up in front of Nicki's apartment building, and Nicki jumped in, bundled head to foot in winter wear. She looked adorable in a white hat, scarf, and puffy coat, shielding her from the blustery wind swirling outside. "I hate this weather," she complained, rubbing her gloved hands together. She leaned over to kiss him, her cold nose touching his cheek.

That slightest contact sizzled through his veins, made hotter by blue, flashing eyes trained only on him.

"I'll turn your seat warmer on." He reached over and pressed the button, then slid his hand up and down her jeans-clad thigh. "I can help warm you up too."

He glanced at her and saw a grin inch over luscious lips.

"That's a dangerous move, Dex, especially while you're driving. You may want to save it for when we're alone. Later."

The veiled promise of another night filled with close encounters sent indecent fantasies skittering across his brain. They definitely escalated his internal heat index.

"You can count on it. We just have to get through the next few hours with my niece and nephew."

"What's your niece's name?"

"Chloe. She's six and loves to play with dolls and doll houses. Not my thing, but I try. I'm much better with Colin. A total boy. Trains, trucks, balls."

"How old is Colin?" She shifted in her seat, her usual smile missing.

"Turning four today. I can't wait to give him his present. He's going to love it."

"What is it?"

"A plastic basketball hoop. We could set it up in the family room. The ball is made of some sort of spongy material, so it can't hurt anything."

Nicki's non-response was deafening.

"What's wrong?"

"Nothing."

He'd been around women long enough to know that "nothing" was "something."

"Are you nervous about meeting my sister and her husband? They're great. You'll love them. And they'll love you."

That brought out a slight smile.

"No. I'm fine with adults." She paused, as if deciding whether to go on. "I'm not a kid person."

He glanced at her to see if she were serious. She was.

Dex reached over and grabbed her hand. "There's nothing to worry about. Kids are so easy. All you have to do is play whatever they ask you to, and they'll love you. I don't know the first thing about setting up her dollhouse, but Chloe tells me what to do." A chuckle escaped. "I guess little girls learn early how to boss men around to get what they want."

At least his little joke elicited a laugh. "Maybe I could talk to your sister. Try to learn all about you from when you were a kid."

"I was a handful after my dad moved out. Until I was matched with my Big Brother. My sister will have stories to make you worry about continuing to see me."

It took a half hour to get to his sister's cape cod amongst a neighborhood of similar houses. Other cars were in the street, indicating the kids' party had not yet ended.

"I hope Janice can scoot some of these people out of here, so we can enjoy time with her kids."

Dex came around and opened Nicki's door. Gloom marred her pretty face. He didn't factor into their date an aversion to children. In fact, it never occurred to him. He thought she was teasing last night when she joked about not wanting any of her own. He loved kids and assumed all women did. Didn't they all want to get married and have a family one day?

Nicki hung back a step as he steered her toward the front door. "They don't bite," he said, trying to lighten her mood. But not even a glimmer of a smile inched over her lips.

The front door was unlocked, so Dex walked in, following the loud voices to the kitchen. He pulled Nicki along. As soon as Janice saw him, she broke away from her friends.

"Dex. I was hoping you'd show up on time." She gave him a harried hug.

"Janice, this is Nicki. I told you about her on the phone."

Janice gave Nicki a broad smile and shook her

hand with gusto. "It's so nice to meet you. Dex couldn't say enough nice things about you."

"Thanks. Same here," Nicki murmured, glancing past Janice as if searching for the kid area so she could avoid it.

"Frank is in the basement trying to corral the kids whose parents are here, so they could leave. It shouldn't take too long. Then we can have our own little family party."

"Uncle Dex." A loud voice pierced the air and a tiny tot charged at Dex, throwing himself around Dex's legs.

"Happy birthday, buddy. How does it feel to be four today?" Dex ruffled his hair.

"Where's my present?" asked Colin, searching the area around Dex.

"I left it in the car. Let's wait until your friends leave. Then I'll get it."

Colin turned to take off, now that he didn't have a new present to unwrap in his immediate future. "Hold on there, kiddo." Dex grabbed his arm and dragged him back. "I want you to meet my friend. This is Nicki."

Colin gave her a quick glance, said "Hi," and disappeared.

Dex let him go. "Sorry. He's a little excited about his birthday."

"Not a problem." Something close to relief accompanied Nicki's statement.

It took at least fifteen minutes for the parents to collar their kids and lead them out the door. The noise level increased exponentially as plans were made for play dates and good-byes were said.

Finally, the last family left, and Dex's stress over

Nicki's discomfort waned a bit.

"Hey, Chloe. You didn't give your favorite uncle a hug." Dex motioned to his niece who was, as predicted, playing in the family room with her doll house.

Chloe slowly ambled over, shy about meeting new people. Before he introduced her to Nicki, he picked her up and gave her a loud kiss on the cheek.

"Uncle Dex, why do you always do that?" Chloe's giggle was contagious, and he tickled her just to hear more of her infectious laughter.

Now that he had her at ease, he introduced her to Nicki. Chloe looked at her with a wary glance but must have decided she looked like one of her Barbie dolls.

"Will you play doll house with me?" Her voice was thin, but she looked up at Nicki with huge brown eyes, clearly hoping to gain a new playmate.

"I'm sorry, Chloe, but I don't..." Nicki's eyes locked on Dex, and there was no mistake she wanted his cooperation in denying his niece.

Dex wasn't going there. "Let her show you how she decorated the rooms. You don't have to do anything." He so wanted Nicki to fit in, to be adored by his niece and nephew like he was. "I'll come with you."

He placed his hand on Nicki's back and guided her toward the doll house. Then he sat on the floor with Chloe, gesturing for Nicki to do the same. She folded her long legs underneath her, stiffly peering into the back of the house.

Chloe rearranged the bed and dresser in the master bedroom. "Do you think it looks better like this?" She looked at Nicki for approval.

Nicki shrugged. "I don't know. Either way."

Dex took over. "It looks much better like that,

honey. You're doing a great job."

A beer appeared in front of Dex. "Here you go," said Frank. "I want to show you our new bar in the basement. I built it myself. Come on."

Dex introduced him to Nicki and Frank offered her a beer, which she declined.

"I'll be right back." Dex squeezed Nicki's arm, giving her a shot of encouragement. It wasn't difficult to interact with a six-year-old girl. And it should be much easier for Nicki than him, given their genders.

The glare Nicki gave him told him he dared not stay long admiring Frank's new bar. So Dex gave Frank the appropriate kudos for doing such an awesome job and headed back upstairs to rescue his forlorn date.

"I'm going to run out and get Colin's gift." He passed Nicki in the same rigid pose she'd been in when he left.

When he arrived back with the basketball set, Chloe was crying. "She broke the leg off my doll."

Nicki held a plastic doll in one hand and a leg in the other. "I was trying to fix her. This leg was backward," Nicki explained, but Chloe's dramatic response got louder.

"I'll put it back together, Chloe." Dex took both pieces of the doll from Nicki's hand. "This happened before. Remember? The leg snaps right back in."

Nicki bit her lip and pushed herself up off the floor. "I told you I wasn't good with kids," she mumbled so only Dex could hear.

They'd been there less than an hour, but after Colin opened his present, and they tossed the ball through the hoop a couple of times, Dex came up with a plausible excuse to leave.

"I have a big day at the office tomorrow and so does Nicki. We have to get going."

Janice protested a little, but she looked exhausted after a day with twenty kids. Unfortunately, she hadn't had a chance to get to know Nicki since she was cleaning up most of the time they were there.

Dex hugged both kids and said he'd see them soon.

Back in the car, he rolled his shoulders and exhaled as Nicki strapped her seatbelt around her. "That was rough." A battle with no ammunition would have been easier.

Their ride back to Philadelphia was eerily silent. Dex frankly didn't know what to say. He wanted the afternoon to be fun, happy. Instead it was disastrous. Nicki clammed up before they even got inside, and once there, hid her friendly, outgoing self. He wanted his sister and her kids to adore Nicki. Yet Colin had no use for her and Chloe blamed her for breaking her doll. Not that Nicki helped the situation.

Breaking the ice, he ventured into territory he wasn't sure was the best, but it was the only way to move on. "You seem so uncomfortable with children. Don't you have any friends with kids?" Since she had no siblings, she couldn't have nieces or nephews.

"Denise has two. She's a friend from high school. And she just took in her nephew. His parents died in a car accident."

"How sad. How old is he?"

"Thirteen or fourteen, I think. Her other two are two and four."

"Do you ever spend time with them?" Perhaps she was better with the children of her friends.

"No. I was there for their christenings and a

birthday party here or there. But I didn't have to do anything with them."

So she wasn't a kid person when it came to other people's kids. "I'm sure once you have your own, you'll feel different."

"What?" Shock shook her voice. "Why would you think that?"

"Because most parents adore their kids."

"I don't intend to find out. I'm not having any."

A laugh escaped Dex's mouth. "How can you say such a thing? How do you know how you'll feel when you're married and settled down?"

"I know." Nicki crossed her arms over her chest. As if that weren't body language enough to shut him down, she turned her head toward the window.

There was a story buried deep inside somewhere, but given Nicki's mood, now didn't seem the best time to question her. In fact, she didn't say another word the entire ride home.

Except to ask that he drop her off at her apartment. Alone.

Chapter Eight

"Thank God you were able to meet me." Nicki slid into the booth at The Continental across from Alyssa, edgy and unnerved.

Alyssa, the most irreverent of her Sworn Sisters, had recently broken off her engagement with her long-time boyfriend, David, and was discontentedly single again.

"You sounded like you needed an in-person visit. And I don't have to work at the hospital tomorrow since I'm on weekend duty. You are giving me the spare bedroom, right?"

"Anything you want."

Alyssa had traveled an hour from Lawrenceville to support Nicki despite her penchant to stay within a ten-mile radius of her residence. It was Thursday night, and Nicki hadn't heard from Dex since he dropped her off on Sunday. Of course, she hadn't called him either.

They ordered drinks, then Nicki dove right into it, unable to stop herself. "I met the most fabulous guy on the cruise I was on in January. His name is Dex. Everything was perfect. We were so in sync. Especially in bed."

"Now, that's what I like to hear. Feel free to share details." Alyssa raised her brows, punctuating her request.

Nicki chuckled. Her high school friends were the

best. Within seconds of meeting, she was already laughing. The perfect medicine for angst.

But she sobered quickly, returning to her dilemma. "We have a major problem." Nicki's stomach plummeted at their divergent life plans. "He likes kids."

Alyssa looked at her as if she had two heads. "Most people like kids, Nicki. So what?"

"Not 'so what.' He's going to want kids. Maybe an entire household full of them. He has such a big heart. You should have seen him with his niece and nephew. He was a natural with them. And he has a Little Brother. Not a real one. He volunteers with Big Brothers."

"How is that a problem? I don't get it."

Tears stung the back of Nicki's eyes. Yet she rarely cried. This was bad. "We're doomed. I don't want kids."

Alyssa spun her glass a few turns before speaking. "I'm sure being pregnant at eighteen and giving your baby up for adoption had an impact on you, but maybe, if you fall in love with the right guy, you'll change your mind."

There it was. Her life-changing past brought front and center. "There's a big 'if' and 'maybe' in that sentence." And Nicki feared she may have met that guy. "I'm not going to change my mind. I can't. I gave my baby up for adoption. I can't have another child who I decide to keep. It's not fair to him. Or her," she amended quickly.

She hadn't told any of her Sworn Sisters the sex of her child. Nor did she disclose the name she had for him. That part was her secret. Her burden.

Alyssa, who was usually so practical and

unemotional, had actual tears in her eyes. "Okay. So you don't ever want to have another child."

Nicki sipped her drink, calling on the alcohol to dull the pain of her past. And her future. "Dex and I had a huge disagreement over children and we've only been dating for a few weeks. What normal, sane guy talks about having kids with a woman he just met?"

"If he's not normal or sane, why are you dating him?"

Leave it to Alyssa to twist her words.

Nicki held back her annoyance. "I'm crazy about him. He's caring. And kind. He's not egotistical. He makes breakfast for me." She paused, musing over his erotic traits. "I know. This is bad." An unwanted tear slid down her cheek.

"Oh, my God, Nicki. Are you in love?"

Nicki wanted to scream her denial, but all she managed was a shrug. "I don't know. But our silence is killing me. I miss him so much. I want to pick up the phone every second of the day and call him."

"Why don't you?"

"This isn't some minor disagreement over what movie he wanted to go see. There's no 'I'm sorry' that will take away the issue. Sure, I can apologize for breaking Chloe's doll or not being the friendliest person to Colin on his birthday. But it won't change our fundamental difference. He loves kids. Wants them when he finds 'the one.' And now I know I can't be the one. Does any of this make sense to you?"

"Who's Chloe and why did you break her doll?" The creases in Alyssa's forehead told Nicki she'd been derailed by her faux pas.

Nicki bit her lip, recalling the disaster. "Dex's

niece. I was trying to fix her doll's leg and it broke off. Dex took care of it."

Alyssa sighed with relief. Jeez, it was only a doll. Hopefully, Alyssa would get back to the important matter at hand.

"Maybe it's your fear of the future getting in the way. Maybe it's too soon to break up over something that isn't on the table right now. As you said, you've only been dating for a few weeks." Alyssa took a swig of her beer. "You're not going to marry the guy tomorrow, thank God."

"Why do you say it like that? You believe in marriage."

"Did. In the past tense. I no longer believe it's in the cards for me. After dating David for ten years and finally getting engaged, his *little indiscretions* have soured me on the whole institution. Thankfully, I learned of them before we tied the knot."

"He was never the right guy for you. I'm glad you finally realized that."

"Why didn't you tell me all those years we were dating?"

"Because you never would have listened, and it probably would have affected our friendship."

Alyssa took another swallow of beer. "True. I don't know how I could have been so blind. I guess I just wanted a wedding—the big beautiful church ceremony with lots of bridesmaids and groomsmen. Me, walking down the aisle in a princess ball gown, looking stunning. David gazing at me with love in his eyes as my father put my hand in his." She sighed. "And then the party. With hundreds of people there to celebrate with us. Dancing the night away, giving us kisses and well wishes."

"Once that day was over, then what? Back to reality where the two of you would have continued to work different shifts and rarely have a night out together. As I recall, you used to say that David was no fun." How Alyssa stayed with him for ten years was a mystery.

"Well, I've moved on and even found someone else to have fun with."

"Really? You have a new boyfriend?"

"No. Not technically." Her sideways glance and Mona Lisa smile told Nicki she had a mysterious secret.

Nicki swatted her with her napkin. "All of a sudden you decide to be coy? Spill the beans. I've been pouring my guts out to you. It's your turn."

"I'm not sure you'll understand. You might hate me." Alyssa's demure playfulness suddenly vanished and her manner became solemn.

Nicki placed her hand on Alyssa's wrist and looked directly into her eyes. "We've been friends since ninth grade. There's nothing you could do to make me hate you. So let's have it. What's your deep, dark secret?"

Alyssa stared out the window toward the street, as if weighing her words. Finally, she turned back to Nicki. "Okay. If I tell you, you have to promise not to judge me."

"I promise."

"I'm having an affair with one of the ER docs."

Alyssa blurted it out so quickly, Nicki wasn't sure she heard her correctly. "What do you mean by affair? You're single, eligible…oh, no. He's not."

"Which is perfect for me. No ties. No drama. I'm having a blast." She made it sound like she had embarked on a thrilling new hobby, like hang-gliding or surfing. "It's so playful and erotic. I can't believe an affair can be so arousing. I get wet just thinking about him."

"Alyssa!" Nicki laughed at her friend's description, despite the seriousness of the matter at hand. "So tell me. Who is this doctor who has you so excited?"

Alyssa stole a glance at Nicki, presumably to see if she was condemning her. A smile crept over her face. "His name is Cole. He started in the ER last year, but it wasn't until three months ago when we hooked up."

"And?" Nicki wanted to hear it all, although it was a bit like watching a train wreck, knowing you should turn away but unable to move.

"He lives in the area, married for five years, two kids." Alyssa kept her eyes on the table as she recited his major flaws.

"How'd you get together?"

"We were both working the night shift. It was quiet, and he said he was going to one of the rooms to catch some Zs. I was in a frisky mood, I guess, and said something to the effect I could think of better things to do. I really meant there were charts to update and meds to order, but I knew he would take it the other way."

"You didn't!" Nicki's eyes opened wider. Alyssa had always been extremely comfortable with the opposite sex, but more like a sister than a siren. Nicki wouldn't have expected her to be such a flirt.

"I did. And he called me on it. He winked and said, 'Come with me, Nurse Beckman. I could use some help down the hall.' I followed him into his room, and as soon as I was over the threshold he closed the door and gave me a kiss that knocked my shoes off. Within minutes, he had the front of my uniform unbuttoned and his hands all over me. I reciprocated of course. His pants were unzipped before we moved away from the door. I was so turned on, he had to hold his hand over my mouth to keep me quiet."

"You've been doing this for three months?" Even Alyssa, who was only having an affair, managed to make it longer than most of Nicki's relationships.

"Absolutely. I can't wait to go to work these days. The planning all night for the right moment; the game of not getting caught. It's a real adrenaline rush when we finally come together."

"Does anyone know what you two are doing?" Nicki assumed there must be rules against work colleagues hooking up, and her job could be in jeopardy.

"Some of the other nurses know, but they're too polite to say anything. At least to my face. And it doesn't happen every night we work together. Some nights are so busy in the ER it's impossible to steal a kiss. But the anticipation is like a drug. I'm addicted."

Nicki totally understood at least some of what Alyssa was experiencing. She felt the same way about Dex. Although they weren't breaking any marriage vows or employment rules.

Nicki was careful with her next question. "Why do you think you're so into it?"

"Because it's different. Cole can't hurt me since he's not mine and I'm not his. And it's kind of naughty." The grin on her mouth and the sparkle in her eyes told Nicki she liked being bad. "We're in this conspiracy together, and we're so in sync. We plot and plan and speak in code. I've learned what a certain look or gesture means, and Cole knows mine. It's this powerful, exhilarating game that only we can play."

"What happens if he gets tired of the whole game?" Nicki didn't want her friend to get hurt, despite claims that she wouldn't.

"Don't be such a downer, Nick." Alyssa's curtness came with a quick smile. "I'm having fun. It's not like I'm in love with him or anything. It's just sex. Head-spinning, mind-blowing sex." A sly smile inched over her mouth.

"What about Cole's wife? Aren't you worried she'll find out?"

Nicki's unending questions were meant to show her friend the potential hazards of dating—no, having sex—with a married man, but Alyssa wasn't catching on; nor did she seem fazed that her life as she knew it could detonate, hurting not only her but innocent bystanders. As a matter of fact, she looked amazingly happy in her naivete.

"She has called him at the hospital after we've disappeared into his room. But the desk nurse takes a message. She's very efficient." Alyssa grinned before adding, "So is Cole. Yesterday, he pulled me into the linen closet. It had about four feet of space and was pitch black. He kissed me. One of those deep tongue kisses that suck the air right out of your lungs. Within minutes, I had an orgasm, without him so much as unzipping his fly. And when he finally did, I was more than ready for him. As a matter of fact, I'm ready for him now." She shifted in her seat.

Nicki knew exactly how she felt. She'd like nothing better than to stop by Dex's apartment, strip them both of their clothes, and do it on the living room floor or couch or table. But Dex wasn't married. "I hope you know what you're doing," she said, sounding not only ineffectual but foolish. "I'd hate to see you suffer again, even though you claim you're just playing."

"Don't worry. I won't. My eyes are wide open. But back to you. I didn't come all the way to Philly to talk about me."

Nicki put her head in her hands. "How would you deal with this kid thing?"

"You seem to be into this guy. It's a new relationship. It may work out, it may not. Time will tell. So stop worrying about this issue now. If the two of you, by some fluke of fate, end up together, either of you may feel differently about children in the future. Why not enjoy the ride until you fall off the rails? You'd be a fool to give up great sex because you're so focused on his liking kids. What is your problem?"

Nicki had to laugh. "When you put it that way, it makes total sense."

"Of course it does."

But it wasn't only great sex she had with Dex. She may be falling in love. Although she'd never admit it out loud. She had a hard time even letting it echo around in her own head. She didn't do love. Her parents had the most incredible, loving relationship, and when her dad died, her mother fell apart. That was not going to happen to her. She was much better off spending time with the guy of the month on her own terms, when she wanted, where she wanted. How had Dex changed her view on this?

She couldn't let him.

Alyssa was right. She needed to stop fretting and

enjoy the ride for as long as it lasted.

Nicki and Alyssa spent the rest of the night catching up on their jobs and their other friends' lives. The pain, so evident in Nicki's mind hours before, had been brushed away by Alyssa's simple common sense and irreverent attitude toward relationships, sex, and marriage. Philosophically, Nicki was right there with her.

Girlfriends were the best.

****

Dex walked over to the bar at the Ritz Carlton after work on Friday. He had sent Nicki an email that afternoon asking her to meet him at seven. She responded affirmatively, but he had no idea what mood she'd be in. Or if she would back out at the last minute. They hadn't talked since Sunday.

His plan had been to give her some space. She was fiercely independent and clearly felt backed into a corner by his conversation. He could only hope five days would be enough to mellow her out.

He sat on a bar stool and ordered a vodka martini, allowing the pressure of the work week to fall away, despite checking email. Unfortunately, the stress over Nicki couldn't be resolved until he saw her tonight. If he saw her tonight.

At seven-thirty, he contemplated leaving. Until her voice enveloped him from behind.

"I'm sorry I'm late. I sent you a text. Did you get it?" She removed her coat without looking at him and sat on the stool beside his.

"No. I guess it didn't come through." He slid his phone into his suit jacket pocket. "I'm glad you made it."

Although his words were formal, as were hers, some of the angst melted away by her presence.

When the bartender came over, she ordered a coke.

He arched his brow. "You either had a difficult week at work or an easy one which doesn't require alcohol."

She laughed, and that melodic sound sang straight to his heart. "I had a few too many last night. My friend Alyssa was in town. The night got away from us."

He clinked his almost empty glass against hers. "To the end of a long week." At least it had been for him. He worked every night until at least nine thirty, guaranteeing he wouldn't pick up the phone and invite her over.

"Cheers. It was definitely a long week."

But she gave no clue as to whether its length had anything to do with missing him.

"How's the Perry Adams launch going?"

Surprise widened her eyes at his interest. "Good. His new CD is coming out next month, and the US tour is starting in May. I have a lot to do before then, but my team is on track." She put a straw in her soda and took a sip. "Are you finished testifying in the divorce case?"

"Yes, thankfully. Now I can get back to my other clients."

"How'd it go?"

"Good. Held up on cross-examination. That's the biggest worry."

"I'm sure you were magnificent." She touched his hand and warmth spread through him. "Is the trial over?"

"Yes. The judge will have a decision within a month."

Should they continue talking about work or move onto more personal subjects? Without going into dangerous territory, of course.

While he contemplated his strategy, Nicki took charge. "Thanks for reaching out to me today. I was planning on calling you this afternoon. I hope we can put our disagreement from last weekend behind us. It's too soon in our relationship to talk about what the future may bring."

Her lips were so distracting, causing that familiar pull in his groin anytime she was near. "You're right." The rest of his anxiety slid off his shoulders. "Things went downhill at my sister's. Maybe we should concentrate on us for the time being."

He'd castigated himself the entire week for pushing the subject. As soon as he realized Nicki was uncomfortable with children, he should have let it go. They had plenty of time to see where things would go with them.

A brilliant smile broke over Nicki's mouth. Beautiful and delicious. "I'd like nothing more. This week was tough without you. I had to go running to relieve some of my stress. I would have much preferred to release it with you. In bed."

He swallowed hard. They needed food and fast.

For he had plans for them tonight that required massive amounts of calories.

Chapter Nine

The next few weekends passed in a romantic haze. As became typical of their time together, they strolled through different areas of the city, dined at the newest restaurants, and indulged in Nicki's favorite pastime with Dex—romantic, erotic sex. Sunday night came far too soon, and the ache in Nicki's heart throbbed as she braced herself to say goodbye. At least until their schedules allowed another interlude.

"I hate Sunday nights." Nicki rose from the couch where she'd been cocooned next to Dex watching a movie. She stretched her arms over her head and twisted her torso to get the blood flowing.

Dex's eyes grew dark. "If you don't pull your shirt down to cover that sexy midriff, I'm not going to be responsible for my actions."

Nicki quickly put her arms down and laughed. "The smallest movements turn you on. I like that." She went into the kitchen. "Do you want anything? Water, juice, wine?"

He followed her. "No. I have to get going. Busy day tomorrow."

Nicki glanced at the clock. "It's only eight thirty." She didn't want him to leave. Not now. Not ever. The realization kicked her in the gut, and she turned away from him to assure he didn't see it written all over her face.

"Are you okay?" His voice was gentle, caressing.

"Fine." Grabbing a glass, she turned on the spigot and drank some water, hoping to wash away this crazy sensation of emptiness before he even left.

Dex came up behind, placing his hands on her hips, pulling her close. "I'm not." His lips brushed her temple.

She turned in his arms and devoured his mouth in a kiss that told him so much more than mere words.

But then the words slipped out. "I…care about you," she whispered. "Too much."

He stilled, pulling his head back to stare at her.

She felt exposed, naked. Although she didn't say the *L* word that struggled to get out, he must see it in her eyes. She bit her lip to keep tears from springing forth. *Say something.*

She tried to pull away, slip from his grasp, needing air and space to diffuse her humiliation at his silence. But his grip tightened.

"I care about you too, Nicki. I don't understand how I can feel so close to you already. But I do."

Nicki's relief came out in a sigh. "I know what you mean. This is something so new, so unexpected. I usually don't…bond." She stroked his unshaven jaw.

He held her hand against his cheek, then kissed her palm. "When can I see you this week?"

She spun through her mental calendar. "Wednesday might work. I have meetings Monday and Tuesday nights. And I have a work event in New York City next weekend, so I won't be around." An unfamiliar melancholy spread through her system.

"Wednesday won't work. I have a committee meeting for Big Brothers Big Sisters." Disappointment creased his forehead.

"What committee?"

"The Big/Little Race. I took your advice."

A smile hijacked her mouth. "You didn't tell me you were doing that."

"I like to keep you guessing."

"That you do, very well." She zeroed in on his eyes. "Do you need any help?"

"You said you wouldn't be on the committee."

"I'm not offering to be. I'm the idea person, remember?"

He nodded and pulled her into a hug. "It was a great idea. I have a fabulous committee so far, made up of colleagues as well as students from Drexel and Penn. We can use your help with marketing the event. I'll let you know when we have more information. We're in the beginning stages."

"When's the race?"

"June. Perhaps you'd like to put together a team and help raise some money."

Nicki laughed as her heart expanded threefold. "You're a great guy. And a good ambassador. I'll see what I can do."

"How about Thursday night?" Dex looked hopeful, but all Nicki could think was it was four days away.

"Good." Would she make it through the next ninety hours without feeding her addiction?

He broke into her thoughts. "What's the event next weekend?"

"It's for Perry Adams. The launch party for his new record is in New York City. We originally contemplated Nashville, but we're hopeful some of his songs will cross over and hit the pop chart. So the city it is."

"I'm available next weekend. Would you like company?"

Up until now, neither of them crossed the line into each other's business dealings. She studied Dex's face to see if he were serious.

"I'd be working a big part of the night. I have to network with Perry's agents and managers as well as the execs at my company."

His offer to accompany her settled in and became an intriguing possibility. Yet she struggled with it. Bringing Dex into her business world was a big deal. She'd be introducing him to her bosses as well as her clients. It meant something to her—to acknowledge Dex as her significant other. Was she ready for this step? Was he?

"That's fine if you don't want me to come." Dex's regret lay just below the surface. "I erroneously thought we might be able to turn your work weekend into a little getaway."

"It's not that I don't want you there. I worry you'd be bored. If you came to the event, you'd be on your own for several hours."

He took her hands into his and smiled. "I could manage to entertain myself while you're doing your thing. It will be interesting to experience your world."

The anxiety dissipated and she laughed. "Then I would love for you to come with me. To be clear, my world is usually working with my team in the office or doing research on a particular group. These parties aren't a huge percentage of my job description."

"So noted." He smiled and gave her a quick kiss. "What's the plan for Saturday?"

"We should leave Philly around noon. I have a hotel room at the Waldorf, which is where the event is. The business part of the night starts at seven with a cocktail party. There will be dozens of people in attendance who you could talk to while I'm networking and managing the high-maintenance guests. The launch party starts at nine and goes until who knows when. We don't have to stay for the whole thing."

"Do I have to wear cowboy boots and a flannel shirt?" He grinned.

"Please don't. A suit would work better." Her smile couldn't be contained. "This will be a first for me. I've never brought a date to a business affair." Yet it felt so good to break that habit.

"I like being first." He kissed her on the nose. "See you Thursday. And Saturday."

At least the melancholy over Dex leaving her on a Sunday evening was buoyed by the tiniest raft that would carry her through the week.

****

Saturday night finally arrived, and Nicki's nerves stretched to their limit. When they arrived at the Waldorf that afternoon, they went straight to the spa for a massage, with Nicki trying to hold onto the calmness for the next few hours. Preoccupied with getting ready for the night to come, she barely noticed Dex flipping through television stations with the remote, no doubt searching for something sports-related.

The edgiest outfit she owned was a tricolor leather minidress with geometric designs. Even though the strappy heels she'd bought to go with it would not be her friends tonight, she ignored the notion and slipped her feet into them.

"Wow." Dex eyed her from the mirror while he knotted his tie.

"Wow, yourself."

Dex looked devastatingly handsome in a black designer suit. He must have his suits tailored, because they all fit him to perfection.

Coming over to her, he gave her a safe kiss on the cheek. "You look amazing. I'm going to have to stake my claim to you early so those country guys don't think you're fair game."

Nicki smiled at his possessive statement. "Since when are you the jealous type?"

"Since right now. Looking at you in that dress makes me think of whips and chains. Very hot."

She picked up her clutch, then took his hand. "Let's go. I need to get the first part of this evening over with."

"Are you nervous?"

She nodded as he pulled the door closed.

"I've never seen you like this. But as they say, adrenaline is good. It will keep you sharp and focused."

They found their way to the small ballroom, where Nicki introduced Dex to a few of the executives at her company. Then she excused herself to do her thing—schmoozing with the band's agents, the tour sponsors, and the band members themselves, including Perry Adams.

Once in work mode, the nervousness disappeared, and she moved from contact to contact with efficient ease. She spent the required amount of time with each, either talking about the general marketing plan, the tour promotion, or how wonderful the band was, depending upon her audience. She drank water instead of wine and refused the *hors d'oeuvres*, unable to eat and talk, and definitely not wanting any green bits between her teeth.

Whenever possible, Nicki scanned the crowd for Dex. Of course, he was fine, moving around the room and engaging in conversations with whomever. But every time she spotted him, her heart thrummed to a beat of its own. He was so cool, so charismatic.

And so damn nice to offer to come with her this weekend. Although taken aback at first, once she warmed up to the idea, she was thrilled to have him accompany her. They were a real couple, sharing up and down time. The way it should be in a relationship.

She caught his eye at one point and blew him a kiss before embarking on a new conversation. He sent her a wink and she melted. Was she in high school?

For another hour she cruised and networked, then it was time to move to the grand ballroom for the main party. Nicki's feet were on fire, and more than once she fantasized about taking off her shoes and walking around barefoot.

She sidled up to Dex. "Do you have a date?"

"I've heard that line several times tonight. You're going to have to come up with something more original, Miss—?"

"Ms. Reading is the name. I'm in charge of this party. So you may want to remember that name for future reference. And exactly how many times have you been propositioned tonight, Mister—?"

"Hanover. But you may call me Dex." The sides of his lips inched up in a delicious semi-smile. "Three, four. It's not important. I only had my eye on one woman this entire night."

Nicki arched her brow. "And what woman was

that, Dex?"

"You. That dress. Those legs. I'm mesmerized."

Nicki beamed from within. "Good. Would you mind buying me a drink at the bar in the lobby? I need to sit for a few minutes before entering the fray in the main ballroom."

"I was hoping I could convince you to forgo the main event and accompany me to our room for our own private party."

"You can convince me. But not yet. I have to make an appearance."

"In that case, let's go get you a drink."

****

Dex ordered a club soda and a vodka and cranberry for Nicki, happy to have her to himself for a few minutes. The past two hours were interesting, but he would have rather been at Nicki's side than across the room making small talk with music people.

Nicki slid onto the stool and crossed her legs, her short dress rising to mid-thigh. His mouth went dry. Knowing it would be another hour or two before he could have her all to himself, he unglued his gaze from her legs.

"My feet are killing me. I'd love to take these heels off, but I may not get them back on."

"Perhaps the vodka will dull the pain." He clinked her glass with his. "Here's to a successful party. You've done an amazing job pulling it all together, and everyone was having a fabulous time at the private reception."

Her smile dazzled. "Thanks. I appreciate your compliment. But you are a biased reviewer."

"True. But I'm also an accountant. I call things the

way I see them."

"Yes, I keep forgetting you're a boring numbers person."

"Boring, huh? I don't recall you yawning the last time we consulted in bed."

"Hmmm. I may need a refresher." Her sultry laugh surrounded him, and he wanted nothing more than to remind her of how combustible their coupling could be.

"You're in charge tonight, Ms. Reading. Tell me the time. I know the place. I intend to impress you with a demonstration of sensory enlightenment principles followed by an advanced course in direct labor efficiency—to test your break-even point." He smirked. "Or perhaps I mean your breaking point."

"*Oooohhh*. I can't wait." Her crystal blue eyes flashed with a mixture of playfulness and need.

"Me neither. So drink up. Let's get the next phase of your required participation out of the way."

They finished their drinks, and Nicki led Dex to the ballroom where the real party was beginning. A DJ spun dance music at a noise level rivaling the sound barrier, although everyone was still talking. The spirit was infectious. This time Nicki didn't go off on her own to network. She held Dex's hand and introduced him to the powers that be at her company.

One of the execs grabbed her arm and shouted, "It won't be long until you'll be joining us in New York."

Dex's shoulders tensed as Nicki's glance slid over to him then returned to the speaker.

"Thanks for your confidence in my talents, Richard."

What kind of answer was that? Dex forced down his concern.

"Keep doing what you're doing. We're noticing your hard work." Richard's words had that controlling tone, where anyone listening would think what he said was gospel.

Nicki smiled, and as if waving his comment off as chitchat, turned to greet another colleague. She was clearly in her element taking charge of introductions, not only for Dex's sake, but for others whom she deemed needed a connection. Her memory of faces, names, and affiliations was impressive, and she worked the room like a pro. So much for the fun part of the night.

Close to midnight, Nicki whispered in Dex's ear. "Let's go."

Finally. Pure desire buzzed through him as they wound their way through a myriad of hallways to get to their destination.

The second they got to their room, Nicki slipped off her heels and practically purred.

"Come here." Dex pulled her to the couch and invited her to sit.

Gorgeous but wary eyes followed him as he removed his jacket, unleashed his tie, and rolled up his shirt sleeves. Then he knelt on the floor in front of her, took one foot in his hands, and massaged it. Her toes were painted a bright pink and looked very appealing at the end of her endless legs. Nicki leaned her head back, closed her eyes, and moaned.

"Would you like to amend your statement about my being boring?"

Her eyes flew open. "I didn't mean you were personally boring."

"I do believe you implied such a slur. However, I

take no offense. So relax."

He continued his assault on one foot, then the other, delighting in Nicki's pleasurable sounds. When she appeared to be totally relaxed, he moved his hands up to her calves and kneaded them before inching up to her thighs. Slowly, he edged under her dress, teasing with trailing fingers, as taut muscles jumped at his intrusion. Nicki's breathing quickened and her lips parted, signaling her shift from relaxation mode to a heightened sense of sexual need.

"Take me to bed," she pleaded, her voice low and husky as she squirmed under his hands.

"My pleasure."

Taking her hands in his, he pulled her up from the sofa and turned her around. Unzipping her dress, he let it fall to the floor. A deep purple lacy bra and panties sent his heart racing.

"Nice," he managed, as he unbuttoned his shirt and removed it.

"I agree." Nicki's eyes wandered over his chest. "Keep going, please."

Her tongue moistened her top lip, and he moved in to capture it with his mouth. He deepened the kiss, mating his tongue with hers, as his hands smoothed over silky shoulders, toned arms, and magnificent breasts. He slipped one strap down and uncovered her nipple, stroking it first with his thumb, then with his tongue. Her groan went straight to his shaft, and he pressed against the V of her legs as his mouth roamed and his hands strayed.

He guided her over to the bed and hastily pulled down the covers so she could lie before him, a feast he was desperate to consume. Her blue eyes darkened, as if a storm brewed under her surface. He removed the rest of his clothes and hers, unable to break from that mesmerizing gaze filled with desire, which pulled at him like a magnet.

Dex joined her with a hot kiss before pulling away. He stroked her face with his fingers, then his knuckles, before trailing a path down her neck to her breasts. Nicki's eyes closed with pleasure and her body arched, begging for his touch.

"Open your eyes," he said.

Her lids flew open in surprise.

"I want to see how I make you feel."

He pulled on her nipple, and her lips parted with a soft gasp. He continued to fondle her as she squirmed. Taking her arm, he raised it above her head, placing her fingers around one of the rungs of the headboard. Then he took her other arm and did the same.

"Keep them there."

He tracked his fingers along the insides of her arms, and gooseflesh appeared as Nicki laughed. "That tickles." Her eyes sparkled with playfulness.

Dex then splayed his hand over her flat belly, gliding from one hip to the other then back, each time moving lower. All glee left Nicki's eyes as need replaced it. She bit her bottom lip and her pelvis inched off the bed.

He watched her face intently as his hand dipped between her legs, teasing her delicate folds. Her lids lowered, but she kept her eyes trained on his. Waiting. Wanting.

She writhed under his massage, pushing into his hand, begging with her eyes for more. He slid his finger inside her, then two, and her groan nearly unmanned him.

"Please," she whispered.

"Please, what?"

"Come inside of me. I need you."

And he needed her.

Without breaking eye contact, he knelt between her legs, holding himself up on his arms. He entered her slowly, deliberately, stroking her walls as the passion, the pleasure, the desire played out in her pupils, her irises. Her beautiful, beautiful eyes.

She released her hands from the invisible bonds and touched his face, his shoulders, his chest, as her lower body came up to meet him with every thrust.

But never once did she close her eyes.

Chapter Ten

The next morning, they made love again as the bright sunshine of the day peeked through the side of the shade. Nicki played with the hairs on Dex's chest, her head on his shoulder. He should be sated and content.

Instead, bleak theories invaded his mind. What if Nicki transferred to New York? Of course, it was only ninety minutes from Philadelphia, but keeping a relationship going on weekends, and probably not every weekend due to work commitments, was not something he relished. He wanted more time with her, not less. If Nicki stayed in Philadelphia, there was no telling where their relationship would take them. But she was a powerful player in the music industry, and he feared the high she got from that could only be bolstered by being in the center of power. And New York City was that center.

"Where are you?" Nicki asked, her hand lazily drifting to his arm.

"Right here with you."

"You seem far away. Is everything okay?"

He pulled her tighter into his arms. "Good. You must be ecstatic about the way things turned out last night. It was a great party, and everyone had a really good time."

Her smile lit up the room. "I am happy. It was very

successful. And I got a lot of compliments from the execs in our main office."

His heart sank at her excitement over the conversation from the night before.

"Who is that guy, Richard?"

"He's the CEO of the company."

Much worse than he thought. "He wants you to join him in New York." He attempted to pull the gloom out of his tone. "Is that what you want?"

"Oh, I don't know. There's still room for me to move up in our Philadelphia office. My boss, Kurt, told me I'm going to be promoted soon, but that won't change my location. I love Philly. And I'm also dating a really great guy who lives nearby." Her eyes sparkled and she grazed his lips with hers. "I couldn't be in a better place."

Not a resounding "No," but at least she acknowledged him as a consideration. He breathed a little easier along with an admonishment to relax. But still nagging at him was the unknown of their future. Unfortunately, it streamed from his pores.

"Is there something at work preoccupying you?" She smoothed his forehead, and he wished that's all it would take to rid himself of the troublesome impression.

Exhaling, he pulled the sheet aside and got out of bed. "No. But maybe we should check out and get on the road. I do have a busy week coming up." It wasn't a lie. Just avoidance of what truly ate away at him. And maybe a little self-preservation instinct warning him to keep a modicum of distance between them.

"Okay." Disappointment marred her beautiful face. Even he was frustrated with himself over how fast he had turned their morning of passion into the reality of the day.

They showered, dressed, and packed their overnight bags, stopping for coffee and bagels before hitting the road.

"Thanks for coming with me this weekend. It was so nice to have you by my side. I know the first part of the night I deserted you, but the rest was perfect." She reached over and rubbed his thigh. "Especially once we got back to the room."

Desire flamed within at the idea of Nicki squirming under his ministrations. "Perhaps we shouldn't talk about that while I'm driving. I may need to pull over at a raunchy motel on the way home and have my way with you again."

Her laugher echoed in the car, and she leaned over and kissed his cheek. "I'd go anywhere with you."

He grabbed her hand and brought it up to his lips, kissing her knuckles. The words "I love you" were so close to the surface he kept her hand glued to his lips for a few moments to prevent them from escaping.

When he finally released her, he took a different direction. "We both work such long hours. It's hard to find time to spend together. We should plan a vacation."

"Oh. Do we dare? What if you go off and find someone else to replace me?" She was obviously joking, but there was a trace of caution in her statement.

He glanced at her and saw the hint of a smile. "There is no chance of that happening. I could say the same of you."

"I am sure I wouldn't take my eyes off you."

Her sincerity warmed his heart, maybe even

squeezed it. Mentally running through his calendar, he settled on a time frame. "I can't go anywhere until the summer. Too busy. What about July?"

"I can do July. It gives me enough time to plan around the week we choose. Where should we go?"

Anytime they spoke of the future it gave him hope. "What's your pleasure?"

"Given the time of year, shall we head north? Maine, Canada. Not too far away. Where we can either drive or get there with one flight."

"What about Quebec?"

"I've always wanted to go there," she squealed. "Let's do it."

Four months away. Too long, but no other options. They had four months to take their relationship to the next level. And plan for an entire week, maybe ten days, together. Without careers interfering.

The anticipation, which some would say is the best part, would surely kill him.

****

Dex pulled up in front of Nicki's apartment instead of heading for the garage around the corner.

"What are you doing?" asked Nicki. "It's only two thirty." She reached for his hand as if to pull him from the car. "We rarely see each other during the week. Let's not cut our weekend short. Come on up."

His odd mood, at times causing him to disengage from her, was interfering with their last few hours of the weekend together.

Nicki leaned over and kissed his mouth. "If you leave, how are you going to collect on the foot massage I owe you?" She ran her hand up his thigh and he stirred. "Come on. This weekend is not over."

He grabbed her hand to stop her from inching higher. "When you put it like that, how can I refuse?"

Nicki smiled and continued her sexually charged remarks until she had him in her apartment—exactly where he wanted to be. Men could be so stupid sometimes. He'd been ready to leave Nicki in the middle of the day, because he was sulking over her move to New York when she hadn't even been offered it—yet. And they would have missed spending the rest of the day together, doing precisely what he wanted to be doing with her, because of that stupidity.

As soon as they crossed the threshold, Nicki tossed her overnight bag and purse onto the couch and moved into his space. Playful hands fluttered over his chest as serious, blue eyes locked on his.

"I missed you today. You've been distracted," she purred, her voice encircling him with lust.

Refusing to acknowledge his idiocy, he pulled her closer, engulfing her lips with his; thirsty for her, hungry for her.

Nicki responded with her own need, deepening their kiss as she pressed the length of her body against his.

Her kisses were lethal, dragging him into a sexual haze of need and desire only she could elicit with such depth. "Let's go to bed," she whispered against his ear, sending fireworks to his private parts. "Unless you'd rather play in the kitchen."

A vision of Nicki sitting at his table not long ago, wearing his robe, which lay open as he poured maple syrup over her beautiful breasts, had him panting. "No time for that," he growled as he pulled her into her room and accosted her mouth with his.

Struggling to rid Nicki of her sweater and slacks, he worked on his own at the same time—not the most efficient use of clumsy hands, but practicality could not break through his dogged determination. The end goal was in sight.

A warm chuckle escaped Nicki's lips at his inept attempt to strip them both at the same time. "Can I help?"

Only then did Dex realize the zipper on his trousers, which he furiously tugged at, was stuck. A groan reverberated in his throat. "Be my guest." He held his hands up in surrender as Nicki's fingers tortured his straining penis while she worked to ease down the metal hasp.

"Just needed a little patience," she preened, shedding the rest of his clothing.

There was no use in responding, since lack of patience in getting Nicki naked and into bed was his main objective.

Dex pulled her onto the bed with him, then covered her body with his as he ground against the juncture of her legs, teasing the sensitive part of her neck with his tongue. Nicki arched her back and spread her legs, giving him more access to her erogenous zones. Soft moans fueled his fire, and he plunged deep into her core as his own groan reverberated around the room.

In an attempt to slow down this exquisite ecstasy, he pulled out slowly, connecting with Nicki's shining eyes. He watched her lids shutter closed as he inched back into her hot center, before picking up the pace. Manicured nails dug into his shoulders as her walls tightened around him, clenching and releasing as her orgasm rocked through her. Within seconds he rocked it right back.

****

They spent the rest of the day and evening lounging in her bed, then the living room, eating delivered pizza and drinking champagne. A perfect match.

Easing off the floor, Nicki brought their paper plates and napkins into the kitchen for disposal as Dex followed with empty flutes and a near empty bottle.

"I hate to end this day, this weekend, but I need to go." Dex placed the glasses in the sink. Nicki's disappointment was mirrored in Dex's eyes.

"I wish we could spend every night together." Had those words escaped her mouth? She had never wanted to give up her freedom, her independence. But Dex held her heart in his hand.

"We can, you know." He placed her palm against his chest. His heart beat strong and clear. "And I don't mean just living together. I want to marry you. I want us to be together forever."

"What?" Had she heard him right? "Really?"

A broad smile took over his mouth. "Really. I adore you, Nicki, and I want us to be together. Permanently."

Pure joy raced through her being trailed by glitter and sparkles and fireworks. She shook her head. "I can't believe I'm saying this, but I want that too."

The muscles in his jaw tightened. "With marriage comes a family, Nicki. Children. Not right away, but in the future."

A bucket of ice water crashed over her happiness. "Is the promise of children a requirement?" Her voice was hoarse, choked.

"Yes."

All light left her body, and imaginary sandbags weighed heavily around her neck, cutting off oxygen. She needed to breathe. With effort, she said, "I have to sit down."

He guided her back into the living room and sat next to her on the couch. Concern etched his eyes. "Nicki, I know you're not a kid person, as you call it, but don't you think you'll view this differently if you have your own? You're such a warm, caring person. You'd make a wonderful mother."

"Can't you be happy with just me?" Hurt wound around her heart.

He stroked her shoulders. "I adore you. You do make me happy. But kids add another dimension." He sighed. "I don't understand your strong aversion. Is there something else driving this? Is there something I should know?"

She nodded. "I'm a terrible mother." She had to tell him the truth. Maybe he would then see what she saw. What she knew. "I had a baby when I was eighteen. Right out of high school. I gave him up for adoption." Tears poured down her face. "I didn't even look at him when he arrived. The doctor tried to give him to me to hold. I turned my head so I couldn't see him. I asked her to take him away." Choking sobs escaped her throat.

She hadn't told anyone this. Her best friends knew she gave her child up for adoption, but she never told them about his birth. They didn't ask questions, because it upset Nicki. Her refusal to hug and comfort her newborn was her dark secret. It made her cold and heartless. Sharing her story with anyone would make them dislike her immensely. Sharing it right now with Dex would make him hate her.

Nicki stood, her goal to get some tissues, but more importantly to get away from Dex who looked shell-shocked.

After she wiped her face and blew her nose, she returned, folding into the chair adjacent to the couch. She waited for him to speak.

"I'm so sorry, Nicki. That must have been hard on you." His voice surrounded her with compassion. "But it was a long time ago. Your son is being raised by adoptive parents who love him. You did what you had to do back then."

All true. But it turned her from the warm, caring woman Dex believed her to be into a cold, horrible person. No reason to point out her flaws, but he surely saw them and would draw his own similar conclusions.

Dex came over to her chair and knelt on the floor in front of her. "People change. You've changed since you were eighteen. You shouldn't let guilt over your actions back then affect your life going forward." He took her hand in his, so warm and comforting. "I love you, Nicki. I want to get married and have a family. I've always wanted four kids." He chuckled. "I'd settle for three, maybe two." His eyes grew serious. "I can't settle for none."

So this was it. The ultimatum.

She could be ecstatically happy with Dex, but only if she agreed to have children. It might seem a simple decision to him, and one she should say yes to, but she vowed to herself and to the son she refused to hold that she would never have another child. It wouldn't be fair to give one up and keep another. To love one and not the other.

With sadness so deep she thought she'd die, Nicki gave Dex her answer. "I can't do it." A tear escaped and slid down her face. "I guess we found our fatal flaw."

Chapter Eleven

"I'm an idiot." Dex stood at his sister's front door on Monday morning, the weight of his and Nicki's parting words pressuring his chest. He rubbed it, trying to dislodge the tight band.

"Come on in." Janice's forehead scrunched in confusion. "What's going on?"

"Are you alone?" Dex followed her into the kitchen.

"Chloe's at school, Colin's at day care, and Frank is working. I'm going to the office at noon." She stopped and placed her hand on his arm. "You're scaring me. Speak."

"Nicki and I broke up." Saying the words out loud tore at his insides.

Janice's face softened. "I'm sorry, Dex. What happened?"

Dex sank onto the bar stool at the counter and stared at the veins crisscrossing the marble top.

"I pushed things too fast. I was afraid of losing her so I asked her to marry me."

Janice stood across the counter, her eyes nearly popping out of her head before valiantly erasing the shock from her face. He had rendered her speechless.

"I know it was quick. We met in January on a cruise of all places. But Nicki got to me." He shook his head, wanting to deny the truth of his confession.

"She's so upbeat and full of life. She makes me happy. And she's brilliant at work, a top-notch marketing expert. When I told her I had a Little Brother but I wasn't making enough of a difference, she honed in on the bigger picture. How I could help make a real difference by bringing in money through a fundraiser. When she presents something, her enthusiasm is catchy. I couldn't not do it. Because of her excitement, I'm chairing a run in June for Big Brothers Big Sisters at Fairmount Park. She helped me with the planning, from getting a great committee together to marketing and advertising." He looked up at his sister, giving her a chance to weigh in, to help him through this dilemma.

"I…I only met her once." Janice's eyes narrowed as if trying to conjure up something nice to say about Nicki. "It was impossible to get to know her. The kids were running around, and guests from Colin's party were still here. I spent most of the time in the kitchen cleaning up."

"I know she didn't make the best of impressions. She was so uncomfortable with the kids, and Chloe had a little temper tantrum when her doll broke, blaming it on Nicki."

A short laugh escaped Janice's mouth. "Nicki couldn't wait to leave. I do remember that."

"It was a tough ride home. We barely spoke. I learned that kids were not on Nicki's list of favorite people to hang out with. It was disappointing, but I assumed she'd overcome it. We decided to spend our time getting to know each other before bringing our families or friends any further into the mix." Dex inhaled and let it out slowly. "Our time together has been amazing. We love doing the same things.

Checking out different areas of the city, trying different types of food at ethnic restaurants, going to museums." *Making wild, passionate love.* The band tightened around his chest.

"Why don't you just continue dating? Why talk about marriage?"

"As I said when I walked in, I'm an idiot. We went to New York City this past weekend for a party her company was putting on for one of their artists. Nicki's a music exec, in charge of marketing and PR for several bands. She ran the event at the Waldorf, and the CEO was extremely impressed with her. Since the main office is in New York, my worry that she might take a job there trumped my common sense. I didn't want to lose her." He hung his head. "But I did just that."

"I still don't get it. Take your proposal back. Tell her you jumped the gun. That you'll be just as happy continuing to see her without getting married." Janice's frustration with his seemingly dense brain came through loud and clear.

"Nicki was willing to marry me." He rolled his shoulders to open up his lungs, which refused to work. "She doesn't want children." His voice strangled in his throat. "And that's a bullet to the heart of our relationship. I want kids. I want an entire, whole, happy family. I want what we didn't have growing up."

"Oh, Dex." Janice took his hands in hers, tears shining in her eyes. "I didn't realize how much Dad's leaving affected you."

"It didn't affect you?"

"Of course, I was sad he wasn't around when we were young, but I barely thought about it once I got to college. Maybe even in high school. I was more into my girlfriends and parties. And boys. When I married Frank after college, I never once said to myself, 'I finally have a family.' You and Mom were my family. I was fine with the three of us."

"But you have kids. You have what we didn't, growing up."

She chuckled. "I wish I'd waited for a while before getting pregnant. It's not easy. I'm exhausted most of the time trying to keep up with Colin and Chloe, the house, my job. I barely spend any alone time with Frank. If I have a night off, I want to go to bed…and sleep."

"I know it's difficult. But that doesn't mean people shouldn't have kids. Everyone manages. And we would too. Except in Nicki's mind, it's not even a possibility."

Janice seemed to ponder his dilemma for a moment. "Maybe she can't have children. Maybe she has a medical problem preventing her from getting pregnant."

"She didn't say she couldn't get pregnant. What she did say is she had a baby at eighteen, and she gave him up for adoption. That's what's coloring her decision now."

Janice's eyes widened. "That must have been tough. Do you think it's guilt over having given up her child that's preventing her from having any others?"

"I don't know. She didn't say that specifically. She said she'd be a horrible mother. She believes this because she wouldn't hold her child when he was born."

"Clearly, she was afraid of bonding with him, knowing it would be that much harder to give him up. And if you take it a step further, maybe she believes it's unfair to love any future child when she didn't keep and love her first child."

"How do you get that from what I just said?" And he thought he was fairly good at understanding women.

"Because I'm a woman and a mother and I know how I would feel." Janice's eyes shared his pain. "So you each drove your stakes into the ground. Unless one of you changes your mind, there can be no resolution since there's no compromise."

Dex smirked. "Gee, thanks for underscoring the obvious."

"I know you adore Chloe and Colin, and you spend a lot of time with your Little Brother, Kenan. I'm guessing they will never be a substitute for having your own?"

He shook his head. "No. Something about sharing a life and shaping that life on a daily basis is important to me. I want to be there for every stage, whether it's holding their hand to help them walk, or teaching them how to play soccer, or letting them cry on my shoulder when they have their first big disappointment. I have so much to give. I also know what not to do from observing our father."

"You're a fabulous uncle so I know you'll make a fabulous father. With as difficult and tiring as it is to raise kids, I wouldn't trade it for the world, so I totally understand your position." She came around the counter and hugged him. "I hate to see you so miserable over losing Nicki. But you'll find the right woman soon who will want all the same things in life you do."

The only way that would happen was if he could exorcise Nicki from his being, for she had seeped under his skin and into his heart and soul.

****

Nicki roamed her apartment most nights after work, a mean depression forcing her to throw things out, reorganize, stay busy. Anything to keep her mind from the devastating last scene with Dex. There was no use in spending one more second agonizing over it. Nothing she could say or do would resurrect their relationship. She wasn't going to change her mind about kids and neither was he.

This was the exact reason why she didn't want to be in a relationship in the first place. The pain of losing the person you love was unbearable. She'd seen it in her mother's eyes when her father died. In her whole being. Nicki didn't want to be that person—so dependent on a man for her happiness she couldn't live without him.

She sat on the floor in her walk-in closet, discarding shoes she no longer wore. In the back corner was a large brown box, securely closed with masking tape. Pulling the box from its resting place, she dragged it into her bedroom. She knew what was in there. High school mementos. She should have thrown them out years ago, not shoved them in the back of her closet. She fingered the tape, vacillating between tossing the entire box in the dumpster, sending it back to its dark burial, or opening it. Curiosity won out and she ripped the tape off.

Several photo albums sat on top. She leaned against her bed and flipped through. Not all bad memories. She smiled as she turned page after page of her and her Sworn Sisters—Denise, Alyssa, and Sam—at basketball games, parties, volunteering at the senior center, Homecoming, the prom, hanging at each other's houses. She couldn't throw these away. They were a precious slice of the past capturing their youth and vulnerability.

She should invite them all over. She missed them individually and as a group. They could reminisce—remembering the days when the slightest snub caused so much drama. When waiting for a boy to ask them to a dance caused so much angst.

Nicki dug farther into the box and lifted her journal. She and her Sworn Sisters had decided to write diaries during their senior year to record their thoughts and dreams before embarking on their new lives at college. They made a pact to hold onto them until they were old—like sixty—when they would share them with each other. It seemed like a good idea at the time; a time before her life turned upside down. Nicki erroneously surmised her senior year could only get better, since she'd already gone through the heartbreak of her father's death. She'd believed her writings would help her get out her emotions, help her through that difficult time. Who knew things would actually get worse?

She ran her fingers over the flowery cover, drew in a breath, and opened her journal.

September 1—Senior Year

We promised each other we'd write weekly diary entries. The Sworn Sisters, that is. So when we're old and feeble, we can look back and relive our wonderful, youthful, fun-filled days while rocking in the activity room at the senior citizens' center. Will the four of us still be friends? I hope so.

What will each of us write? Just the good times? My problem is everything isn't as wonderful with me as it is with the others. Or am I assuming that?

No one will want to read my diary if I write about my depressing thoughts, but I need to write what I feel, not what I think we might want to read in the future. Maybe I'll write in two diaries. One will have the good stuff I'll share and one will have my secrets. Obviously, this entry must be the start of my secret diary, since I can't tell my Sworn Sisters I'm keeping anything from them. To make sure I don't get them mixed up and share the wrong diary, I'll call this one "Nicki's Journal" and the second one "Nicki's Diary." Not very creative, but it'll work.

Maybe I'm just sad these days because it's the year anniversary of my father's death. It's hard to be upbeat when Mom barely drags herself around the house. She's tried to function normally, but this month it's as if she's been pummeled by a heavyweight champ.

I look at her and wish I could make things better, but I can never take my father's place. They were such a great couple, doing everything together including working at the same real estate office as a team. I wondered how they could spend so much time together without getting sick of each other, but they became even closer. They were able to get a lifetime in by most other couples' standards.

Seeing Mom barely able to cope with her loss has me thinking it might be better to not love someone so desperately; so fully. That way, when they die, it won't make me unable to live.

What a smart young girl. Tears streamed down Nicki's cheeks. Words of her seventeen-year-old self cautioned her against love. Although Dex didn't die, he might as well have. He was gone from her life, and the hole in her heart hurt so much she couldn't breathe. Why didn't she remember her mother's overwhelming sense of loss when she jumped blindly into this relationship? She clearly remembered it for all those other men who breezed through her life in the past. Her string of casual relationships. Never getting too close, never opening up. And when things fell apart, she hardly cared. She convinced herself she was happier on her own.

Until Dex. Damn Dex. He had gotten under her skin and wormed his way into her heart. Into her soul.

She stuffed the journal into the bottom of the box and tossed the photos on top, then retaped the flaps, pushing the box deep into her closet. Memories were not her friends.

She needed to get back to her strong, independent self, the one who'd learned how not to love.

Chapter Twelve

Nicki turned left into the driveway at seven on Friday evening, the last weekend in May, gravel crunching under the tires of her little red BMW. Behind her were Denise and Alyssa, whom she'd met at the convenience store on Route 35 in Crescent Beach, before heading to Sam's little getaway for the summer.

They were here on a mission of mercy.

Sam flew out through the screen door, letting it bang behind her. "Oh my God," she squealed as she took in not only Nicki, but her other Sworn Sisters. Tears escaped as she ran to each friend, hugging them. "What are you all doing here?"

Denise responded for the group. "We got your email invitation but didn't realize it was an emergency until Nicki called us the other night. She told us you and Tom had separated. If we can't drop everything for our Sworn Sister in need, then we're not the friends we thought we were." She gave Sam a lopsided smile. "How are you holding up?"

Sam spun around to take them all in. "Much better, now that you're here. Welcome to Crescent Beach."

Sam grabbed Nicki's suitcase from her trunk, straining from the effort of lugging her "overnight" bag. Nicki couldn't go anywhere without a full contingent of possibilities, no matter how depressed she was.

Nicki followed Sam to her bungalow, with only her

handbag to carry. "Where'd you find this little cottage by the sea?"

"One of my friends at the law firm. He and his family don't use it until August, so he offered it to me when he learned about my forced leave of absence. It was really nice of him, since I'm sure he could have rented it for a small fortune. But I guess he recognized my mental health was worth the price of rent. I've only been here a week, but I can see why he likes it so much. You're removed from the crazy pace of everyday life. It's like a little refuge."

"Does it come with seven dwarfs?" Alyssa tossed her duffel bag next to the couch.

"I gave them the weekend off. But they are fun to have around." Sam glanced toward the kitchen. "You must be starving. I don't have much to offer. I thought only Nicki was coming."

"You're in luck," said Denise. "I made stuffed mushrooms, bruschetta, and a Mexican dip. I know they don't exactly go together, but I wanted to make sure everyone had their favorites. I'll be right back." She headed out the door and toward her car, no doubt having a trunk full of provisions.

Denise was the best, always considering her friends' culinary preferences, believing food was the panacea for all ills. And Nicki knew Sam could sure use any comfort she could get, whether from her Sworn Sisters' presence or bruschetta.

"I brought wine and beer," chimed in Alyssa, following Denise out to the driveway.

They worked together with little effort, pouring drinks, assembling assorted appetizers on plates, and taking it all to the living room where they covered the coffee table. With wine in hand, beer for Alyssa, they got down to the business of catching up, tiptoeing around the reason that brought them here.

"Nicki, how's the music business doing?" Alyssa tipped her beer bottle to her mouth and took a long pull. No ladylike glass for her.

"Great. But a little too busy. I'm at work six days a week and on Sunday I can't drag myself from bed." Of course, there were other reasons for that.

"How'd you get away this weekend?" Sam's concern that Nicki couldn't spare the time showed through.

"I told my boss I was going out of town. I'm sure he assumed I was flying to Vegas or somewhere equally decadent, but no need for him to know the details. I'm entitled to a vacation day here and there."

Sam relaxed back into the sofa. "Thanks. To all of you. I'm sure it wasn't easy to get away on such short notice." She raised her wine glass, and they all followed suit.

Alyssa made a toast. "To the Sworn Sisters. May we always be there for each other."

Nicki should have assembled them when she and Dex broke up two months ago. But at the time, she didn't want to talk about it. Obviously, Sam did.

"Not to bring this party down, but we are here for a reason." Nicki zeroed in on Sam. "We know you and Tom are separated, but we don't know any of the details. If we're going to slice and skewer him, we need specifics."

Sam's fleeting smile faded, and Nicki admonished herself for honing in on the problem at hand so quickly.

"I guess I should put it all out there." Sam inhaled,

then put her wine glass down. "The sooner I get through this, the faster you can all weigh in and then we can move onto other, much more pleasant topics." She sat at the edge of the sofa, clearly angst-ridden. "Tom called me at work one night to meet him for a drink uptown. I thought it was such a nice gesture. We rarely did that, and I was more than happy to get out of the office a little earlier than normal and enjoy the spring weather." Sadness peppered her words. "When I got to the bar, he was already there, and his usual smile was missing. I assumed he had a bad day and wanted to discuss it. I ordered a drink and we sat down in a booth in the back. It didn't take long for him to blurt out he was going to San Diego for the summer for work—with the company's comptroller. Who, by the way, he's having an affair with."

"Oh my God, Sam, how awful." Denise scooted closer to Sam and gave her a hug.

Sam's eyes watered, but she kept it together. "It was awful. At first, I thought he was kidding. I know Sherry really well. We used to go out with her and her fiancé for dinner once in a while. She had gone to the movies with Tom and me not too long ago." Sam's shoulders slumped. "Once I realized he was telling the truth, I felt like such a fool, but worse I was actually nauseous. I couldn't believe he had invited me out to tell me this news. Do you know what he said? He didn't want to be alone with me. He didn't want me to beg him to stay. He had moved out that day and was going to be staying in a hotel until he left for San Diego." Sam's voice escalated with the retelling of Tom's hurtful words.

Nicki knew the feeling. Although Dex didn't leave

her for another woman, he left her just the same. She felt Sam's pain clear down to her toes, re-experiencing the last night she spoke to Dex.

Alyssa filled the silence. "What an ass. How could he be so insensitive? You're better off without him, Sam. You deserve better."

Nicki couldn't help but note the irony of those words coming from Alyssa, who was having an affair with the "insensitive" husband of another woman. Despite that, the heartfelt sentiment of those words, while true, would not help ease the agony Sam experienced.

Unfortunately, Nicki couldn't speak over the lump still prevalent in her throat, so she let Denise and Alyssa do all the talking, their murmurings echoing around her as if she were in a vacuum. Being the good friends they were, they appropriately shredded Tom and coddled Sam, so focused on their job they didn't notice Nicki's near silence at first. When they did, they dragged her into the fray, which was better for her, since skewering Tom was a whole lot easier than grieving over Dex.

"This conversation is exhausting," Sam pointed out after at least an hour of pulling apart the inner workings of her marriage.

"I'm sorry, Sam." Denise stood and cleared away some empty plates on the coffee table. "We're here to support you, not make you miserable. Let's change the subject. I'm going to put the mushrooms in the oven. Can I get anyone anything?"

"I'll take another beer," said Alyssa, draining the last sip in her bottle.

"I'll get the wine." Nicki stood with her glass. "All

this talking is making me thirsty. Did I tell you I ran into Matt last month in Philadelphia?"

And just like that the conversation veered from Tom to reminiscing about their high school days.

"Did he look the same as he did back then? He was so hot." Denise returned to the group with a beer for Alyssa while Nicki brought a cold bottle of wine.

"He looked good. Remember he came on the trip we took to Notre Dame senior year to see Denise's brother?"

"What a trip!" Sam poured wine into her empty glass. "Nine of us in a van on the Pennsylvania turnpike in a blizzard and needing gas." Sam chuckled at the predicaments they had gotten themselves into. "I guess no one checked the weather before driving to Indiana for a weekend."

"Why wasn't I invited?" chimed in Alyssa, as if anyone would have given their left tooth to live through the experience.

Denise volunteered the answer. "You had to work a few Saturdays a month at the movie theater. You lucked out."

Alyssa considered her prior schedule and accepted Denise's logic. Since they rarely did anything apart, if one of them wasn't present for some remembered event, there had to be a good reason.

"You never missed a beach weekend." Nicki pulled her long, blonde hair into a pony tail and secured it with the band around her wrist. "Remember that day, Sam, when you and I took a walk and the lifeguards called us over?"

"Oh my God." Sam slapped her thigh and laughed. "They asked us if we would stop at the next lifeguard stand and see if they had tape in their first aid kit. We went from stand to stand because no one had any."

"And were checked out by twenty lifeguards before the last two let us in on the joke."

Nicki laughed at the memory. "But we got invited to the lifeguard party at night. Remember all those gorgeous, muscled bodies? And am I fantasizing, or did they all have streaked blond hair, blue eyes, and perfect white teeth?"

Alyssa's memory wasn't as unspoiled. "They were not all gorgeous surfer boys. One of them, and I distinctly remember he had black, curly hair and not a blond halo, kept pouring vodka into my cup. When I started swaying, he offered to take me to his room, so we could 'relax.' Thank God Denise was close by. She swooped in and said we were leaving. Then she gathered the troops and we were outta there."

"It was you who ruined the night," teased Nicki as she clinked her wine glass against Alyssa's beer bottle. "I could have met the man of my dreams."

"Then you wouldn't have met Dex."

Alyssa's innocent statement chilled the air around Nicki. The last time she'd spoken to Alyssa, she'd told her she and Dex were doing great, especially after Alyssa's advice to enjoy the relationship and not project too far into the future. She hadn't shared her heartbreak with any of her Sworn Sisters, although she suspected his name was bound to come up over the weekend.

"True." She left it at that, hoping no one picked up on her melancholy.

Sam studied her for a second, doing her own diagnostic test, and must have decided to save that conversation for later. Sam reached over to the end table and grabbed a book. "Have any of you read your diary lately? I've been reading mine. The entries really take you back."

Another landmine. What was going on here?

"I don't care to read mine," stated Alyssa. "There might be something in there I don't want to remember." She raised her eyebrows as if considering the deep, dark secrets contained therein. Then she started laughing. "Who am I kidding? My sex life in high school was pretty much nonexistent. Maybe a kiss here and there, a little groping. But nothing X-rated. It's got to be boring as hell. I didn't even have a real diary. I used a black and white marble notebook."

Sam looked at her red silk journal and rubbed her fingers over with the word "Diary" embossed in gold. "Mine's pretty."

Alyssa knelt next to Sam and took her hand. "Yes, it is, Sam. Very pretty. You always had prettier things than I did."

Sam pulled her hand away in mock annoyance. "Oh, here we go again. Poor Alyssa had to wear hand-me-downs from her sisters, while I got new clothes. Blah, blah, blah."

By now the entire group was howling at the familiar scene being replayed as if they were back in high school. It was a perfect antidote to Nicki's doldrums, as well as Sam's.

And the best thing about the night was the continual laughter generated by story after story about house parties (and the secret stash of liquor), minor fender benders (and whose fault they were), silly pranks (putting a bra on the statue of the Virgin Mary at school), ensuing detentions (when they had to clean the classrooms), and who got away with the most (St. Denise, for no apparent reason to the others).

With their mouths finally tired and their eyelids drooping, they collapsed in their respective sleeping quarters, with Alyssa sharing Sam's queen-sized bed, and Nicki and Denise in the guest room with single beds.

Tonight was the first night in a long time Nicki went to bed with a smile on her face. Spending time with her Sworn Sisters was the perfect antidote to her overwhelming misery.

If only this feeling could last.

****

Nicki awoke at nine to an empty room. She rarely slept this late and felt surprisingly refreshed. Voices from the kitchen beckoned and she headed down.

As she entered the kitchen Alyssa said, "I have to be at work by noon. What time is it?"

Denise responded, "Almost nine. I'm sorry, Sam, but I have to go soon too. I can't leave Ben with all three kids all day."

"No problem," said Sam. "I'm so happy you were able to get away last night. After we got past the first hour dealing with my issues, I had a blast. At times I was laughing so hard I was crying. I can't remember the last time that happened."

"Me neither." Denise put her coffee mug in the sink.

"Don't think you have the rest of the weekend to yourself. I'm staying." Nicki opened a few cabinets before finding the one with coffee mugs.

"Who wakes up looking like that?" Denise stared at Nicki with her mouth open, then looked down at her own plaid boxer shorts and T-shirt.

Nicki frequently wore pretty lingerie to bed and had on a white, spaghetti-strap, silk and lace nightgown. "Just because we're not sleeping with a guy doesn't mean we should wear flannel." Nicki leaned against the counter as she sipped her black coffee, winking at Denise. "Not that there's anything wrong with your shorts."

Alyssa weighed in. "I never wore anything like that. How much does a silk nightgown cost?" Alyssa's practicality with money bordered on miserly.

Nicki ignored the question. "What about you, Sam?" Nicki frowned at the cotton nightshirt Sam sported. "You must have some nice lingerie. You're a New York City gal."

Sam chuckled. "Where a person lives doesn't dictate what they wear to bed. Although, I must say, you look beautiful. If I ever have a man in my life again, maybe I'll try it."

"You don't need a man in your life to make yourself feel sexy or beautiful. You should do it for yourself."

Denise, who'd started the conversation, remained mum. "Denise. What about you?"

"I have one or two sexy nightgowns hidden deep in some drawer. Having two kids under four does not play well with silk lingerie. Their little hands are always pulling and tugging at whatever I have on, and Johnny still spits up on my shoulder." Denise cringed. "Now that Bobby's living with us, I can't walk around like that. He's fourteen. Lingerie and children do not go together."

"What about when the kids are in bed and it's you

and Ben? Surely you want him to see you as a sexy, vibrant woman. Someone other than his kids' mother."

Denise rolled her shoulders as if to ease the tension of the conversation. "It's not something I worry about these days. I'm usually too tired when I drop into bed. And if I'm not, I'm not going to waste time looking for my well-hidden silk teddy. I'm okay with Ben ripping off my flannel shorts and T-shirt. And he's okay with it too."

Denise was so steady. So easy to get along with. Nothing ever bothered her. And she had a great personality that rarely got ruffled. Nicki shouldn't criticize her over what she wore to bed. Denise and Ben had been together since high school, so whatever Denise did, it obviously worked for them. She needed to keep her mouth shut.

For the next hour, the women drank coffee and bounced from subject to subject until Alyssa and Denise had to leave.

Sam walked them out to their car to say good-bye while Nicki stood in the doorway, not wanting to go outside in her night wear. It truly was amazing how the four of them had remained so close over all these years despite their different career paths and lives.

She smiled as she watched them, thinking girlfriends were the most important people in her life.

Much more important than a man.

Chapter Thirteen

After Denise and Alyssa pulled out of the driveway, Sam came back to the house, her shoulders sagging a bit. "I'm so glad you're staying." Sam's eyes shone with tears. "I miss you." She hugged Nicki, and it felt so good to hold onto a friend.

Nicki hadn't left Philadelphia for the past two months except for business. She had this death wish to run into Dex on the street as she jogged for miles, incorporating the blocks in and around his apartment and office building into her weekend exercise routine. It never happened. Besides, Sam needed her now, and Nicki admonished herself to snap out of her funk and do what she came here to do.

Nicki moved her mouth into what she hoped mirrored a genuine smile. "You are not a mush woman. You are going to tell me all the reasons why you are better off without Tom. Understand? And you are going to believe them."

"Why don't we put on our bathing suits? We have all day to labor over my sad story at the beach."

"Do we have to go to the beach?" Nicki glanced out the window checking the weather, hoping for clouds and eventual rain. No such luck. The sun was blinding. "I'm not in the mood, and I don't want to subject myself to getting more wrinkles around my eyes. I'm not keen on skin cancer either."

"There is sun screen. And you could wear a hat. I even have a beach umbrella you could sit under."

Nicki considered this for a moment, but before she could respond, Sam came up with alternatives.

"Never mind. If you don't want to go to the beach, we can sit on the porch. Or we can ride bikes around town." She paused, waiting for Nicki to express interest in any one of her suggestions.

Nicki should do whatever Sam wanted, but she had become so dull after her breakup with Dex, nothing appealed to her. Yet she had to bury her melancholy for Sam's sake.

"We'll think of something. Let's get changed." Nicki headed for the stairs.

Sam glanced at the clock on the wall. "It's almost eleven. I'm starving. How about going out for lunch? We can go to The Reach. It's a few blocks up, across from the beach. Then you can at least see the ocean, without actually going near it."

"Now that sounds like a good idea. I'll go get ready."

Nicki took a quick shower and stepped into a blue, silk, flowered sundress and strappy sandals. Gold bangles and hoop earrings were next. Then she brushed her long, blonde hair until not one strand was out of place. Grabbing her favorite designer bag, she swung it over her shoulder.

Sam's mouth dropped open as Nicki descended the stairs. "Where do you think you're going?"

"To lunch. I need to look good in case I meet the man of my dreams." It was time to put Dex behind and move on. At least that was the message she wanted to give Sam, so she better be able to follow her own advice.

"This is the beach, Nicki! People don't dress like that. They wear shorts, or a bathing suit and cover-up. You look like a million bucks."

"Thanks. That was the goal." She swung her hair over her shoulder and posed.

"And what do you mean about meeting the man of your dreams? What about Dex?"

"We broke up." Nicki's voice caught, but she covered it up quickly. "I'll fill you in at the restaurant. Let's go."

"I'm so sorry, Nicki. What happened?"

Nicki picked some imaginary thread from her dress. "We'll talk about it later. Come on." She paused, looking Sam up and down, taking in her beige shorts and white tank top. "You can't wear that."

"Why not?"

Nicki grabbed Sam's hand and led her upstairs to her room, then rummaged through Sam's closet, reminiscent of their high school days.

"What are you doing?" Sam sighed.

"Looking for something a little more appealing." She pushed aside one hanging garment after another in her quest. "There's not much here to work with."

Sam's beach wardrobe didn't contain silk dresses or designer handbags. Just some tops, shorts, and pants.

Nicki ultimately pulled out a white slim skirt and a black and white halter top. "This is better. Meet me downstairs when you're ready." Nicki left Sam to follow her command.

When Sam appeared, Nicki pounced. "Is this a halfway decent place we're going to? Might I meet a gorgeous, gainfully employed stud?" Her sole goal now was to move on. Replace the emptiness that threatened to consume her.

"It's a popular spot, and yes, I believe there will be men there."

Nicki motioned with her arm and her jewelry jangled. "Lead the way."

Noisy chattering filled the popular restaurant. No reservations meant waiting at the bar, but since Nicki had no plans of stepping foot on the beach, this was an acceptable alternative. Air conditioners and ceiling fans mercifully kept the heat at bay, while floor-to-ceiling windows allowed a view of hundreds of bodies lying near a wave-pounding, blue backdrop. Summer at the Jersey shore had begun.

Ignoring Sam's request for an iced tea, Nicki ordered two margaritas.

She sipped at hers, hoping the tequila would lift her out of the funk she found herself in way too often these days. Since Sam seemed to want to avoid talk about her despicable husband for the time being, and Nicki wasn't ready to talk about Dex yet, she caught Sam up on some of the more mundane aspects of her life. Sam nodded and asked a question here or there, but her focus wavered. It wasn't until the second drink when Nicki decided enough was enough. The time had come to discuss the state of Sam's marriage.

"I thought Tom was one of the good guys. I can't believe he did that to you."

Fresh pain washed over Sam's face, a pain Nicki knew well, but Sam stoically kept the tears at bay as the words came pouring out. "I can't believe it either. Some days it feels like I'm living a nightmare, and some days the pain is so acute I can't get out of bed. I thought he loved me. I can't believe I took it for granted. Took him for granted. I assumed he was happy."

"Time heals all." Hope sprinkled with skepticism peppered Nicki's remark. "And it looks like you have the time."

"It's hard to admit this out loud, but after Tom left, I could barely function at home, much less at the office. I went through the stages of grief—denial, bargaining, anger. Now I'm just depressed." She inhaled and blew out a long breath. "My personal problems were interfering with my professional life. Before this happened, I was on track to become partner in September. Now, I'm not so sure. I got the impression our managing partner thought I should have sucked it up and moved on." She fingered the condensation on her glass. "And you know, I've felt the same way about some of my divorce clients who wallowed in their sorrow. Now I know what it's like."

Nicki nodded her understanding.

"Worse yet, clients were calling to complain I wasn't being responsive to their needs. That kind of bad press does not bode well for positive votes from the partners."

"Maybe the rest of the partners don't know." Nicki gave it an optimistic spin. "In the scheme of things, a ten week leave of absence is a drop in the bucket compared to the time you've spent in the office over the past seven years." She traced the wood grain of the bar, hoping her analysis was true but knowing intellectually a break in service, no matter the reason, would impact Sam's rise in some way. "Why did your boss give you so much time?"

"He must have determined it was a bargain

compared to the prospect of upping the firm's malpractice insurance if I stayed." Sam chuckled without mirth.

"I'm glad to see you've kept your sense of humor through all this."

"I'm all cried out. But don't worry, there's always tomorrow." Sam sipped her drink. "Tell me, what happened with you and Dex? And don't tell me it's no big deal. I can see it in your eyes."

Nicki contemplated spilling her guts but wasn't sure it was the right time or place. "I didn't know him well. We met on a cruise, dated for eleven weeks, then broke up. No harm, no foul." Even Nicki couldn't believe she condensed her story to this lie. But what was the sense in discussing her heartbreak on top of Sam's? Instead she switched gears to sidestep the subject and began relating hysterical tales of diva behavior by the artists her recording company signed. And thankfully Sam let her do it.

After sitting at the bar for forty-five minutes, they were seated at a table by the window.

Having ordered, Sam brought the conversation back to Nicki. "It seems you're ready to jump back into the dating scene."

"Absolutely." The lie stuck in her throat like a kernel of popcorn. "But I don't want a relationship. Just a stable of guys to do things with on the weekend." She picked up her glass and drained it.

"You not having a boyfriend? I don't believe you. I can't remember a time when you've been without a partner—significant or otherwise. You attract men like bees on honey."

"Not the right ones. I don't think there are any right

ones." Nicki's eyes widened at the size of the burgers when delivered. After taking a bite, she segued right back to their conversation. "I'm sticking with what works for me. I don't get too involved." She leaned over the table as if to share her secret. "Anything over three months and they're history."

"That's a short period of time. How can you ever get to know a guy well enough in three months?"

"It only takes a night." Nicki's mind wandered back to the cruise. An immediate attraction had sprung from one drink at the bar and grew into a full-fledged compulsion during their day in Key West. She shook her head to dispel the memory. "The point is, I don't want to get to know them well. I learn a little bit about the guy while going to nice restaurants, plays, sporting events, wherever. But I make sure they know my philosophy. No strings. No commitment. Just sex. Just fun."

Sam held her burger halfway to her lips. "Fun. I could use that. How does one go about meeting someone like that?"

Sam was assuming Nicki was out there dating around now. And she didn't want to disabuse her friend of that notion. She was here to bolster Sam's self-confidence, which had been shattered by her selfish, egotistical husband. It was Nicki's job to show Sam the way out of her dark hole. No sense in advising her Nicki was still trying to climb out of her own.

"You work in a predominantly male world. You can easily meet eligible bachelors at your bar association functions or Chamber of Commerce events. But make sure you don't form any attachment."

"What happens if you fall for one of them?" Sam

seemed skeptical of Nicki's plan.

Nicki swallowed. *You die a slow death.* "That won't happen if you stick with the plan. Your life can become uncomplicated by the ups and downs of a relationship. I love my career as a music exec. I get to travel. Meet talented artists. I come and go as I please, without compromising or bending to someone else's will. It's great to be uncommitted." Four truths and a lie. Not bad. Hopefully, Nicki wouldn't be struck by lightning.

Sam scrutinized Nicki's face as if performing some lie detector test. "Are you really happy, or are you trying to convince me, as well as yourself, that everything's perfect without having a meaningful relationship?"

"Just because you have a bachelor's degree in psychology doesn't mean you can analyze me." Nicki grimaced at Sam's perceptive question. But she had no intention of backing down from her stated philosophy. "Do you truly believe I need a man to make me whole? Well, I don't. As a matter of fact, I'm much happier now than when Dex and I were together." Was she actually saying this and pulling it off? "And my guess is, once you get over the pain of losing Tom, you're going to find you can be happy on your own too."

"Maybe I'll try it your way. When I'm ready." Sam wiped her mouth with her napkin, looking pensive. "It sounds good…but I'm not sure I can live my life as a single, independent woman forever."

"Why not?"

"I always pictured having a family one day. Children."

Oh, here we go. That pesky child conversation.

Sam was the ultimate career woman—a workaholic reaching to become a partner at her law firm. She had no time for children.

"Have you lost your mind? Why in the world would you want kids? They mess up your career, ruin your body, and throw up in your hair."

"Charming, Nicki. But if it's that bad, then why does everyone want kids?"

"Everyone doesn't want them. Some people think they want them until they have them. Some people don't think about it, they just do it. I for one wouldn't even consider it."

"I pictured myself having a loving husband, a beautiful four-bedroom house in the suburbs with a pool, and two little adorable kids calling me Momma and telling me they love me."

"It sounds dreadful," Nicki said. "Stop making it appear so idyllic. You should know better than anybody. You're a divorce lawyer, for God's sake." She leaned toward Sam, making sure she had her attention. "And wasn't Tom the perfect husband at one point? What if you had kids with him and lived in that great big house with the pool? Then *poof*!" She snapped her fingers. "He's gone. What do you do then? Sell the compound and drag those little rug rats into the city to live in a two-bedroom apartment because you can't afford the mini-mansion anymore? You try to juggle your career with day care, and you're always late picking up the kids, while Tom flies in once a month from San Diego to do the daddy thing."

"Enough." Sam held up her hands in mock defeat. "I get it. Children make things harder. And you're right. I'm glad I don't have them with Tom. But someday…"

"Never," responded Nicki, almost to herself.

A sharp knife pierced her heart as she uttered that word. Her undoing. What Dex wanted the most and she wouldn't consider. Not even for love. She needed to terminate this conversation before she broke down and started sobbing.

Nicki held up her hand to get the waitress' attention to distract herself. "May we have some more water, please?"

As soon as their glasses were refilled, Sam broke through Nicki's haze. "I'm sorry if I raised a bad subject. It couldn't have been easy for you to have a baby at eighteen and give it up for adoption. I didn't mean to be so insensitive." Sam pushed her half-eaten burger away. "I'm not thinking clearly."

Nicki waved her apology away. "Don't worry about it. You don't have to tiptoe around me."

Unfortunately, Sam was intuitive. She linked Nicki's philosophy concerning children to her guilt over abandoning her child. Yet Nicki refused to acknowledge the connection out loud. She would stick with her outward persona; strong, independent, and free. She didn't need a man or a family to make her whole. At least that's the face she wanted to project to the rest of the world, including one of her closest friends.

Sam folded her napkin and placed it on the table. "Let's get out of here. It's beautiful outside. How about a little walk on the beach? You can't be at the shore for a weekend without at least feeling some sand through your toes or dipping your feet in the water. We won't stay out long enough for you to ruin your sensitive skin. I promise."

"I guess I could use some exercise to burn off this alcohol before we start again tonight." Nicki was bent on getting Sam out of the house and into a club—or at least Crescent Beach's version of a club—to show her the possibilities out there.

They paid their bill and left the cool atmosphere of the restaurant, running smack into a wall of heat. Winding their way toward the ocean, they made a path through a maze of beach blankets, careful not to kick sand on the well-oiled bodies worshiping the sun. Nicki's bracelets jangled as she slung her bag over her shoulder and transferred her sandals to her other hand.

"I should have brought my hat." She shielded her eyes from the blinding sun.

"You must have a pair of sunglasses in your purse." Sam continued her trek toward the ocean. "If you don't, you can borrow mine."

"No, I have some." Nicki stopped to rummage through her bag. Three little boys came barreling by, spraying sand and water from their bodies. Nicki let out a curse.

"Nicki! This is a 'G' rated beach. Could you watch your language?"

"That little sand rat almost knocked me over. And he splattered me with dirt and water." She brushed off her dress in irritation.

"It's not dirt. It's sand. This is the beach. Come on. Let's go feel the water."

Nicki inhaled, trying to bury the foul mood she was strewing on friends and strangers alike. She tried valiantly to brush off her relationship with Dex as nothing more than a fling that had run its course. Only Nicki knew better. He had reached in and caressed her heart, warming it, protecting it. Until she'd pushed him away.

Nicki dipped her toe into the remnants of a wave. "It's freezing," she said as she backed away. "How could all those people have their full bodies in this ice water?" A strand of seaweed deposited itself right at Nicki's feet. "Ick." She kicked it away. "And it's dirty too. Lord knows what diseases we're picking up wading in this pollution."

"I wouldn't call dipping your foot in the ocean, wading." Sam studied Nicki's face as if to check on her seriousness. "Is there anything about the beach you do enjoy?"

Nicki needed to lighten up. She scanned the area and focused her attention on two young men passing a football to each other. "Now there's a scene I can enjoy. Look at those abs. And those shoulders. Maybe we should consider getting wet and sandy with them. You can have first choice."

Sam followed her gaze. "Watch out!" she yelled, as the football came hurtling toward Nicki. Nicki dropped her shoes and purse and raised her hands just in time to deflect the ball from her face.

"Sorry," said one of the hunks who came running over to get the ball. "Are you okay?"

Nicki looked down to see one of her shoes being carried away by the tide. She screeched and pointed. The young man dashed into the surf and scooped it up, holding the water-logged sandal by a strap. Nicki glanced at her kid leather purse lying in the wet sand. "On no!" A water stain seeped up its length. She leaned over to pick up her other shoe and bag. "They're ruined." She grabbed the shoe from the stranger and held the designer items up for further inspection. They looked worse from this angle.

"Sorry about that," said the second guy who had jogged over to take responsibility along with his friend.

Nicki deflated even more, if possible. "I guess I shouldn't have had these at the beach."

Sam rolled her eyes but didn't comment. Wise choice given Nicki's surly demeanor.

"Maybe we can take you and your friend out to dinner later to make it up to you," said the culprit.

Nicki perked up and leveled her eyes on Sam. Maybe this weekend was the perfect time to restart her own dating plan while showing Sam how it was done.

"Uh...I don't know." Sam's eyes told Nicki "no."

So Nicki came up with a more acceptable suggestion. "You can buy us a drink later. Where will we be tonight, Sam?"

"How about The Bentley House?" Sam offered with little enthusiasm.

The taller one spoke up. "Okay, we'll see you there at ten. By the way, my name's Ken and this is Jeff." They shook hands, and the women introduced themselves before the men apologized again. Then they sprinted off toward their prior positions and continued tossing the ball, ignoring the havoc they had wreaked.

Nicki held her wet shoes and purse away from her like they were live crabs, and she and Sam began to walk. "Do you think they'll show tonight?"

"Who cares?" Sam stole a glance at Nicki.

"True." Disappointment wound through her being—whether over her ruined accessories or because she couldn't move on, Nicki wasn't sure.

"Let's go back to the house and see if we can clean

and dry off your stuff," Sam suggested in a clear attempt to ward off Nicki's funk.

Little accidents and dwelling on the past could sure affect a mood.

Chapter Fourteen

"Earth to Sam." Nicki dragged her suitcase down the stairs on Sunday evening as Sam sat on the couch sipping iced tea, looking sad, desolate.

The weekend had been a series of ups and downs, but they got through it, capped off with Sam's argument with the cop last night, earning her not only a parking ticket but a disorderly person summons.

"Do you have to go?" Sam rose and came toward Nicki.

"You'll get through this, Sam." Nicki hugged her. "But you should deal with it now. There's no use dragging it out."

"What do you mean?"

Nicki wrestled with sharing her painful experience, coming to the conclusion it might help Sam get through the pain faster. Why she waited forty-eight hours, she didn't know. "When Dex and I broke up, I kept thinking he'd change his mind. He was crazy about me and I was crazy about him. But he wants to marry and have children. I was good with the marriage part. Not so much with the children part. I didn't believe something like that could get in the way of us being together forever. I kept hoping he'd come to his senses eventually and see it like I saw it. That we could be happy—just the two of us. I couldn't move on. Because not only was part of me thinking he'd change his mind,

I also hoped I'd change mine. I wasn't at all sure I had made the right decision. And I miss him so much."

Nicki sighed. "But I haven't heard from him in two months. He hasn't come to the conclusion he can't live without me. And I haven't decided I'll have children so I can be with him. When it's over, it's over. Move on. Don't spend your nights crying over what could have been. Don't question his decision or believe he might change."

Sam nodded, a bit in a daze. "Are you telling me to file for divorce?"

"Don't look so shell-shocked, Sam. You know I'm right. Tom left you for another woman. Even if he does dump her, are you going to want him back after what he's done to you? You're strong, Sam. You can do it. You'll find your way."

Sam wasn't there yet, but Nicki hoped she'd at least consider her advice.

"Thanks for listening to me, for letting me vent. And for the advice. I guess." Sam shrugged. "You know. Maybe I am getting stronger. It still hurts that I failed at marriage. I never thought I'd be in this position. But the pain is duller. And less frequent. I can breathe again."

"This is a good place to get away from it all. You're lucky you were able to take a leave of absence. When Dex and I broke up, we were in the middle of a merger with Yukon Music. I couldn't take off the weekend, much less ten weeks. But we all get through it, one way or another." Although if truth be told, Nicki was far from through this. She just didn't want to let on to Sam how difficult the road ahead would be.

"You're right. I've said the same thing to my

clients over and over." She sat on the arm of the sofa and straightened, as if pulling courage into herself. "It's been a good weekend, in an odd sort of way. Having my Sworn Sisters here to support me means the world. Thanks for coming, Nicki."

Nicki smiled. "Any time, Sam. But next time, you should be a little nicer to the cop giving you a parking ticket."

"*Ugh*. I can't believe I lost it like that. Now I have a disorderly person ticket on top of it." Sam shook her head. "I'll let you know if I get thrown in jail when I go to court to fight it."

"You do that. I'll send you bail money." Nicki rummaged through her purse looking for car keys.

"Oh, I almost forgot." Sam perked up. "Did you get the invitation to our fifteenth high school reunion?"

"No. And please don't tell me we've been out of high school for fifteen years."

"It came by email. Perhaps the committee doesn't know how to reach you."

"I'm not offended. I have no desire to reminisce with anyone about high school days, other than with my Sworn Sisters."

Sam played with her ring, an odd look on her face. "I know senior year was tough for you, Nick." She glanced up, a sadness playing around her eyes. "There's something I've been meaning to tell you all weekend, but I kept putting it off, given all our other issues."

There couldn't be more bad news. "Go on," Nicki encouraged, wanting Sam to get out whatever seemed to be bothering her.

Sam sighed, picking at a thread on her shorts. "Remember Michael McCain?"

Nicki stopped breathing and sank down at the other end of the sofa as lightheadedness threatened her stability. "Yes." Her voice deserted her and it came out as a raspy whisper. "He disappeared the night of Alyssa's party. A few weeks before graduation."

"Well, I ran into him the other day. At the local coffee shop."

"What?" Nicki barked.

Sam jerked her head up at Nicki's reaction. "Are you okay? I didn't mean to shock you."

Nicki swallowed, trying to tamp down her racing heart. She stared at a candle on the coffee table, gathering her focus. After a few seconds, she peered at Sam. "What was he doing in Crescent Beach?"

"I don't know. I never asked him." Sam's sheepish look confirmed her unbelievable answer.

"What do you mean you never asked him? We thought something bad had happened. That he might be dead. Yet he shows up here fifteen years later, and you didn't ask what happened to him the night of Alyssa's party? What he's been doing for the past decade and a half?" Nicki's voice got shriller with each word. She needed to calm down.

"It was a weird coincidence seeing him there. I was stunned…and embarrassed. A few days earlier, I had hit him with a volley ball. I was walking on the beach and this ball plopped in the ocean right in front of me, spraying me with frigid, sandy water." Sam continued babbling about this stranger calling her *lady* when he asked her for the ball. "I hate that term lady. It makes me feel old and crotchety. I threw the ball hard, hitting him right in the chest. At the time, I didn't know it was Michael. He looked different and I wasn't focusing on him. I was deep in thought about Tom. And Sherry." Sam inhaled, as if back on the beach evaluating her marriage. "Then I ran into him in the coffee shop."

A chill, then heat, then pressure hit Nicki all at once, compressing her vocal chords, making it impossible to speak.

Sam filled the air and space. "I know we all assumed something bad had happened to him. He had that fight with Carl Nixon the night of Alyssa's party. And his father was so abusive... Since I didn't get any information before leaving the coffee shop, I googled him the second I got back to the house. The latest mention was that he was a partner at a New York City law firm. That was last year. I don't know if he's still there or moved on, since I don't know why he was here in Crescent Beach."

"I can't believe you found him so easily on the internet." *And ran into him in person.* Nicki sounded unreasonably shocked, so she dialed it back a notch. "We hadn't talked about him or heard from him in ages." Nicki gaped at Sam, still unable to process this information.

"Are you feeling okay?" Sam got up and went to sit on the sofa next to Nicki.

"I...I can't believe he's in the area. That none of us ever heard from him." Especially Nicki. Her voice cracked, and she stood and walked into the kitchen for a glass of water.

When she came back into the living room, Sam got up and gave her a hug. "I'm sorry I dumped this on you right before you were leaving. I knew it would affect you; I just didn't gauge how much. You spent a lot of time with him senior year. I remember that summer being so worried about him, speculating about what might have happened. I guess he didn't want to be found."

"I guess not." A dull ache throbbed at the base of her skull. Nicki wasn't sure *she* wanted him to be found.

"I never considered looking him up sooner. I hadn't thought about Michael in years. Running into him took me off guard."

Nicki did think about Michael once in a while, wondering what she would say to him if he showed up after all this time.

"I have to go." Nicki picked up her suitcase and headed for the door.

Sam did a double-take, then moved between the door and Nicki. "No, don't go yet. You're upset. Let's talk. I'm sorry. I didn't mean to shake you up."

Nicki didn't want Sam to blame herself for divulging this shocking news. Sam had no reason to believe it would affect her so much.

"I'm okay." Nicki gave her a wobbly smile. "I have a long drive and a busy day at work tomorrow. I need some time to let this sink in. I'll be fine. The ride will do me good."

Sam hugged her again. "Call me when you get in so I know you've arrived safe."

"Will do."

With that, she headed out the door and fled to the privacy of her car. It took only seconds for the dam to break.

****

As soon as Nicki got to her apartment, she ran to her bedroom closet and pulled out her box of memories.

Ripping the tape she replaced two months ago, she dug down to the bottom and retrieved her journal. Hastily flipping through pages until she got to the right entry, she sat on the floor against her bed and read.

Senior Year—Saturday, May 15

Dear Diary,

I can't seem to stop crying. Although I did hold it together tonight at Alyssa's party, I had to tell Michael I was pregnant. My secret was killing me, and I haven't been able to tell my Sworn Sisters. After graduation. When things calm down. Then I'll tell them.

I don't know what I thought would happen when I told Michael. I'm so emotional about everything. Which didn't help. When he asked if I wanted to get married, I just about bit his head off. He was going to carry through with the fight with Carl, and I want nothing to do with a person who beats up on other people.

Not that I want to marry him. I'm not in love with him and he's not in love with me. We're friends. Friends who let their emotions make bad decisions. He seemed to believe me when I blurted out that I was going to get an abortion. Probably because that's what he wants to believe.

The whole marriage idea had me freaked. I suppose he was trying to say the right thing. He apologized over and over—as if that was going to do anything. Besides, it was half my fault. I'll never forgive myself. I'm smarter than allowing this to happen to me—and to some poor child who's going to grow up believing his or her mother didn't give a damn. I do. I just can't raise this child.

My mother is going to have a coronary. She's still in a deep depression over my father's death, and that happened almost two years ago. She goes to church every morning, but it doesn't seem to be helping. I can only hope her prayers help us both get through this new revelation.

I'm going to lie to her about what really happened. Since I went to an out-of-town party with my cousin last month, I'll convince her that someone put something in my drink and I passed out. When I woke up, I was in a strange bed with half my clothes off. I'm not going to use the word rape. My mother will call the police. I have to make it sound like it was partly my fault, like I drank too much. That will send her in another direction but it's worth it. She can't know it's Michael. I don't want her and his father conspiring to marry us off.

I can't believe I'm in this position. Everything in my life is going to change because of one night when I felt sorry for Michael. When I felt sorry for me.

And now I'm going to feel sorry for this baby who will be given away to some stranger.

Nicki stared straight ahead as she recalled that night and its aftermath. Michael had gotten into a fist fight with Carl. Then he disappeared.

It was an awful time for Nicki and for their graduating class. He'd been their friend. Her friend, despite their last encounter at Alyssa's party. The police interviewed dozens of students, including everyone at the party. The rumors ran rampant that Carl's thug friends from Trenton had gotten hold of him. Though a distinct possibility, Michael's father was also a strong suspect. He'd abused him for months after Michael's mother and sister moved out.

But no evidence of foul play ever surfaced, and the police concluded he'd left town under his own power and will. He was eighteen and an adult in their eyes. He had the right.

Nicki went ahead with her plan to put the baby up for adoption as soon as he was born, and although she tried hard to avoid looking back, she was unable to let it go completely. It was one of the momentous events in her life that colored how she dealt with relationships, refusing to get close to anyone. Until Dex. Yet the end result was the same.

She turned back to her musings on Michael. Until that fateful night, they had supported each other through their hard times. Michael was there for Nicki in helping her deal with her father's death and her mother's depression. She was there for him in dealing with his mother's desertion and his father's abuse. Heavy issues for two teens to handle alone.

Why hadn't he ever reached out to her to see how she was? Sure, they were just friends. Not romantically involved, except for that one night when they both lost their heads.

Her sigh reverberated around the room. It was all water under the bridge. A lifetime ago. They had both moved on and become successful despite their issues in high school.

And their big mistake.

Chapter Fifteen

"Hope I'm not too early." Dex stood at Janice's front door at six p.m. on a Saturday night.

"Are you kidding? You can never be too early to babysit. I need time to finish getting ready and the kids won't leave me alone." Janice had her robe on, eye make-up on one eye, and half of her hair straightened.

Dex walked into the house behind her. "Nice look. Which half is done?"

"Very funny. Just wait for when you have kids."

The kick to his gut hurt more than usual.

"Sorry. I didn't mean to raise a sore subject. I meant…"

"I know what you meant. Don't worry about it."

Janice walked with him into the kitchen instead of straight upstairs to her room to finish her makeover. "I hope we didn't ruin any big plans you had for tonight. Usually, the girl around the corner babysits, but she just broke her ankle and we were desperate for a night out." Her face showed sympathy, which he didn't want or need.

"I already told you, I had no plans for tonight and I'm happy to see Chloe and Colin whenever I can. I'm really glad you called."

She studied his eyes. "You are telling the truth. I thought for sure a handsome bachelor in Philadelphia would never be idle on a Saturday night."

He chuckled. "I work six and a half days a week. When Saturday night rolls around, I love nothing more than relaxing at home with take-out and a bottle of wine."

Janice squinted at him. "That, I don't believe. Why aren't you out meeting someone?"

"You think I'm going to walk into a bar or night club and the perfect woman will be sitting there waiting for me?"

"What about online dating? Meeting for coffee? A drink? You can't sit holed up in your office all week and then stay in on the weekends. You'll never meet anyone like that."

Janice was right. He and Nicki were over. There was no bridge to cross to meet halfway, no gap to fill with compromise. And if he truly wanted a family as he'd professed to Nicki, he better start doing something about meeting the right woman.

"Maybe I'll check one of those sites out. Next week." Agreeing with his sister was his best bet in getting her off this subject.

"If you don't like dating sites, I know someone you can meet." She said it matter-of-factly, catching him off guard.

His jaw tightened. "You know I don't want to be set up. Especially with one of your friends or acquaintances. Nothing good can come of that." This wasn't the first time she'd tried to play matchmaker.

"I understand you're worried about my friendship falling apart if you and someone I know don't work out, but I don't expect you to be an ass. If you don't like her or things don't work out, it won't affect my friendship if you're at all civil. And I know you will be. What's the harm? One little date for coffee in Philadelphia after work." She looked at him with her crazy, unbalanced eyes, and he had to laugh.

"You better finish getting ready or you'll never get out of here. Don't you have dinner reservations?"

"Yes. But it won't take me long to turn into a princess, since you're here now to distract the kids. So I have a few minutes to tell you about Kylie."

He groaned, acknowledging he'd never get out of this conversation, so he might as well have a seat, listen to Janice's pitch, then dismiss her with a vague promise to think about it.

"Okay. So tell me about Kylie. In two minutes or less. I have a date with Chloe and Colin. Where are they by the way?"

"They're downstairs in the playroom. They must have found something to do together without torturing each other since I haven't heard a peep in the last fifteen minutes."

This was his chance to exit. "Or they could be getting into real trouble. I better get down there." He stood to escape, high-fiving in his head over his clever plan.

"Sit down, little brother." Janice pointed to his vacated stool, using the stern voice she used on the kids when they were not following instructions.

He sat.

"I know Kylie from my Pilates classes. She's a lawyer in Philadelphia at some big firm but lives in Cherry Hill and commutes."

One strike against her. What young, single woman would want to live in the suburbs when she could be living in and experiencing a vibrant city? She must be a total bore.

"I know what you're thinking, Dex, but she's not a loser just because she doesn't live in the city. Kylie's sister and her three kids live in Cherry Hill, and her sister's husband died last year. So she moved out of Philly and into a rental condo here, so she could help out when she can."

Whoa. Was I wrong. Janice had his attention now. But he still held reservations. "If she works for a law firm and helps out with her sister's kids, then she won't have much time to date."

"She doesn't have the time to waste in looking for her perfect guy. Which is why she's perfect for you. She's gorgeous, smart, hard-working, loves kids, and wants to be in a relationship. You have the same qualities and want the same things. Maybe you're meant to be together."

"If she's so perfect, then why isn't she already in a relationship?"

"She and her previous boyfriend broke up because he didn't want to commit. She wants to get married and have kids. Not immediately but when the time is right."

Kylie did seem to be in the same situation as Dex. Maybe it would be worth spending an hour or so having a drink after work to see if there could be a spark.

Intellectually, Dex understood he had to move on. And he wasn't getting any younger. Sulking or waiting for Nicki to come around and all of a sudden want his children did not seem the wise thing to wait for. It wasn't going to happen no matter how much he wanted it.

He glanced at his sister's hopeful expression. "If I say okay, will you please go and put make-up on the other eye? You're looking a little scary."

Janice jumped up and down and clapped like a little kid. "Yes, yes, yes." She pulled her phone from her robe pocket—convenient—and texted him Kylie's contact information.

"Will you call her tomorrow? If not, when? I want to give her a heads-up so she's not taken off guard."

He should bite the bullet and go for it. Why wait? If she was "his person" then the sooner the better to get to know her. If she wasn't, the sooner the better to move on.

"I'll call her tomorrow."

He shook his head and slid off the stool, heading down to the basement to see what trouble his favorite niece and nephew were getting into.

****

"The accountant is here."

Nicki's head shot up as she zeroed in on Cheryl. "Who?"

Her heart practically beat out of her chest. Was Dex here?

"You have a ten o'clock appointment with the company's accountant, Brendan Moore. Remember?" Cheryl's frown told Nicki she was losing it.

"Of course. Yes. I remember. Sorry. I was deep into the marketing presentation for The Bobby Strong Band." Nicki rose and flattened her suddenly damp palms against her skirt. "Is the conference room available?"

"It's all set up. I left the expense reports and cash flow statements along with the other documentation he requested. If you need anything more, let me know."

Nicki swallowed to push down her utter

disappointment. Yet how could she believe Dex would come to see her? He had never come to her office in the past. If he wanted to see her, and he obviously didn't, he'd call and invite her out. Or over. Or something.

So much for moving on.

She picked up a few pads of paper, her calculator, and a pen. She'd never met with the company accountant before. It wasn't part of her job description until her recent promotion. Not knowing what to expect or how long the meeting would last, she pushed all extraneous thoughts from her mind and strode to the conference room.

"Mr. Moore." She entered and extended her hand to shake his.

"Please, call me Brendan." His height, build, and green eyes reminded her of Dex. So not fair.

He held her hand a little too long as he took in her features. She couldn't be annoyed. She did the same with him. "What do you need to know?" She sat down and invited him to do the same, getting right to business.

Business took the better part of the day, but she got to know Brendan, at least on the surface, and he was funny, smart, and easy to work with. It would have been perfect if he didn't remind her of the one man she wanted to forget.

"Thanks for your time today, Nicki. I know you're new to this role, but you made my job easy."

Charming too.

"I didn't know what to expect. I'm glad we were able to give you everything you needed." She stood, sensing the heat of his gaze on her. "I guess this is it for now." She shook his hand.

"For now." He smiled, a smile Nicki was sure would melt the panties off most women. But not her. She wasn't interested in meeting, dating, or otherwise engaging with men since Dex walked out the door.

Now that three months had passed, shouldn't she be getting back to normal? Back to having fun? The no-strings kind of fun?

"We'll be meeting once a month," Brendan informed her with a sparkle in his eye.

"Sure. Let Cheryl know the dates, and we'll have everything ready for you."

He gathered his belongings and left, leaving Nicki unsettled and questioning.

"Wow," said Cheryl as she came cruising into the conference room. "I wouldn't mind being locked in a room with him all day."

Nicki smiled. "Undeniably easy on the eyes. Nice too."

"Did he ask you out?"

"Of course not. He's the company's accountant. There must be some policy prohibiting fraternizing with our consultants."

"There isn't. I looked it up. Just in case." Cheryl studied Nicki as if under a microscope. "Are you going to ask him out?"

"No. Why would I?"

"Because he's gorgeous, has a good job, and is single."

"How do you know?"

"No wedding ring. I checked."

"A guy not wearing a wedding ring doesn't mean he's not married."

But Nicki knew he wasn't. They'd had hours to

chat in between his review of their records, and she'd found out plenty. Brendan had recently become a partner at his firm, lived in Society Hill alone, had gone to the University of Pennsylvania, her alma mater, for his bachelor's degree and Wharton for his MBA. He enjoyed playing soccer in his free time, as well as listening to music—classical music. He was on the board of the Symphony and had played the cello when he was in high school. Typical boring accountant.

But of course, she knew better than to stereotype. Dex had never been boring—especially in bed.

"Is he?" asked Cheryl. "Married?"

Nicki paused, making Cheryl wait for the answer she wanted to hear. "No. Not married."

"Don't you think it's time to move on?" Cheryl cloaked her question in empathy.

Nicki looked up, surprised at her bluntness.

But she had no answer. Because the only person Nicki wanted to move on with was Dex.

****

"Nicki. It's so great to see you." Denise hugged her before she got through the door. "In Princeton on business again?"

Nicki moved into Denise's living room, discarding her suit jacket. "I had a meeting at the Hyatt with one of our execs from New York. Since I was in town, I decided to see if you were home, catch up a bit."

Although she did have an ulterior motive. Unable to get Dex out of her heart, she started wondering if she could change her mind. Perhaps Denise would help. She adored her own kids as well as her adopted child, Bobby. Maybe Denise's spin on things would encourage Nicki to move away from her aversion to having children. Or at least make her more open to the possibility.

Denise started picking up toys from the floor. "Good timing. Johnny is down for his nap. And Jennifer and Bobby are at camp."

Nicki sat. "Don't clean up. Come and sit. You look exhausted." Denise's olive skin had a grayish tint. "Is everything okay?"

Denise plopped on the couch beside her. "No." Tears sprang to her eyes.

Nicki sat forward, taking her hand. "What is it?"

"Bobby has leukemia." The words fell between them like a grenade ready to explode.

"Oh my God. When did you learn that?"

"A few weeks ago."

"Why didn't you tell me?"

She couldn't remember if she'd spoken to Denise since they all met in Crescent Beach. Nicki moved in her own little, sad world, working six days a week and trying to sleep through the seventh. Her sole goal was to purge Dex from every corner of her memory.

Denise shrugged. "Ben and I have been trying to process it ourselves. Getting a second opinion. Coming up with a plan for treatment. I couldn't have a conversation about it."

Nicki hugged Denise. "I'm so sorry. Is there anything I can do?"

Although nothing could take away the pain of having a sick child. Wasn't this a resounding reason not to have children? And here she'd come to Denise to find a reason to change her mind.

"No. I don't think so. Sam is doing whatever she needs to do to obtain the adoption records from when

Ben's brother and sister-in-law adopted him. If we can find out the names of Bobby's birth parents, we'll reach out to them to see if they're a match for a bone marrow transplant. Neither Ben nor I are."

"When will you hear?"

"Sam said it shouldn't take too long. Maybe two more weeks. Apparently, with the change in the adoption laws, it's easier now, but there are still some hurdles, depending on the case. I'm leaving it up to her to wade through the details. I just want the end result."

"What if you can't find them or they don't want to get involved?"

Denise spun her wedding band, then looked up at Nicki. "Why wouldn't a parent want to help their child if we can find them?"

"Of course they would." Nicki took Denise's hands in hers and squeezed them. Why had she even raised those negative questions?

Silence hung between them, as if words were the enemy.

Finally, Nicki dared to ask another question. "Is Bobby feeling sick?"

"No. He's doing okay. But once the chemo starts, it will be a different story. Ben and I are trying to be positive to keep his spirits up. And of course, Jennifer and Johnny don't understand what's going on. I'm living in disjointed worlds." Denise looked at Nicki with pleading eyes. "Let's talk about something else. Take my mind off Bobby. How are you doing? How are things with Dex?"

Nicki inwardly cringed. Yes, she wanted to help Denise take her mind off Bobby, but she didn't want to shine a spotlight on her miserable existence. So she'd revert to her rote answers. "We broke up. Turns out we weren't right for each other."

"What do you mean? You were crazy about him."

Nicki's stomach plummeted. "I was." She dug deep for a smile. "It didn't work out. He was too serious for me." *He wanted to marry me. Have kids*. Only Nicki could find fault with that. "And way too conservative." *Although not in the bedroom*. Nicki's face burned remembering their steamy encounters. She needed to erase those images from her mind completely or she'd spontaneously combust. "You were right. A cruise ship romance could never work out." She fought back the urge to cry. "But it was fun while it lasted. I didn't want a serious relationship anyway." She deserved an Oscar for this performance.

"What's wrong with being serious, Nicki? Don't you want to settle down, have a family?"

How should she answer this? Nicki's real reason for dropping by was to learn about the joys of having children. But after what Denise shared, her question became irrelevant. Bobby had leukemia. How does any mother get through that trauma?

"I'm not ready to settle down." But she was. With Dex. Just no kids.

"I guess its best then that you broke up before either of you got too attached."

All Nicki could do was nod, for the clog in her throat prevented further words on the topic.

"How's work?" Denise must have sensed a change of subject was in order, and she clearly didn't want to go back to the subject of Bobby.

"Good. Busy." Thank God. It kept her from going insane thinking about what she'd thrown away. "My accounts are heating up. Three of the four artists we signed in the past year have new releases, which I've been working on. I have my hands full."

"Your job sounds so exciting. I can't believe you know Perry Adams. I love his music."

"He's a great guy. Very talented and it hasn't gone to his head. Yet."

"Why don't you date him? He's single. And I'm sure you had his head turned when you were in Nashville."

"I don't date clients. Besides, you can't trust those music types to be faithful. Too many beautiful women throwing themselves at them."

"You said you're not ready to settle down. You don't want to get serious. He'd be perfect. And then we can get good seats to his concerts when he's in the area."

Denise was right. She *did* say she had no intention of getting involved in a relationship. She *did* plan on dating many and dating often. No strings to bind her. Free as a bird. Yada, yada, yada, blah, blah, blah. That would assure her heart wouldn't get broken. But right now, she was more talk than action. She'd used the same rhetoric with Sam, hoping to help her out of her funk. And maybe she would follow her own advice someday. But right now, she had to get over Dex.

"I should get going. It'll take me an hour to get back to the office, and I have a million things to get done today." Nicki stood and picked up her purse. "I'm truly sorry to hear about Bobby."

"Thanks for coming by. It's so good to see a friend at a time like this." Denise's eyes glazed but she didn't cry.

"Stay strong and positive, Denise. Like you always are. Hopefully, Sam can find Bobby's birth parents, and one of them will be a match. If not, you have so many friends. I'll get tested. I'm sure Sam and Alyssa would as well."

That brought out the tears. "I'm so lucky to have you. All of you. I'll let you know what happens."

Nicki hugged her and left.

Children could bring such pain.

Chapter Sixteen

The efficient receptionist at Snow Leopard Music called Nicki in her office. "There's a Samantha Winslow here to see you."

Sam? I wonder what brings her here. Nicki strode to the reception area where Sam was perched on the edge of her seat, alternately crossing and uncrossing her legs, twisting at her fingers, and compulsively checking her watch. She must be late for something.

"Sam? Hi." She went over and hugged her friend. "Is everything okay? Do you need to be somewhere soon?"

Sam brushed at the air. "No. Nowhere. I decided to come into Philadelphia today. I'm going crazy at the beach. I hoped you wouldn't be caught up in some important meeting."

"Any other day this week and I would have. This is perfect."

"So show me your office."

Sam's voice seemed tight and her smile forced. Perhaps some new development with her soon-to-be ex-husband had her jittery.

"Sure. This way."

Nicki led Sam through a series of hallways where the decibel level was high and the activity bee-like. She loved the energy at her home away from home.

When they reached Nicki's office, Sam closed the

door before she sank into the chair in front of Nicki's desk.

"What's up?" asked Nicki, waiting patiently for Sam to explain the reason for her visit. "Is something wrong? Did you hear from Tom? You seem edgy."

"You know Denise's son Bobby has leukemia, right?"

"Yes, I know. It's so awful. That poor kid. Losing his adoptive parents in a car accident and now this." Nicki sat forward in her chair, worry worming its way through her system. "Have you heard something new? Has he taken a turn for the worse?"

"No. No. He's the same," Sam reassured her. "But they've decided on a course of treatment after speaking to the specialists. Chemo, then a bone marrow transplant. I represent Denise and Ben. And Bobby. I filed an application. To obtain his adoption records." Sam's short sentences and halting delivery were so odd. "I got the original birth certificate yesterday."

Relief spread through Nicki. "That's great, right?"

Sam bit her lip. "Nicki, you're Bobby's mother."

The words hung between them, suspended. Nicki couldn't have heard her correctly. She moved her lips to comment, but no words came out. Her brain froze and her muscles tensed. The silence in the room magnified itself in sharp contrast to the blur of noise on the other side of the door.

"Could you repeat that?" she croaked, the hairs on the back of her neck standing in almost painful attention.

This couldn't be. It was impossible.

Sam nodded to affirm the words Nicki had heard.

Her dulled mind spun through the past—the

hospital where she'd refused to hold her son when he was born, believing it would dim the pain of turning him over. The social worker giving her one last chance to say hello and goodbye, before taking her baby to his adoptive parents. She hadn't wanted to meet them, hadn't wanted to know who they were. She fast-forwarded to Denise's in-laws' death in a car accident, to Denise and Ben taking in their nephew as their own. Adopting him.

Nicki buried her face in her hands, and something akin to a primal scream emerged.

Sam hovered over her, stroking her back, giving an awkward hug. This couldn't be happening. Bobby wasn't her son. But Sam wouldn't be here telling her this if it weren't true.

Nicki's wracking sobs couldn't be controlled. She spoke through her tears, but only incoherent words came out. She lifted her head in search of a tissue and mopped away the tears and running mascara.

Finally, Nicki had the strength to speak. "You probably need to know who the father is." She couldn't look Sam in the eye.

"No father is named on the birth certificate. You said you were drugged at a party and didn't know who he was."

"I wasn't drugged. I made it up." Her heart thudded and she could barely breathe. "I was with a classmate, and I didn't want anyone to know. The father is Michael McCain." Nicki's throat closed around her words, as she watched Sam sit back on her heels, her face ashen, her eyes wide.

"But...you mean you lied to everyone?"

Yes, Nicki had lied to her best friends fifteen years

ago and never corrected her statement. Not that she ever raised it again, and if it came up, she brushed it aside. The reality that she'd had a baby and given him up for adoption was in the past, and Nicki tried hard to keep it there. It had been so unsettling when Sam brought it up in Crescent Beach. Even worse when she'd spoken about Michael McCain.

Sam reached for Nicki's hand. "Why didn't you tell us you were involved with Michael in high school? We shared everything."

Nicki shook her head. "We weren't involved. We were friends. He felt sorry for me because I was so upset about my mother's depression after my father died. I felt sorry for him because his father was abusive. I wanted to be there for him, listen to him. He was so angry his mom left with his sister and not him. We talked about that a lot—with me trying to come up with excuses for her desertion so he wouldn't hate her." Nicki looked out the window. "The more time I spent with him, the more time I wanted to spend. I wanted to be there for him, to help him. I wasn't in love with him, but he needed me, and it made me feel good."

Nicki reached for another tissue and dabbed at her swollen eyes.

"One night, I was with him after his father had beaten him up for some minor infraction. I remember that night so clearly. I touched his bruises, trying to erase them. Before I knew it, we were kissing. Then it went further. I felt so incredibly close to him. Like we were the same person. We were both in so much emotional pain." A sob escaped. "He probably didn't feel anything but lust. His real emotions were wrapped up in his dysfunctional family. And I had lost my father, spiraling my mother into another world." She glanced at Sam, a flush of embarrassment heating her face. "He was sweet to me. He cared about me. As a friend."

"Did you tell him you were pregnant?" Sam's voice came out in a whisper.

"Yes. The night of Alyssa's party. The night he disappeared."

"Did he tell you he was leaving?"

"No!" Nicki's adamant tone underscored her statement. Michael's disappearance that night had the entire student body wondering if he had met an untimely death, either at his father's hand or Carl's, that awful kid he'd gotten into a fight with that night. "I was as shocked and upset as everyone else. I thought something bad had happened to him."

Sam's skepticism was barely hidden. Nicki couldn't blame her. She'd lied to Sam. To all her Sworn Sisters.

"I know you must feel betrayed. We told each other everything. I'm sorry, but this was too personal. Too much a part of the bad side of me. I didn't want to share it. I couldn't."

Sam reached out and touched Nicki's shoulder, a reassuring gesture that told Nicki no matter what, she'd always love her. "Nicki, you don't have a bad side. You were young and afraid. Your mother wasn't there for you. But we would have been by your side no matter what."

Nicki nodded, acknowledging at age thirty-three what she didn't know at eighteen.

"How did Michael react to your news that night?" Sam's voice cracked, as if she were afraid to hear the answer.

"It was not a good night for him. He had a new black eye, courtesy of his father, and had been arguing with that ass, Carl. But I couldn't keep it to myself a second longer. I needed to tell him; to share my fears. I think my confession pushed him over the edge." Nicki bit her lip, remembering. "He said all the right things—after he suggested an abortion. When I balked, he told me not to worry, he'd stand by me, marry me if I wanted to keep the baby. That was not my plan either. I wanted to talk more, but he was so distracted. I begged him to forget about Carl, but he wouldn't hear of it. He wasn't going to be called a coward for failing to show up for the fight. I was scared for him, scared for me, scared about the future. He must have been too." She paused, replaying that night from so long ago. "I was angry this thing with Carl seemed more important than what I had told him. I blurted out I would do what he suggested and get an abortion. That he didn't have to worry about it; I'd take care of it. Then I left." Nicki looked at Sam and whispered, "I couldn't believe he disappeared." As if to say it out loud would make it more real.

Sam sat on the edge of Nicki's desk. "We all worried about what might have happened to him."

Nicki nodded. Although she and her Sworn Sisters participated in the theories running rampant in the aftermath of Michael's disappearance, they were also dealing with the news of Nicki's pregnancy. Never knowing there was, or could have been, a connection between the two.

"Did Michael ever try to reach you?" asked Sam.

"No. I never heard from him. At first, I convinced

myself he'd be back. Or at least call me. He wasn't the kind of person who'd leave me to deal with the problem on my own. But when he didn't resurface, I assumed what everyone else did. He'd met up with his fate." Nicki continued. "I went to speak to the officer in charge of the investigation, convinced they'd overlooked something, someone. But they hadn't. In their eyes, he was a missing person who wanted to disappear. And after the officer explained their findings, I began to believe that too." Anger poked through Nicki's words. "Don't tell Michael he's Bobby's father."

"I have to, Nicki. I have a legal obligation to Denise and Ben. And Bobby."

Fresh tears sprang into Nicki's eyes. "Oh my God. I can't believe I know who my child is. I saw Bobby at a party at Denise's. When Ben's brother and his wife were still alive." Nicki's voice broke and pain reached down to her toes. "I'll be the donor. He can have my bone marrow. There's no reason for Michael to be told." Nicki continued to resist, throwing out whatever possible solution came to mind as guilt and angst collided.

"What if yours doesn't match? What if there are other problems? From what I understand, it's not easy to find a perfect match, and Bobby deserves all the help he can get."

"You don't care what your best friend wants?" Nicki used their friendship as a weapon to bolster her plea, despite its unreasonableness. Especially given that Nicki hadn't trusted *her best friend* with the truth in the first place.

She reconsidered. "I'm sorry, Sam. But I don't

want to face him. I lied on the adoption papers about not knowing who the father was. And I've tried to bury that awful chapter of my life. It's helped me survive giving up my child, our child, for adoption. I don't ever want to see him again."

"I understand your anxiety over bringing Michael into this. And of course, he'll be shocked. But he's the boy's father and Bobby needs as many chances as possible to help him get well. You don't have to see Michael. You don't have to talk to him. Any and all tests can be taken independently of each other."

Nicki's fight leaked out of her system and fresh tears streamed down her face. "Of course we both need to help." Nicki turned her back on Sam.

Sam reached out and hugged Nicki to her. "Don't worry. I'll help you get through this. I promise."

****

Nicki sat holed up in her office long after Sam left, long after everyone in the office left. All strength and emotion drained and puddled around her on the floor. The questions had no answers, yet they kept taunting her. How could this be happening? Of course there were coincidences, but how could Ben and Denise's relatives have adopted her child? How could Ben and Denise now be his parents? And how could he be so sick? The ache in her gut kicked up ten notches when she dared to dwell on that question.

There was no history of cancer in her family. Of course, she didn't know about Michael's. He probably didn't even know.

Poor, poor Bobby. Leukemia. Now that she knew he was her child, it sounded like a death sentence. Yet Sam seemed so hopeful. All he needed was a bone marrow donor. A parent. Was it really so easy? Could he be cured?

She eventually pushed herself to turn toward her computer, moving the mouse in a circle to wake it up. It had been hours since she'd moved, and her body hung heavy with lethargy. She typed in the offensive word. Four common types of leukemia popped up. Then there was the treatment, but that depended on the type. Then the benefits and risks, depending on the treatment that was dependent on the type. She slammed her fist on the desk—the greatest physical effort she made since Sam left. What type of leukemia did Bobby have? The worst? The most curable? This measly bit of research was making her crazy.

She hadn't asked Denise when she first learned of Bobby's illness. At the time, Bobby had been a near stranger. Now he was her birth child. How soon would he need the transplant? How sick was he? She needed to talk to Denise. But she had to pull herself together first.

How ironic that Sam had recently discovered Michael was alive. Was it all a coincidence or were the fates punishing her for giving up her child for adoption?

She'd done the best she could under the circumstances. Getting the needed help and support from a local adoption agency assured her baby would be loved and cared for by a couple who couldn't have children. She trusted the agency to choose the right parents. It was their job. And they guaranteed an anonymous transaction, which was sure to help her forget about this traumatic experience in the long run.

The workers at the agency didn't make her feel guilty about her decision. She took care of the guilt on her own. They understood she wasn't ready to become a mother. She had goals. Ambitions. The first of which was to attend college. The University of Pennsylvania deferred her admission until the next year, and she hoped by then she'd be able to put this whole nightmare behind.

Yet she mourned her loss for months; even longer. She cried every day until she had no more tears to shed. The rest of the Sworn Sisters all went off to college, and though they kept in touch, they were in a different world. Dating, partying, studying. While Nicki barely drifted from day to day, her overwhelming sadness pushing her to despair.

Her mother finally got her to a counselor, although how her mother recognized Nicki's depression was a mystery, since her mother lived in the same state from the time of her father's death. Therapy saved her life. But she also built barriers. Barriers that sheltered and protected her and assured she'd never encounter the sharp knife of pain again.

How was it possible that in the course of a few weeks she'd been brought back to those days she worked so hard to forget? Pain and loss washed through her anew, as if it hadn't been fifteen years. A sob escaped, and she held her hand over her mouth to prevent another. But who would hear? She was alone, left to cope with her past.

And that's how it was meant to be.

Chapter Seventeen

The aggravating buzz of her condo intercom set Nicki's teeth on edge, and she had half a mind to pretend she wasn't home. She'd gotten in from work five minutes ago after a crazy day and expected no one. Further, she was not in the mood for harassing canvassers or charity do-gooders. For she was not in a charitable mood.

Over the past few days, between marketing reports and meetings, she'd surfed the internet researching leukemia and its cure. At times she'd felt encouraged, knowing the bone marrow transplant would work for Bobby. At other times she'd been downright depressed, fearing he could die. It had taken all her courage, but she finally called Denise. And now she was emotionally exhausted.

Despite her best attempts at ignoring it, the buzzing continued, and answering it seemed the only way to make it stop.

"Who is it?" she called through the intercom, her annoyance floating through the wires.

"Michael McCain."

A dizzying rush nearly downed her, and Nicki inhaled, closing her eyes. She put her hand against the wall for support, waiting for the spell to pass. The buzzer sounded again.

She didn't answer but hit the button to allow him

entry.

Didn't he have a telephone? An email account? How had he gotten her address? Sam. Of course. Nicki was going to kill her. But now that he was here, what was she going to say to him? After all these years. How was she going to explain she'd lied to him about getting an abortion? That she'd lied on the adoption papers? Her stomach flipped, and she placed her hand on her abdomen in an attempt to quell the nausea.

Nicki stood by the closed door and waited for her unwanted visitor as her insides continued to somersault to the beat of her pounding heart. She didn't have to wait long.

At his knock, she opened the door and there he stood, a ghost from the past. Dressed in a suit and tie, looking ever so different than she remembered. His eyes caught hers and held them; sadness or perhaps discomfort etched his face.

"May I come in?" His voice had a deeper, richer timbre than she remembered.

Moving back, she gestured for him to enter.

He came in a few feet. "Thanks for letting me in. I know I gave you no warning."

She nodded, struggling to find her voice. "Didn't Sam tell you I didn't want to see you?" It didn't come out mean or hostile, but the question held its own censure.

"Yes, she did." He stared at the rug. "I'm sorry. I had to talk to you."

"How did you know where I lived?" Sam was so not off the hook.

"I knew you lived in Philadelphia. I looked you up."

Ugh. No one had privacy with the internet.

"Come on in." She moved toward the living room. "Sit down." Since he was here, there didn't seem to be a way out of this conversation. And she was sure there was more than a nice discussion coming her way. She'd lied. Big time.

He sat on the edge of the sofa, leaned his arms on his thighs, and looked up at her. "Aren't you going to sit?"

Moving to an armchair across from the sofa, she slipped her heels off and drew her legs up underneath her, trying to get comfortable. It wasn't going to work.

"What brings you here?" As if she didn't know. Yet she attempted to keep her cool, her voice calm.

"Come on, Nicki." His tone couldn't be considered cool or calm. "Drop the semi-polite aloofness. We have to talk. We have a child together. A sick child. A child I didn't know about. Why did you lie and tell me you were going to have an abortion? Why did you tell me not to worry about anything?"

Heat rushed to her cheeks, and she was ready to pounce, but she held herself in place by squeezing the arms of her chair. She didn't expect him to start the conversation with blame. "How dare you question me after all these years? I had to do what I had to do to protect myself. You disappeared. Even if you hadn't, you weren't serious about getting married. You didn't love me." Her voice grew louder and more accusing with each sentence. So much for cool and calm.

"You didn't love me either. It wasn't the best solution, but I wouldn't have abandoned you." His tone, a little more controlled than hers, was just as resentful.

"Yet that's what you did." The cutting words fell

on the floor between them, and Michael stared at her, then shook his head.

"You told me you were getting an abortion. I believed you." He scruffed his hands over his face. "I knew Carl's friends would be coming for me after I beat the crap out of him. My father would have added to the mix. You, of all people, knew what I was going through at home. You encouraged me to leave. To go live with my mother. You predicted the next time my father raised a hand to me, one of us was going to end up in the hospital. Or worse." He stood and started walking around the room; as if the intensity of the subject wouldn't allow him to keep still.

Yes. She'd known.

She turned her head to follow his movements as the bluster leaked out of her. She reached into the recesses of her brain to respond. But what could she say? So much time had passed. Decisions had been made.

"The police said you didn't go to Ohio to live with your mom."

"No. I was afraid my father would find me there and make me come back. I went to New York City, figuring I could get lost in the millions."

"By yourself?"

He nodded.

How could an eighteen-year-old with no relatives, money, or job survive? But he did and even succeeded in life.

He walked over and stood before her. "Nicki, I'm sorry. In hindsight, I should have let you know where I was. Reached out to you in case you needed me. I was young and immature and fighting for my life." He shook his head. "When you said you wouldn't marry me because I used my fists to settle fights, it terrified me. I didn't want to become my father. I hated him. I had to get away. Then you told me you were going to get an abortion. I wanted to believe you. It made things simple. And it allowed me to do what was best. To disappear."

Nicki fought the lump taking over her throat as tears welled up in her eyes. She looked down so he wouldn't notice, but they betrayed her and spilled over her cheeks. She was such a fool. Crying for the scared kid she'd been. Crying over the guilt for giving up her child. And now crying for the eighteen-year-old boy who'd needed to hide out in New York City.

She sighed. "I guess it was for the best. I couldn't have handled your problems while I was trying to handle mine. Although I decided against having an abortion, I couldn't keep the baby. I was too young. Too immature. Too selfish." She sighed and swiped at her tears. "I met with a social worker from the adoption agency who promised to find a good home. It was the right decision. The baby would be happier with a family who wanted him." Over the years when she thought about her son and her choice, she'd been able to lessen the guilt based on this. "Besides, I had my life to live, which was going to start with an Ivy League education. Hell, even now I know I wouldn't be a good mother. I'm not cut out for the job."

The tears continued to flow down her cheeks, and she didn't try to stop them. The release, after years of stifling her emotions, felt almost cathartic.

Michael crouched in front of her and took her hands into his. "Please don't cry."

She smiled through her tears. "Why is it guys can't

deal with crying? It's an emotion that comes out through our eyes. It's healthy." She brushed her hand against her cheek.

"Maybe I should try it then."

His eyes were so sad, his face drawn. He must be as tortured over all this as she was. And he was reaching out to her. To share it. And to move forward.

"It might make you feel better. I hope I do."

He nodded.

"I need some tissues. Excuse me."

Michael stood to let her by, a hint of relief shadowing his face. "May I take off my jacket?"

"Sure."

When she came back into the living room, she carried a box of tissues. "Would you like something to drink?"

"I could probably use something stronger, but water would be great. Thanks."

She went to the kitchen and turned on the tap. She had to admit it took a tremendous amount of guts for him to show up here. Especially since he'd known she didn't want to see him. Despite everything, he'd been the bigger person. He'd done the right thing. Clearing the air.

Nicki turned off the water and headed back to the living room, handing him the glass. "I guess I sound unreasonably angry for something that happened so long ago." She set the glass on the table before him.

"No. I left you to deal with a problem we both created." He rubbed his hands over his face. "Not that I want to characterize Bobby as a problem. You know what I mean. If I knew you were going to have the baby, I wouldn't have left."

She nodded. She'd forgotten her cruel words to him the night of Alyssa's party. God, she'd been so mean. Obviously, he hadn't forgotten. "You did what you had to do. Things were so bad with your father. You had to get away from him."

Michael grimaced. "In retrospect, it was stupid of me to believe you would get an abortion. We went through twelve years of Catholic school together. But there's no accounting for my stupidity. At least back then. I hate to use it as an excuse, but I had a lot on my mind." His lips formed into a thin line of disapproval and possibly disappointment in himself. "I'm sorry for being so accusatory when I first arrived tonight."

She spun the bracelet on her wrist. "I shouldn't have said back then that you were going to be like your father. I was your friend." She swallowed. "What now?"

"We move forward. On the same page, hopefully. To help Bobby."

The familiar ache squeezed her heart every time she thought about what that young boy, her son, was going through. What he still had to go through. "We have to have blood tests. See if we're a match. Have you talked to Denise yet?"

"No. I wanted to discuss this with you first." He pushed his hand through his hair and sat back, looking as weary as she felt. "Did you?"

"Yes. It wasn't much of a conversation. I asked her for the information I needed to get tested. We were both in shock about the news and neither of us went any deeper. I still can't wrap my head around the fact that Denise and Ben have known our child his whole life. First as their nephew and now as their son. They've been to his christening, his First Holy Communion, his birthday parties. And now they're sitting in doctors' offices discussing methods of treatment, watching, waiting for his symptoms to worsen." Her throat clogged and she tried to swallow the painful lump. "I called and scheduled the blood test. You should do the same."

Michael nodded. "I'll call Denise tomorrow." He picked up his glass of water, then put it down without drinking, sighing at the same time.

"What?" she asked.

"I don't want to meet Bobby. It can't be a good idea. How must a kid feel when he knows his parents gave him up?"

"I've been agonizing over the same thing. It would be awful for him to learn the woman who abandoned him is one of his adoptive mother's best friends." Nicki had analyzed it to death over the last forty-eight hours, looking at the pros and cons. She contemplated asking Denise not to tell Bobby anything until she thought it through. "Maybe we shouldn't tell him we're his birth parents. Denise can tell him we heard about his illness, and we're willing to submit to a blood test to see if we're a match."

"But Bobby knows Sam obtained the records." Michael leaned forward, his arms on his thighs. "He must know she's reaching out to his birth parents."

"She can say she can't find them. Or they won't help."

"That would be worse, don't you think? Besides, Sam wouldn't lie."

Michael's authoritative statement about Sam puzzled Nicki, and her radar kicked in. "How do you know so much about Sam and her case?"

Michael stilled, then his eyes caught hers, and he held them for a moment before speaking. "I ran into her a few times in the beginning of the summer when she came to Crescent Beach. I live there now. At first, we didn't recognize each other. Soon after we did, she came to municipal court over a parking ticket. I'm the prosecutor there."

A laugh escaped Nicki's mouth, and she held her hand over it. "Oh, no. I was with her when she got that ticket. Two actually. She was so angry I thought she was going to end up in jail that night."

"Well, I didn't do her any favors in court, and she was ready to bite my head off after being found guilty and charged with fines and costs."

The sparkle in his eyes told Nicki he got a certain amount of satisfaction from bringing Sam down, but she couldn't help asking. "Why didn't you give her a break?"

"It wasn't up to me. It was the judge's call." Michael chuckled. "But if you could have seen her that morning. She was in full litigator mode—power suit, commanding voice, prepared to plead her case with conviction. Then the judge shut her down. It was too amusing to watch." His grin got wider.

Nicki could picture it and she chuckled too. "How did you get from adversaries to friends?"

Michael's smile faltered and his jaw tightened.

Then it hit her. "You're more than friends?"

This question prompted Michael to loosen his tie. Interesting. And telling. Nicki frowned, waiting patiently for his response.

He cleared his throat. "Yes and no. I didn't know

her well in high school. But I learned over the past few weeks she's a very special person. Kind. Caring." He paused. "She's going through a tough time with her divorce. The last thing she wanted to do was take a leave of absence from work. But although she's not in the office, she's been helping her clients on a daily basis. And she took this case on for Denise. It can't be easy for her to be in the middle of it all. I admire her."

Nicki nodded. "Don't forget she's gorgeous too."

His face reddened. "Yes, she's gorgeous."

"I can't believe her husband's having an affair with a co-worker. And went to San Diego with her for the summer. Sam didn't deserve that."

"People change. Relationships change."

Nicki didn't know whether Michael was making a general statement or talking from experience. So much time had gone by since they'd been friends that she didn't know him at all anymore.

He seemed to key into her thoughts. "It's odd to be sitting here talking to you after all these years. We were so close back then." He shook his head. "And now we're like two strangers."

It was sad. But time marches on. And if truth be told, she was glad to be far away from her high school years and all the drama those years brought. She was in a much better place now if she overlooked the heartbreak over Dex. She had a great career. A fabulous apartment in the city. And good friends who would get her through anything.

Then her heart hammered. And a sick child who needed her help.

Nicki studied her old friend. "I guess we'll be seeing a lot more of each other in our effort to help

Bobby. And if you're friends with Sam, we're bound to run into each other. At least for the next month or so while Sam's staying in Crescent Beach." A shadow crossed Michael's face. "Sam's a great person. And a wonderful friend. She could use a little male attention right now. Just don't hurt her." She wagged her finger to make her point. As if she had any control over it.

His jaw tightened. "That's not the way it's going to go down. She'll be leaving to go back to New York."

"What goes around comes around," Nicki blurted out.

The pained look on his face was more telling than words, and she wished she could take her glib statement back. If she was reading him correctly, she was seeing a little more there than admiration for Sam.

Could he be falling for her?

****

After Michael left, Nicki roamed her apartment, moving by rote through the living room, dining room, bedroom, and kitchen. She looked for things to put away or clean, but everything was in its place, as usual. The perfect home for the perfect life.

She stopped at the picture window, ignoring the row homes before her, and instead focused on the treetops from a park a few streets over—black silhouettes against a gray-smudged, stormy sky. Their leaves shook in the wind like a hundred birds flapping their wings but going nowhere. It was so quiet in her condo, but she could almost hear the rush of wind stealthily moving through branches, twigs, and needles, defying those leaves to fall from grace. But they held on, clinging to life. Strong and resilient in the face of adversity.

Was she like one of those leaves or was she barely holding on?

She exhaled, then threw herself on the couch and hugged a pillow into her chest. For years she'd avoided dwelling on her actions surrounding her child. That self-defense mechanism had shielded her from emotions which would bring her down. Make her weak.

Now, with every turn she was pummeled with her past, compelling her to deal with unwanted feelings. Not able to label them, she spun through the list of possibilities. Anger, sadness, hurt? No. Happiness, relief, hope? Maybe relief.

Relieved that Michael forced her to face him and the past. She'd believed it was all behind her, a slice of life she tried to bury. Yet even if this new development hadn't occurred, what did happen fifteen years ago affected her in the present. Because of her child, who now had a name and a face, she couldn't move forward with Dex.

She squeezed the pillow harder. Hollowing it in the middle. The exact way she felt. Like a shell with no center. No real place for feelings.

When had she become a shell? It started before she'd given up her baby. When her father died and her mother's true spirit disappeared. She'd built the shell, layer by layer, until it was so thick nothing could get in, and nothing could get out. She banished her emotions, refusing to allow them to chip away at the inner casing. And she refused to let anyone else do the same.

Yet Dex had peeled away a layer and had been working on more. Until she'd shut him down. One in a string of relationships doomed from the start.

She was incapable of loving unconditionally. And

she was incapable of having another child.

Along the way she had lost her soul.

A lead weight sank in her stomach. She'd gone from questioning her problem to labeling it. But it all made sense. Everything she'd done over the past fifteen years contributed to her independence, as she liked to call it. But once she met Dex, things had changed.

A tear slid down her check, then another.

She had built the perfect, independent life that wasn't so perfect after all.

Chapter Eighteen

"Nice work, little brother." Dex's sister, Janice, tapped him on the shoulder, beaming as she took in the scene. Runners, joggers, and walkers milled around the registration table for the first annual Big/Little Race at Fairmount Park. Dex's pride was overtaken with angst, so he was thrilled with the distraction.

Dex squatted to hug his niece, Chloe, dressed in a pink tutu over her pink shorts, and his nephew, Colin, dressed as batman. "You guys look great! Thanks for coming." He looked up at his sister. "Is Frank here?"

"Yup. He's parking the car. He'll have to walk a mile before the race even starts. But the kids and I wanted to find you to see if you needed any help, so he dropped us off. Right kids?"

Colin spun around, making his cape fly out. "Right. Uncle Dex, I wanted you to see my costume."

Janice chuckled. "Okay. So maybe they don't want to help."

Dex ruffled Colin's hair. "I bet that cape will make you run even faster than you usually do. You'll definitely have an advantage in the under-five age group."

"What about my costume, Uncle Dex? Do you like it?" Chloe tried to stand on her toes in her light-up sneakers, then did a few jumps with her arms over her head.

"You're the prettiest ballerina here. All the other girls will wish they had a tutu just like yours." He kissed her on the cheek, then stood. "Where's your costume, sis?" He couldn't help the grin.

"You know we can't get out of the house without them wearing something interesting. There's no use fighting it. Chloe wore her leotard, tutu, white snow boots, and a strand of pearls to the grocery store the other day. Of course, everyone we passed made her feel special, so she's never going to dress normally again." Janice rolled her eyes, but amusement made them glow.

She was a great mom, and she loved that job even more than her career. A pang of jealously pinged his heart.

"So do you need any help?" she asked as Colin tugged on her arm, begging for popcorn from the vendor he just noticed.

"Actually, everything is under control. I have the best committee ever. The students from Drexel and Penn have been incredibly organized and helpful, and they brought their friends to do all the legwork this morning. I've been working at the registration table for the past hour, but they really don't need me there."

"Good. Then we have a few minutes to catch up." Janice wasted no time in getting to the topic she apparently wanted to talk about. "I hear you've seen Kylie a couple of times." Her smug smile held an "I told you so."

He swallowed his impulse to keep his private life private. After all, she did facilitate their meeting. "Yes. And you were right. We're very like-minded."

"Are you going to see each other again?" Her eyes gleamed at the possibility.

"As a matter of fact, we are. We have a date tonight."

Before his sister could continue her interrogation, Janice's husband, Frank, jogged up behind her and pecked her on the cheek before picking up Chloe and tossing her in the air. A squeal escaped along with contagious laughter.

"Daddy, put me down."

But her face covered in glee said otherwise.

Frank held her in one arm while he tickled Colin with his other hand. "You have quite a crowd here, Dex. How many people registered?"

"Four hundred twenty-six preregistered, but a lot more are showing up this morning. I guess they wanted to see what the weather was like before committing."

"For your first event, you did an incredible job."

Dex looked over the crowd, a sea of blue T-shirts sporting the event logo, made up of college students, Big Brothers and Big Sisters with their mentees, young professionals—some from his accounting firm—and families, all here to support an organization that meant so much to him. Last year, pulling something like this together would have never crossed his mind. His excuse of being too busy always trumped any involvement in a fundraiser.

And then Nicki had come along. Energetic, exciting Nicki. Ideas had poured out of her head, along with an enthusiasm that made him take note. And the start of his spiral death dive into torturous waters.

He recalled their date at the Barnes Museum and lunch afterward where she'd raised the idea of this very event. What had seemed an insurmountable task was made simple by her words.

It's not hard if you have a big committee and are good at delegating. I'm sure there are people from your firm who would be interested. You went to Drexel, right? There are thousands of students there, some of whom are community minded and some who may need to get involved for credit. Either way, you could populate your committee quickly with volunteers from just those two places.

She'd gone on and on. Her celestial blue eyes flashing as she explained to him how to get participants by creating a flyer to post at all the local colleges and gyms. And more importantly, how to get sponsors by crafting a heartfelt letter to send to corporations around town. Although she refused to be on the committee, when he took her advice and jumped into unchartered territory, Nicki had used her creative abilities behind the scenes.

The one person who was instrumental in making this fundraiser happen wasn't here. His initial happiness at the success evidenced before him slumped into a sadness so deep, he had trouble breathing.

"I'll be right back." He dodged behind the registration table, needing to exorcize the memories by jumping into a helpful task.

He snuck a look over at Janice to see if she was observing his hasty retreat, but she and Frank were entertaining their kids while waiting for the main event to start, broad smiles on everyone's faces. Frank leaned over and kissed Janice on the cheek, a sweet, intimate gesture amid the chaos.

His heart and soul ached with longing for something so small but meaningful. Nicki's presence came back with a vengeance, threatening to bring Dex to his knees. He inhaled.

"Hey, boss, what do we do with the cash?" A Drexel student from the committee who had taken charge of registering walk-ins held a wad of bills. "We were only expecting checks and credit cards. I don't want to be responsible for this." He handed the wad to Dex.

Good. A responsibility. "Thanks, Henry. Just mark on the forms who paid in cash so we can reconcile it later."

This was going to be some massive administrative and accounting job after the event was over. Sending thank you letters and amassing a mailing list for next year would take a huge chunk of time. Funny, Nicki never mentioned that. He smirked as if to acknowledge the joke she had played on him. Yet instinctively, he knew she'd say, "Don't worry. It's easy. Divide the work amongst your accounting majors and business majors. They'll get it all organized and done in no time."

He smiled to himself, despite the gut-wrenching sadness her memory brought.

If she were here, would she see the bond between parents and their kids, or the connections between the "Bigs" and "Littles" as they put on matching shirts and did warm-up exercises together while the DJ spun dance songs? Would she embrace the love as he did; the smiles, the laughter, the excitement?

His Little Brother, Kenan, came bounding over with one of his school friends. "Dex, when is the race going to start?"

Dex looked at his watch. "Ten minutes. Are you ready, buddy?"

Dex had picked Kenan up at six a.m. this morning to get to the park to set up. Kenan had been so excited to help, to be a part of a major event like this. This is what it was all about. Raising a child to not only become independent, but to help others.

"I'm ready." Kenan bounced up and down like a champion boxer, gangly and getting taller by the day. "Why aren't you running, Dex?"

"I have a lot to do back here. As the runners come in, we have to greet them, record their time—at least for the front runners—and make sure everything goes smoothly. I'm counting on you to keep your eyes open while you're on the course. You have your phone, right? Let me know if anyone needs help."

Although Dex had volunteers posted every tenth of a mile and water stages along the way, he needed to be aware of any accidents so help could be sent immediately. EMTs were at the ready as were security teams engaged for the event. It was Dex's responsibility to make sure everyone was in place and available to do their jobs. But giving Kenan a job to do while he participated made him feel special, and he needed that in his life.

Kenan beamed at his assignment. "Will do, boss." His big, toothy smile melted Dex's heart. He had obviously heard some of the college kids call Dex boss and wanted to be a part of the team.

Dex gave him a thumbs up.

Grabbing the bullhorn by the registration table, Dex stood front and center and shouted, "Will everyone please move to the starting line."

Young and old, singles and families, walkers, runners, strollers with babies—they all moved as a hive of bees, buzzing with excitement and camaraderie, making this event a success, not only monetarily but by pulling together as a community. Today, they were one big family here to help kids who needed a mentor.

Pride and satisfaction streamed through him like a parade. Pushed to the edges of his consciousness was the only thing that could ruin this day—the bittersweet thought of Nicki.

****

Standing on the front porch of Denise's house, Nicki trembled as her finger hovered over the doorbell before pressing it. On the drive from Philadelphia to Princeton, she concentrated on other things—the marketing campaign for Azelea Williams, the logistics of getting her apartment painted, where she might go for a week's vacation now that she wouldn't be spending it with Dex in Quebec. Anything but the conversation that would occur once she arrived.

She assumed Denise would be home on a Friday after Bobby, Jennifer, and Johnny went to camp, or whatever it was kids did during the summer. If Bobby was well enough to go to camp. She had no idea what she would find, but she couldn't bring herself to call and have this conversation over the phone. So she took the risk.

The door opened, and there stood Denise in yoga pants and a tank top. Her black, shiny hair was perfectly in place, and her dark eyes with thick lashes needed no make-up to enhance their beauty. Those eyes widened as she acknowledged her visitor. Then they filled with tears.

"Nicki. What are you doing here?"

"We need to talk and it's best if we do it in

person." Nicki tried to find a smile, but there was none available. This whole subject was so shocking and painful and sad.

Denise nodded and drew Nicki into the house.

"Are the kids home?" Nicki asked, her voice hoarse with worry.

"No. Bobby's at a soccer camp and Jennifer's at her preschool camp. My parents picked up Johnny to take him to a petting zoo near their house."

Nicki breathed a sigh of relief. She didn't know if she could see Bobby right now without staring at him or breaking down. "Good."

"Come on into the kitchen. Do you want iced tea or something else to drink?"

"Iced tea would be great." She followed Denise, her feet heavy with trepidation despite the sunniness of the room.

"Have a seat," invited Denise, so formal in her delivery, so polite.

It wasn't usually like this with them. They'd been friends since ninth grade. They hugged the moment they saw each other and just started talking, as if picking up on a conversation they'd left off weeks before.

Denise placed a glass of iced tea in front of Nicki and sat down across from her with her own.

Nicki took a sip, needing a moment to gather her thoughts. "Where to start." She avoided Denise's eyes as guilt over her huge lie to her best friends sat between them. Nicki opted to skip over that for now and get straight to the most pressing matter. "I had the blood tests done, and I'm not a match." She twisted her bracelet around her wrist as she choked out the words.

"I'm so sorry."

Nicki dared to glance at Denise and saw a tear slip from her eye. That's all she needed to see before the torrent she'd kept dammed up flooded forward. Denise came around to Nicki, and the two of them hugged each other tight, saying nothing as they cried on each other's shoulders for what seemed like forever.

Finally, Denise broke away and spoke. "Maybe Michael is." Her optimism was never-ending.

Nicki nodded, praying Michael would be that little boy's savior. "I'm sure you were shocked to learn I'm Bobby's birth mother. I was shocked too. It couldn't have been easy for Sam to deliver the news to either of us."

Denise nodded, giving Nicki the floor to continue.

"I know I told you and the rest of our Sworn Sisters I didn't know who the father was, that I'd been at a party and someone slipped something into my drink. If I didn't come up with something plausible, my mother would have guilted us into marriage. I wasn't going to allow that to happen. I told Michael I was pregnant the night of Alyssa's party. I told him I was going to get an abortion." Nicki shuddered at the notion.

Becoming pregnant on the heels of her father's death was such a low point in her life; it was hard to relive.

She continued. "Who would have thought Ben's brother and sister-in-law would be the ones adopting him? I didn't want to know. I didn't want my child to know about me. It would be best for him. Now this." Her heavy sigh echoed around the room, but it didn't lessen the weight of this new problem, which now rested atop old regrets.

"I don't know what else to say, Denise. If you have any questions, throw them out there. If you want to make a statement, go ahead."

The worst of all was not knowing how Denise would react to her deceit. She steeled herself to be pummeled.

"Oh, Nicki. I'm at a loss." Denise's eyes shone with unshed tears. "I'm sorry you didn't believe you could tell us the truth back then. We were like sisters. We shared everything. For you to have gone through that alone makes me so sad. I remember how affected you were by Michael's disappearance. We all knew you were a good friend of his, so we attributed it to that. If we had known he was the father of your child, maybe we could have done more to help you deal with it. You kept us at arm's length that summer and we let you." Denise shook her head. "In hindsight, if we had been more insistent in talking about what had happened, maybe you would have shared what you were going through. You must have been even more devastated than we believed over Michael's disappearance. We shouldn't have listened to you when you continuously told us you wanted to be alone."

"You were all going away to school at the end of August. I had to defer my admission. It was too much for me to hear about how excited you were to start the next chapter of your lives while I was staying behind. Yes, I lied about the father. But that had nothing to do with the way I was feeling that summer around you."

"Why didn't you tell us the truth?"

"Honestly, I don't know. Back then, I believed if I told one person, my mother would find out. She would have told Michael's father, which would have been disastrous for Michael and me. After he disappeared, it was senseless to change my story. What good would it have done? I wanted to give birth, give the baby up for adoption, and move on. I believed my story would keep the drama to a minimum and allow me to try to forget about it."

"What do you want to do now?" asked Denise.

"What do you mean?"

"Do you want Bobby to know you're his birth mother?"

"No!" Panic tripled her heartbeat.

"What do you want me to tell him?"

"That I'm one of your friends and I want to be here for you. For him."

Denise nodded, as if turning her request over in her mind. "Bobby knows we received the adoption records. He knows we're looking for his birth parents. I don't want to lie to him."

Whoa. Nicki didn't expect that response. She assumed Denise would go along with her plan. "It can't be good for Bobby to know one of your best friends gave him up for adoption."

"Bobby's been seeing a counselor since his parents died. And now that he's sick, he's dealing with that through therapy as well. I'll ask his counselor how best to deal with it. But you have to promise me, if her answer is to tell Bobby, you have to allow it. He's been through so much in his short life. I want to do what's best for him."

Nicki swallowed. "You're right. Of course." How could Nicki fight this if it was best for Bobby? "Let me know what the therapist says."

A commotion and voices sounded at the back door.

"Johnny and my parents are back." Denise got up to let them in.

Nicki hadn't seen Denise's parents in a few years, and she mustered up the appropriate greetings. Kisses and hugs preceded a short catch-up conversation about her career and love life. Not much to say there.

They didn't stay long since they had lunch plans and a game of bridge at the senior center. Johnny buzzed around the kitchen before sitting down with his peanut butter and jelly sandwich, allowing all talk of Bobby and its attendant tentacles to fall by the wayside.

Denise grabbed her keys and wallet. "I have to pick up Jennifer at camp. Will you please stay with Johnny? I'll be gone less than a half hour."

"Me? You want me to babysit?" Nicki didn't mean to sound so stricken, but there was no overlooking her flustered alarm.

"Yes, Nicki. It will be fine." Denise's calm voice helped a bit. "Johnny will take the next fifteen minutes to pull apart and finally eat his sandwich. Just wash his hands and face when he's done, and go with him into the family room. He'll most likely play with his trains or trucks. I'll be back before you know it."

Denise didn't give her more time to protest. She left through the back door, got into her car, and drove away. How could she trust her precious son to Nicki?

Nicki watched Johnny decimate his sandwich, first dissecting the crust from the bread, then pulling apart the slices and licking the jelly off one side. His cheeks and chin had purple smudges everywhere. Once one slice was nearly jelly free, he attacked the peanut butter side with the same enjoyment. There seemed no need to talk to him while he mangled his lunch, and by the looks of it, he might still be sitting here when Denise arrived back with Jennifer.

All at once, Johnny tossed the slice of bread on the table, jumped out of his chair, and ran out of the kitchen.

Nicki sprang from her chair and grabbed him around the waist. "Hold on there, kiddo. Let's wash those dirty hands and face."

She carried him, holding his body away from hers, trying to avoid the sticky mess finding its way onto her suit. She intended to get to the office sometime today, hopefully free of food smears. Putting him down in front of the bathroom sink, she turned on the water, grabbed a washcloth, and held his hands under the warm water as she did her best with a wiggling two-year-old. After squeezing out the washcloth, she wiped his face with it as he dodged and weaved to get away from the offending material. Water dripped on the floor as well as onto Nicki's skirt, but she refused to let Johnny out of her clutches until he was clean.

Sweat dripped down her back by the time she was done, but a huge sense of satisfaction enveloped her.

"Okay. Now we can go play."

"Let's make a house." He took Nicki's hand and showed her to his blocks.

"When I said *we,* I didn't mean you and me. I meant you should play and I'll watch."

Her explanation was lost on him, and he directed her to sit on the floor. She removed her suit jacket and did as she was told. He then dumped out a whole container of giant blocks and laughed at the mess he made.

Deciding it would be best to join in, Nicki began

building a house, guiding Johnny to help by showing him what blocks to put where. As soon as the house was almost finished and looking quite good, Johnny swung his arm, knocking it to the ground. His delight came through with his adorable laugh.

Nicki feigned surprise but had a smile on her lips. "Why did you knock it over?"

"It's fun." His huge brown eyes crinkled with glee.

"Shall we do it again?"

"Yes, yes, yes, yes, yes."

He would have kept going, but Nicki playfully put her hand over his mouth and said, "Okay."

Before long, Denise arrived back with Jennifer. Nicki swore she saw a look of surprise flit across Denise's face, but she didn't say anything. Jennifer knelt down and started to help as well, adding to the noise level as she and Johnny disagreed over what blocks should go where.

"I'll let you two figure it out. I have to get to work." Nicki unfolded from the floor and brushed the wrinkles from her skirt, then picked up her jacket from the couch. "Thanks, Denise."

"For what?"

"For not giving me a hard time about lying to you so long ago. I was dreading this conversation, but you made it as painless as it could be." Nicki went over to hug her.

She was preparing to leave when the back door slammed shut and a fourteen-year-old boy walked in.

Nicki froze in her place, her blood chilling and the hairs on her arms standing straight up. Bobby.

Denise's head spun toward Nicki with a silent plea in her eyes, but Nicki was clueless as to what it meant.

"Hi," he mumbled to Denise, dropping his backpack on the floor by the door.

"Don't leave it there, Bobby," said Denise in her reasonable tone.

Some snort of protest came out of his mouth, but he bent over and picked up the backpack. "Where should I put it?"

A small smile inched over Denise's lips. "In your room, please. The same place I ask you to put it every day. But before you go upstairs, I want you to meet a good friend of mine. This is Nicki Reading. We went to high school together."

Bobby gave Nicki a cursory glance. "Hi," he said before opening a cabinet, removing a bag of cookies, and grabbing a few.

His hair was dirty blond, a combination of hers and Michael's. But his eyes were the same color blue as hers. More of an icy blue, whereas Michael's were bluish green. He was taller than Denise by an inch or so, but shorter than Nicki. At that gawky stage, his limbs seemed too big for his body, yet he was a cross between handsome and cute, and Nicki wondered if he had a girlfriend.

All of a sudden her eyes teared, and she blinked fast to ward them off. She wanted to talk to him, say something, anything, but her tongue was paralyzed.

Unaware of the storm barreling through Nicki, Bobby headed out of the kitchen, passing her as she stood there like a statue.

"Are you okay?" asked Denise after Bobby was safely upstairs.

Nicki nodded, then took in a calming breath. "I don't know what happened. It was like I had a stroke or something."

Denise came over to her, putting her arm around her shoulders. "I'm sure it's hard to see Bobby for the first time after learning he's your son."

Those caressing words and the full recognition that she'd seen her birth son were her undoing, and the floodgates lifted. "Oh, Denise. This is so hard."

"I know. But it's done. You did it. It has to get easier each time, right?"

Denise, the eternal optimist. But Nicki wanted to believe her, so she nodded as a plea to make it happen.

Jennifer ran into the kitchen. "Can I have a cookie, Mommy?"

Johnny was right behind. "Me too."

Denise picked up the bag of chocolate chip cookies Bobby had just left on the counter. "You can have two each. I'll get you some milk."

"Nicki, do you want one?" asked Jennifer in the sweetest voice.

"No, thanks." But she didn't want to sound dismissive. "I haven't eaten lunch yet, so I can't have a cookie until after."

"You can bring one with you," offered Jennifer.

Nicki smiled at the little girl, who she had made friends with a short time ago because they built a house together. It had been so easy. "Thanks, Jen."

Nicki turned to Denise. "Can I come visit again soon? Would that be okay?"

"Of course." Denise's smile made it to her eyes. "Whenever you want."

"You can play with me and my dolls next time," offered Jennifer.

A flashback of Nicki holding the plastic leg of

Chloe's doll while she wailed about Nicki breaking it shot through her mind, but she pushed it away.

"Do you have a doll house?"

"No, but I'm going to ask Santa for one for Christmas."

Johnny chimed in. "I want a tree house."

Denise rolled her eyes. "Christmas is very far away, and I don't think Santa can fit a tree house in his sleigh."

Undeterred by Denise's response, Johnny insisted he could.

The banter continued, with Jennifer calling her brother dumb and Denise lecturing on the rudeness of name-calling. The tightness in Nicki's chest eased a bit. Perhaps she had thwarted a panic attack.

Or maybe, just maybe, her heart was expanding.

Chapter Nineteen

Michael was a match.

On hearing the news this morning, Nicki was ecstatic. Michael wholeheartedly agreed to the life-saving procedure, and everyone involved was cautiously positive over the outcome.

As energy whizzed through her being, her apartment got the benefit of being wiped clean of imaginary dust and vacuumed of nonexistent dirt. She usually went to the office on Saturday mornings, but to celebrate, she gave herself the day off.

Finding a pair of errant earrings on her bedside table, she opened her jewelry box to put them away. A shiny glint caught her eye, and she picked up the silver bracelet with blue chalcedony insets Dex had given her in Key West. A swath of regret mixed with pain cut through her as she slid the cuff onto her wrist, remembering that day seven months ago when Dex had made the impulsive purchase; a simple gift holding the promise of a future. A video played in her head of them laughing over everything. Nothing could ruin their day. They had both escaped their plus ones. It was decadent, freeing. And exciting. Embarking on an adventure they knew not where it would take them…an adventure that must have been doomed from the beginning.

Too perfect, too extraordinary. They liked the same things in art, music, films. And in bed. Just the thought of Dex flitting kisses down her spine made her tingle. She wanted that again. More. Please.

Dragging her mind from the erotic playfulness of Dex, she moved from her bedroom to the kitchen. But even there, she saw him. Feeding her bacon with maple syrup dripping over her lips, his mouth covering hers to lick it off. And then…oh my…and then…

She couldn't go there. It was too hot, too wonderful, too painful.

In the months since they broke up, she'd dreamed he'd change his mind about kids. Hoped he'd realize he couldn't live without her and kids be damned. It didn't happen. It never would.

But now that she began to make a connection with Bobby and Denise's two other children, maybe she'd consider a mind-blowing about face on this issue. The reason she never wanted another child hadn't changed. But now she knew Bobby was loved tenfold. By one of her best friends. Knowing that, could she move past her promise to her newborn and perhaps love another child she brought into this world?

The concept hurt her head.

She went over to her laptop on the dining room table and woke it. Going directly to Gmail, she typed in his name. His address popped up after the first three letters. D-e-x. Who else had that name?

Her fingers hovered over the keyboard. She walked away. Came back. Sat down. Then put her head in her hands. *What are you doing? You have nothing to say.* But maybe she did. Maybe she had a story to share with him. An opening to a discussion.

Convincing herself she had nothing to lose, she quickly typed an invitation for a drink after work on

Monday evening. Now, for a reason. She couldn't tell him in an email what she'd learned recently. Nor did she want to give him false hope that she'd changed. She was a work in progress. But those words wouldn't inspire him to leap at her invitation. She typed, deleted, typed, and deleted. Then she settled on *something's come up. I need to talk to you. Please*.

She aimed the arrow over Send but hesitated. Would this lead to more pain? She bit her lip, stared at the bracelet on her wrist, then closed her eyes and clicked the button. Her message flew away, through air and space. Or somewhere.

It was done.

Then panic set in. She needed to undo it. But how? She googled the question and came up with an unacceptable answer. In limited circumstances, yes. In hers, no.

Her inbox pinged with a message. Could he be declining her invitation so quickly? She opened the email. An auto-reply message. He was out of the office until Monday afternoon. Forty-eight hours from now.

She groaned and closed down her computer, the beginning of a headache forming at the base of her skull. She should have called him, but not after sending an email. She'd appear too desperate. Nicki massaged her head, squeezed her eyes shut, and exhaled all the negative energy zooming around her body.

The wait would surely kill her.

****

Dex checked his work emails throughout the weekend, despite the getaway with Kylie. His clients demanded attention seven days a week, but it didn't interfere too much with their visit to his colleague's beach house in Spring Lake. Sitting in a sand chair in front of the ocean scrolling through and deleting messages wasn't the worst thing he could do on a Saturday afternoon in the summer. Usually, he was in the office.

Dex's eyes stopped at a message from *nicki.reading* and his heart pumped an erratic rhythm. Heat swarmed to every extremity, and a bead of sweat trailed down the side of his face.

He glanced over at Kylie, a dark-haired, dark-eyed pixie, who was the exact opposite of the blonde, blue-eyed, lithe Nicki. Thankfully, she was engrossed in a book, unaware of his comparative inventory of her physical characteristics.

Swallowing, he opened the email and read the scant words she'd typed. Concern took over his brain. Was something wrong? Should he call her?

He stood and started walking toward the ocean.

Kylie stopped him. "Where are you going?"

"For a walk." He couldn't ask her to join him.

"With your phone?" A grin covered her mouth. She already knew his workaholic ways.

He raised his hand with the phone in it. "I have to call…someone back. I don't want to disturb anyone." He nodded toward the couple they were visiting.

He berated himself for lying, knowing he gave the impression that *someone* was a client. "I won't be long." He forced a smile and turned back toward the ocean, putting distance between them.

Rereading the message to assess its urgency, he realized it was simply an invitation for a drink—to talk. Yes, she said something had come up, but it didn't sound as dire as his first impression. He shouldn't call her.

He walked along the surf, staring out at the horizon, but his mind was back in Philadelphia, back in Nicki's apartment, lying in her bed, tangled up in her. Every part of her. Sure, the sex was hot, so hot, but even better, her heart had been his—at least when he could slide through a crevice of the brick and mortar she erected to protect herself. He misjudged his agility to creep through and stay. Dex erroneously believed she would do anything for him, as he would have done anything for her.

But she had her limit, and her limit was having a family with him. Proof her love had restrictions. A tight band squeezed his chest and he tried to rub it away. But it was internal and beyond reach. He thought he'd moved on. Kylie was perfect for him. He should be happy.

But one little email sent him spiraling backward.

All the hurt and anguish he worked so hard to rid himself of the past four months washed through him with a vengeance. His fingers ached from clutching the phone in a vise-like grip, as if he could transfer these unwanted emotions to the device that woke them. He slid the phone into his pocket and flexed his hands.

He couldn't allow her to bring him back there. Dex was moving on. Kylie wanted the same things he did. Stability, marriage, a family. He made sure before he spent more than one date with her. He wouldn't make the same mistake again—investing his heart and soul without doing his due diligence.

Sure it was a cold way to enter a relationship, but he was no kid anymore. A partner at his accounting firm, he'd reached his professional goal and was doing well. Now it was time to add to his accomplishments. It's what everyone wanted at his stage of life. Everyone but Nicki.

Dex intellectually understood Nicki's guilt over giving her baby up for adoption. Her truth that it would be unfair to heap love and affection on a future child when she didn't do it for her first made sense. But instead of carrying guilt around for her entire life, she should have allowed him to help her erase it; not turn her back on the wonderful future they could have had.

Perhaps if she had opened her heart to his needs, she would have understood and changed. Coming from a single parent home since the age of nine had Dex focused on the perfect family and what it would be like. He wanted that perfect family from the time his father deserted them. And he was going to be the father his own dad never was. He would help with homework, coach sports, attend recitals, go to doctor's appointments, give advice. Whether boys, girls, or both, he wanted children with whom he could spend time, teaching, consoling, loving. Even during those difficult years.

A chuckle escaped as he reflected on his Little Brother, Kenan, soon entering high school. He was a challenge, always questioning the system. Why did he have to take math? He'd never use it again. Why couldn't he wear his pajama bottoms out in public? They were comfortable. Why did he have to clean up his room? He was the one living in it.

Dex took great pride in having rational and reasonable discussions with Kenan. Explaining to a young teen that he didn't know everything often fell on deaf ears, but Dex persisted, knowing his years of experience should at least be considered. Kenan was a good kid, and Dex saw the positive influence he was having on him. He wanted to do the same with his own children.

A heavy sigh punctured his thoughts. He'd been walking far too long and had to rejoin Kylie and their friends. Damn Nicki for ruining his relaxing weekend. Now all he'd be thinking about was whether he should meet her or not.

Although he already knew the answer.

****

Nicki poured herself into work on Monday, eager to make the day speed by, at least until the afternoon. By three, she was dragging. She checked her email every five minutes, starting at noon. It was exhausting.

Thankfully, she had a meeting at three thirty, which would force her to focus on something else. At least that was the expected result. Instead, she checked her watch so it became noticeable, and her colleague commented that Ms. Reading must have something very important to attend to other than the current matter. Nicki denied it, mumbling about her watch needing a new battery, then made it her mission to concentrate and participate.

But when the meeting came to an end, she nearly flew out of the conference room and back to her office. A dozen emails populated her inbox, but she scanned them quickly and saw the only one she cared about.

She was ready to click it open, but fear stopped her.

What if he was too busy to meet her tonight, or he couldn't see her for a week? What if the answer was no?

Nicki sank into her chair and laid her head back, staring at the ceiling. She pulled all the positive energy she could from every cell in her body. Then she leaned forward and clicked the arrow.

A short reply, two sentences consisting of ten words stared back at her.

Meet me at Hanna's at six thirty. I have an hour.

It wasn't signed. Cold, curt, to the point.

At least he'd agreed to meet her. That had to mean something. He could have denied her this one hour he seemed willing to give. Maybe not willing. Maybe resigned? Curious? Indifferent?

Deciding to walk, Nicki kept a steady pace, using the time and fresh air to help her figure out what in the world she intended to say.

And more importantly, how she intended to end her story.

Nicki stood in front of the large wooden door of Hanna's at six thirty.

Curtains up.

She walked in and scanned the bar.

There was Dex, standing toward the right, dressed in an impeccably fitted dark suit, narrow tie, white shirt. Gorgeous.

She walked over to him and touched his arm in greeting. "Hi."

His eyes darkened and his jaw muscle clenched. Dangerously gorgeous.

"What would you like to drink?"

You, she sighed to herself. "A vodka gimlet," she said aloud.

He raised his brows. "New drink?"

Dex ordered her request, along with his usual

vodka martini. "How's work?" he asked politely but with zero warmth.

"Good. We merged with Yukon Music. I got a promotion. I've been swamped. But that's been a good thing." She accepted the drink from him. "How about with you?"

"Fine. The summer is a little quieter than the rest of the year." He sipped his drink. "What do you need to talk to me about?"

She studied the ice in her glass, searching for an intervention from anyone, divine or otherwise. "You remember I told you I gave up my baby for adoption."

The planes in his face gentled and he nodded.

Better. It allowed her to breathe a little.

"I also told you about my best friends from high school, Denise, Sam, Alyssa." She studied his eyes for recognition.

"I remember. Denise has two kids, lives in Princeton. Sam's a lawyer in New York City. Alyssa's a nurse who lives in Lawrenceville."

Wow, he really had listened. She was unexpectedly flattered.

She leaned against the bar, needing support before she continued. "I have a surprising, maybe shocking story to tell you."

His brow furrowed but he remained silent, apparently waiting for her to go on.

"Denise and her husband, Ben, adopted Ben's brother's adopted son, Bobby. I told you before that Ben's brother and wife were in a fatal car accident last year."

Dex nodded. "I remember. That poor kid."

"Worse yet, they just discovered he has leukemia."

221

This was much harder to tell than she'd predicted. Perhaps it was the compassion so evident in Dex's eyes, or the fear she had over whether the bone marrow transplant would be successful, but her voice cracked. "My friend Sam represented Denise and Ben in obtaining his adoption records. They needed to identify his birth parents so they could hopefully find a match for a bone marrow transplant."

She studied Dex's face to see if there was any glimmer of recognition as to where this story was going. None. His sole focus was on Bobby's dilemma, not some unimagined consequence. All she could do was plow on.

"Bobby is the boy I gave up for adoption."

****

Whoa. Dex was at a loss for words. What hellish coincidence would place the child Nicki gave up for adoption with one of her best friends from high school?

He wanted to reach out and hug her, but he kept to his own space. "How long have you known?"

"Two weeks. Sam came to Philadelphia to break the news."

"That couldn't have been easy for either one of you." He was careful in selecting his words. "How did you react?"

"I think I screamed. It's all a blur. Then I cried for hours." Her eyes glistened in the retelling. "I spent days on the computer researching leukemia, but I didn't know what kind he had."

"Did Sam stay and help you process it?"

"For a while. But I was catatonic throughout most of the day. I finally told her I needed time to myself. But she's been great. Always there to talk." She lowered her lids. "I was hoping I was a match for the bone marrow transplant, but I wasn't." Her voice caught in her throat.

Dex took her hand and warmed it with his. "What about the father?"

Nicki nodded and a small smile escaped. "He's a match. He's going to do it." She exhaled her relief. "The reason I wanted to share this with you is to let you know this might change things for me." Her words were vague and cautious.

"What do you mean, change things for you?" Was she referring to what he hoped? She could let go of the past? Or was he misreading this whole thing? Which wouldn't surprise him since he'd thought they were on the same page in the past.

"You know, about maybe having a child sometime in the future."

That statement should have made him happy. But there were two qualifications in the sentence that made for distrust. Yet she seemed to be expecting a positive reaction from him. He took a gulp of his drink, trusting the alcohol would change the ambiguousness of her words.

He zeroed in on her eyes, those beautiful, crystal-blue eyes that shot Cupid arrows straight to his heart. In her mind, she was saying what he wanted to hear. In his, it was far from that.

"I was hoping…" She trailed off, then bit her lip.

He found his voice. "Hoping we could get back together because you might want to have a child sometime in the future maybe?" Unrestrained sarcasm punctuated his sentence, but he couldn't help it. Did she really believe he could live through that torturous pain again on the off chance she might say yes to kids?

Just getting an email from her catapulted him into full Nicki mode, not allowing him to enjoy the weekend due to unending dreams of their time together. Seeing her again tonight was sure to upend all the progress he'd made in dispelling her from his heart. From his soul.

He had to protect himself.

Making a show of checking his watch, he pushed aside all thought of crushing her in his arms and assaulting her mouth with kisses that would claim her, change her. Make her his. Forever. With no conditions, no maybes, no indefinite timetable.

But Nicki wasn't prone to caveman persuasion. She was independent, strong…and stubborn.

"I'm very sorry to hear Bobby has leukemia. But I'm glad you feel better about having given up your child for adoption, knowing Bobby is being raised by your wonderful friends. All of this news must have been a shock." He stood. "I wish the best for Bobby. I have to go. I have…an appointment."

He put his glass down on the bar, picked up his change minus a tip, and walked out the front door. If he'd looked at that hopeful, beautiful face one more time, he would have surrendered.

And that wouldn't have been the best move for either of them.

Chapter Twenty

Driving to Lawrenceville on a Saturday in August when she should be working wasn't the smartest thing, but Alyssa had invited her, and she needed a friend's shoulder to cry on. At least Alyssa had the entire weekend off for a change, so the two of them could talk, relax, whine, cry, or be silent, depending on their mood.

"Hey girlfriend! Glad you finally got here." Alyssa stood near her front porch, watering a host of wild flowers she had growing in her front yard.

Nicki took in the idyllic scene. "How could you grow such beautiful flowers?" She bent over to smell something purple and big. "They're spectacular."

"Thanks. I like to garden. It doesn't take much talent, and there's something to show for it." Alyssa turned off the water. "How's Bobby?"

Nicki swallowed her angst. "Good. He and Michael are doing the bone marrow transplant next week. I'm going to the hospital with Denise and Ben for the surgery. Unless they need me to take care of Jennifer and Johnny."

"Since when have you ever volunteered to babysit? Don't they know you hate kids?"

Nicki gave Alyssa a playful punch. "I don't hate kids. I'm not compatible with them. But I've been helping Denise out ever since I learned Bobby's the child I gave birth to. And it's been good. I don't mind it."

"Not minding it and liking it are two different things. But it's nice of you to help. I'm sure Denise and Ben are grateful."

"It's the least I could do, given the circumstances. And the interesting thing is, the more I'm around the kids, the more I'm enjoying it."

"Isn't it hard, knowing Bobby's your son?"

"It was at first. But although I gave birth to him, he's not mine."

"Does Bobby know you're his birth mother?"

"Yes. After Denise spoke to Bobby's counselor and got some advice, I sat down with Denise and Ben and Bobby. Denise told him." Nicki still suffered a stab to her heart recalling Bobby's confusion. "I explained that I was young, scared. That I wanted more than anything for him to have a good home, good parents. I told him I couldn't do that for him. We all cried. But it was good."

"Did he accept that?"

"Cautiously. He didn't warm up to me. And of course, I'm not the warmest soul around kids either. But we'll work it out. I'm going to try to visit once a week. My plan is to drop by tomorrow after I leave here. They're only twenty minutes away."

"I'm proud of you, Nicki."

"Yeah. Thanks. But wait till you hear what stupid thing I did."

"That doesn't sound good. What?"

"I emailed Dex. Asked him to meet me for a drink."

"Uh oh. How did it go?"

"Not well. I don't understand."

"Understand what?"

"Men. How could Dex have walked away from me? I practically told him I would have his child."

"You did not." Alyssa's open mouth and wide eyes were probably the appropriate reaction.

"Not in those exact words. But I did say I would consider having a child someday. Or something to that effect."

"And he didn't jump at the chance to get you pregnant?"

"Stop being so sarcastic." Nicki scowled at Alyssa for effect. "I was trying to tell him I've changed. That meeting Bobby allowed me to consider the possibility. And spending time with Denise's other two kids wasn't so awful."

"I hope you didn't use those words. If you did, I wouldn't blame him for sprinting in the other direction."

"Why are you being so mean?" Nicki batted back tears watering her eyes.

Alyssa put the hose down and drew Nicki over to the porch steps where they sat. "I'm sorry if I'm sounding callous. But you need to work on your delivery of what you consider a positive change. From what you told me, Dex fell in love with you and you fell in love with him. But as soon as he talked about a family, children, you pulled the plug. Does that sound like a fair assessment?"

Nicki nodded, miserable over the truth.

"Why did you think he would be ecstatic and want to get back together when you gave him a lukewarm semi-offer?"

"I didn't intend for it to come out like that."

"I hate to be so analytical, but you need to convince yourself you changed before you can convince someone else. I'm one of your best friends, and although I believe you're turning a corner, even I don't think you're there."

Nicki rested her elbows on her knees and held her head in her hands. Why was this so difficult?

Alyssa nudged her with her shoulder. "While you're waiting for the mom gene to kick in, I would highly recommend the casual affair."

Nicki chuckled. "Are you still seeing what's his name?"

"His name is Cole, and the answer would be a definite yes." Alyssa's smile took over her mouth.

"Why would I choose to have an affair?"

"An affair will take your mind off what's bothering you. In your case, Dex. In my case, my stagnant life. There is no down side."

"Since I'm not keen on ruining someone else's marriage, I hardly need an affair. I only need a man who I don't care about and who doesn't care about me, to have hard-core, mind-blowing sex."

"That would work."

"Do you have anyone in mind?"

"Sorry. There's not much to choose from in this small town. But you live in Philadelphia. There must be hundreds of eligible, good-looking bachelors seeking sex."

"You make it sound so enticing." Nicki grimaced.

"If you don't like that idea, what about match.com or going to one of those speed dating events?"

"Neither would work. I wouldn't be good company

if I did manage to snag a date. I can't stop thinking about Dex." She sighed. "I know I'll get where he wants me to be in the kid department. I need to deliver the message better, as you said."

They sat for a while in companionable silence before Alyssa spoke. "If you're serious—and make sure that you are before you ruin both of your lives—what about this idea? Stalk Dex. Not in an obvious way, though. Go to the gym where he exercises and run into him. Go to the grocery store where he shops and pass him in the aisle. Go to the restaurants or bars where he goes, with a date of course, and wave across the room. You get my drift. Don't have a conversation with him, just get under his skin. You must look fabulous every time you see him and you must seem unfazed by the interaction."

"Have you actually done this before, or have you been reading *The Single Woman's Guide to Stalking Without Getting Arrested*?" Only Alyssa could be that devious.

Could Nicki? Maybe it would work.

****

Although she originally discounted it as insane, Nicki thought long and hard about Alyssa's stalking strategy. It wouldn't really be stalking. She needed to go to the gym anyway. It was much too hot to run outside in August. And Dex belonged to a gym called Innovation. Since it wasn't far from her apartment, it wouldn't be considered a stretch if she went there as well.

Signing the contract one night after work, she took the tour, keeping her eyes trained for Dex. She didn't see him that night, or any of the next seven nights.

229

Maybe he quit. Or maybe he started going in the morning before work, and that was not something she was willing to do for love. At least not yet.

On the eighth night, fate was on her side. She saw him using the weight machines as she clocked ten miles on the elliptical. Generally stopping at five, she persevered despite her screaming joints and pouring sweat. Not the picture of classy elegance she wanted to leave him with as she waved from afar. Certainly not the advice Alyssa had given. Should she bother to run into him nonchalantly, looking the way she did?

Nicki cooled down for a few minutes, stepped off her machine, tested her legs to assure she wouldn't fall to her knees, then wiped her face with a towel. He was heading to the men's locker room, so she darted toward the adjacent women's locker room.

"Dex, hi." Nicki tried for cool disinterest with a hint of cheer.

"Nicki. What are you doing here?" He actually smiled. Good.

"It's too hot to run outside so I joined the gym. Not far from home or the office." Her excuse sounded plausible, genuine.

He nodded. "I was running outside too, but I agree. Too hot." He used the towel around his neck to wipe his forehead.

Nicki ached to stay and talk longer, but Alyssa's words reverberated in her head. *Avoid long conversations, just get under his skin.* "It's nice to see you, Dex. I have to run." She ducked into the women's locker room and stopped to catch her breath. Her heart galloped to a triple beat knocking into her ribs.

Alyssa would have been proud of her performance,

although Nicki was not at all sure she liked this game. It hurt too much.

She continued to run into Dex every few days, becoming an exercise fanatic in the process. The one good thing coming from all this was a very toned body. Although she tried the grocery store idea as well as local bars with male colleagues, she never ran into Dex at those more sensible venues.

Every time she saw him, she smiled, was polite, courteous, and short on conversation. How was this ever going to work if they didn't exchange more than pleasantries? Right now, all she managed to be was some ex-girlfriend who didn't hate him.

She knelt to retie her sneaker before moving from the elliptical to the free weights.

"Nicki, can I talk to you?" Dex's voice melted over her, although it was a mere request he could have made to anyone.

She looked up, and there he stood, fresh out of the shower, with his dress shirt unbuttoned at the top, his sleeves rolled up, his suit jacket slung over his shoulder and hooked on his finger. Hot, sexy, powerful. Nicki swallowed and stood, feeling a whole lot less than sexy in her gym shorts and tank top.

"Sure. What's up?" She couldn't disconnect from his gorgeous but intense eyes. One of his best features. One of many.

"What are you doing?"

"What? What do you mean?"

"Why are you here at the gym every day? When we dated, you said you couldn't understand why people paid to exercise when they could go to the park and run."

Pride forced her to come up with a plausible excuse. "When we dated, it was winter, almost spring, and the weather was perfect for running outside. I have to admit I can't run outside in this humidity." She worked to keep her voice steady. "Although, I was wondering why you're here so much. You also denounced gym rats." She raised her brows and gave him a coy smile. "Perhaps you're here for ulterior motives." Was she accusatory enough to make him squirm?

He narrowed his eyes, then shook his head. "You nearly killed me, Nicki. I'm not that much of a masochist to lance the wound by searching you out."

Apparently she was, because that's exactly what she was doing. Her clogged throat prevented her from responding.

He continued. "I thought you were it. Sure, we had this whirlwind romance. It was crazy, it was so fast. But we were so good together. So in sync. Until I asked you to marry me. So many times I've replayed that day, wishing I hadn't gone there. Wishing I'd given us more time to connect on every level. I've wondered if it would have made a difference. Then when you told me about Bobby and how you felt, I questioned if we'd been together through that, whether things between us would have moved us in the right direction. But people don't change. I know that."

A tear slid down Nicki's cheek, and she quickly wiped it away. "What if I can?" Her voice was hoarse, rough.

"I'm with someone now. She wants the same things I want. Marriage. A family."

Oxygen whooshed from her lungs as if punched in

the chest. "No, Dex. That's impossible. You can't love her like you loved me. She can't love you like I love you." She touched his arm, electricity singeing her fingers.

His eyes flashed and he pulled his arm back. "I told you, I'm with someone else. We're engaged. I'm getting married in six weeks."

With that he turned and walked away, and her world crashed and burned around her.

Chapter Twenty-One

"I can't believe you convinced me to come to Philly this weekend." Alyssa dropped her duffel bag by the door of Nicki's apartment as she entered; not her usual exuberant self.

"What's wrong?" Nicki had hoped for irreverent, full-of-life Alyssa, not sad-faced, surly Alyssa.

"I'm in love with Cole." The words were strewn with disbelief and laced with melancholy.

"Oh. No." Nicki's mind rummaged for appropriate words to say. "But you said it was a casual affair. How did it become more?"

"We've been spending some time together outside of the hospital. Kind of like dates. We've been getting to know each other better." Alyssa's sad smile peeked through. "Neither of us saw the harm in it, and we were having so much fun. Playing tennis together, escaping to Atlantic City for an overnight, taking walks on the beach." A tear slid down Alyssa's cheek. "I didn't intend to have feelings for him. It was supposed to be fun. Exciting. Meaningless. Why did I ever believe we could remain sex partners with nothing more?"

"You didn't tell him you love him, did you?"

"Of course not. What good would that do? He's married."

"And here I thought we'd only be dwelling on me." Nicki invited her friend into the kitchen and filled two mugs with coffee. "I guess we need to cheer each other up."

"I'll say. Although I'm not sure either of us will be successful."

"Does Cole feel the same way about you?"

"I think so. But he won't leave his wife. They have two young kids."

Nicki bit her lip as she dispensed her next question. "Have you considered ending it?"

Alyssa's eyes widened. "That would kill me." She reached for a napkin to blot a few rogue tears. "I would prefer that he divorce his wife and be with me."

Reminding Alyssa that the wisdom of having a casual affair was flawed wouldn't do anything to help the situation. Neither would her saying, "I told you so."

"Despite the way you feel, are you going to continue seeing Cole?" Perhaps questions would help Alyssa sort this out.

"I can't not see him. I work with him in the ER, side by side. My entire existence at the hospital is wrapped up in him. I love my job because of him. I can't wait to go to work. And I can't wait to make plans with him outside of work."

"Then I guess the answer is to be happy doing what you're doing."

"I wish I could. But I'm so jealous of his wife. He goes home to her. I know I should be happy with the time we're able to spend together, but I want more. That craving colors the times we do meet up. I don't want to be that needy person, but I can't help it. The heart wants what the heart wants."

"Maybe you're idealizing what it would be like if he divorced his wife to be with you. The grass isn't always greener. You know that."

Alyssa nodded, then blew her nose. "I'm sorry to walk in here and highjack your day. I'm supposed to be trying to cheer you up, not the other way around. What plans do you have for us today?"

"How about the Museum of Art or the Rodin Museum?"

Alyssa shrugged. "I don't care. Both. Neither."

"I know you're miserable too, but this is my day to be suicidal. You can at least pretend to take care of me on the day Dex is getting married."

"You're right. I'm sorry, Nick." She came over and gave her a hug. "I'm surprised showing up at the ceremony and objecting isn't on your agenda."

"Very funny." Nicki tried for a smile but found none. "If I thought it would work, I'd do it. But Dex made it clear at the gym one night we have absolutely no future together."

"Then it's time to embrace your singlehood. Or work on finding someone else. What's your plan?"

"I think I'll try speed dating as you suggested. After a few minutes with ten different guys, I'll know there's no one else out there for me."

"It was a bad idea and I was only kidding when I suggested it. You can't know if someone is intriguing in three minutes. Besides, you'll look desperate. You'd be better off letting it happen. Don't look for someone. You'll be disappointed. When you least expect it— zing."

"That's what happened on the cruise. With Dex. It didn't work out so well for me." Nicki sighed. "I never wanted a relationship. It's too painful when things don't work out. It's better to go through life on my own."

This was not a new revelation. It had been her strategy since her father died, leaving her mother distraught and lonely. Until Dex slanted her world view.

"I can't say I picture you being alone, Nicki. Ever since I've known you, you've had a guy on your arm."

"That's exactly it. A guy who didn't matter. Before Dex, I dated around, had fun, no strings. It was perfect. I need to go back to not caring. It works out better for me."

Then why did the thought of it make her so sad? Dex had changed her. What she'd believed she didn't need—butterflies and violins—she now craved. Saying his name sent her into a tailspin, yearning for that blissful connection. Could she ever go back to that place of heartless dating? Where the destination was more important than the escort?

"You know what I can't understand?" Nicki stood and hit the counter with her palm. "How he could meet someone so fast, fall in love, and get married. It's only been seven months since we broke up. I can't imagine falling in love with another guy right now. Does it mean he never loved me?" Her voice clogged in her throat.

"Of course not, Nicki. He must want to be married. Some people need marriage. That's what I wanted with David. Before I found out he was cheating on me. Now, I don't know. But Dex is different. He obviously wants to be in a committed relationship."

"He wants kids. A family. So now, that's what he's going to get."

Nicki was perilously close to crying, but it wouldn't change anything.

Coffee turned to wine which turned to hard liquor.

They didn't make it to either museum. In fact, they didn't make it out of the apartment. They talked for hours, ordered in from the local Chinese restaurant, watched reruns of *Sex and the City*, laughed, cried, and passed out.

The perfect way to celebrate Dex's wedding day.

****

Since her gym membership became a casualty of heartbreak, running became Nicki's passion. Perhaps not so much a passion, but a necessary evil to rid herself of tension, stress, depression, melancholy or any host of emotional states flitting through her body on any given day. Her career was sailing along, going in the right direction, with the promotion to Vice-President in charge of marketing. Of course, it wasn't surprising, given the number of hours she put in.

On this particular Saturday, she had gone to the office in the morning to finalize a marketing plan for one of her label's new artists. Her sense of satisfaction in completing the task buoyed her spirits. And the sun helped. She was near the end of her five-mile loop and for the first time, she wasn't fatigued. She was getting stronger, physically and mentally, and that acknowledgement motivated her to add an additional mile.

The playlist on her phone was on shuffle, and Alicia Keys was singing her heart out to "Girl on Fire." Appropriate and inspiring.

Abruptly a hand gripped her upper arm. Adrenaline kicked in as she yanked away from the unwanted intrusion. She turned. And there was Dex.

She stopped breathing, then inhaled a lungful as demanded by her racing heart. "You scared me," she managed between breaths.

An amazing, gorgeous smile broke out over his face. "No one has ever accused me of that before."

Nicki shook her head and chuckled. Of course not. Dex was a lover, a seducer, a charmer. She took in his clothing. He was also running. And looking too magnificent for words. "I see married life agrees with you." The stab to her heart made her wince.

"I'm not married."

It took several seconds to process those three simple words. Still, she wasn't sure she'd heard him correctly. "What?"

"I couldn't go through with it. After our last conversation."

Nicki dialed back to their meeting in the gym, and she inwardly groaned. She'd been needy and vulnerable. So unlike her. And it was all too embarrassing. Yet joy bubbled through her. Dex was not married. She wanted to jump and scream and shout out her ebullience. "I guess that's a good thing." She tread with care. "You wouldn't have wanted to make a mistake."

"Like with you?"

Ouch. That stung more than necessary, and all reason encouraged her to start running in the other direction. But instead she stood rooted in front of Dex, trying to figure out where to go with this conversation. She bit her lip and looked to the right, seeing only a blur. *Do not cry*, she scolded. *You're on fire. Remember?*

"That was unfair. I told you I've changed. Clearly not enough for your requirements, but change takes time. You made it obvious in our last conversation it wasn't worth it to you to give me that time. You had moved on."

He avoided her eyes. "I thought I had. But I couldn't stop thinking about you. About the possibilities."

"That was two months ago." She struggled to keep calm. "Why didn't you call me? Talk to me?"

"I needed to straighten out things in my own mind. Figure out whether I was marrying Kylie for the wrong reasons. Because we both wanted a family." He zeroed in on her eyes, holding her captive. "I realized being married to her and having kids could never make me feel the way I feel with you. You destroy me, Nicki. I can't think or function with you on the fringes of my life. The email you sent me over the summer hijacked my brain the entire weekend. Seeing you at the bar for a drink when you told me about Bobby had me wanting to surrender. Running into you at the gym was pure hell."

"Gee, thanks. I was trying to make you remember us as something good."

He kicked at a stone, shaking his head. "You did. And I knew I wasn't being fair to Kylie, so I broke it off. You managed to tilt my world. For years, I knew what I wanted. Then you came along and proved to me that even if I got it, I'd be wondering my whole life if I'd given up love for a dream that came from my father's desertion. I had a lot of thinking to do. I didn't want to cloud my judgment with…you."

Was that good or bad? She was having a hard time interpreting Dex today. Maybe it was her oxygen-deprived brain. "If we hadn't literally run into each other right now, we wouldn't be having this conversation, would we?"

Dex seemed to consider his answer, perhaps to let her down easily, although why start now? The last two conversations she'd had with him had been a huge blow to her ego and a poison arrow to the heart. This one had the same potential.

"No."

When was he going to learn to sugar-coat his words?

Nicki nodded. "It was good to see you, Dex." Then she picked up her pace and started jogging again. Away from him. Away from the one source of all her pain.

"Wait, Nicki." He ran up behind her and tugged on her arm. "Let's walk awhile. Talk."

She'd be cutting off her nose to spite her face if she refused. When it came to Dex, her heart wanted what her heart wanted, as so eloquently phrased by Alyssa. And a popular song.

They walked in silence. Nicki's mind spun, trying to figure out what to say. She didn't count on this meeting. She wasn't prepared. Maybe she should let it go at that.

Then Dex found his voice. "I miss you, Nicki. The eleven weeks we were together were the best of my life. Our breakup was devastating."

Nicki's throat constricted. His words could have been her words. "I felt the same way. I still do."

He stopped and turned her toward him, but she couldn't look at him. Couldn't get drawn into those passionate eyes. That would be her undoing and her goal was to stay strong.

"Let's try again." His husky words zoomed straight to her heart, and she found herself staring into her hopeful future. That's what she'd wanted to hear when she met him at Hanna's, when she stalked him at the gym. She still wanted it.

She swallowed, then nodded as fireworks burst around her. "Yes."

He lowered his head and possessed her mouth with his. She could barely stand through the welcome assault, and her arms snaked around his neck, burying her fingers in his dark hair, holding on for dear life. She dreamed about his kisses, so hot, so erotic. How he could do this to her with only his mouth on hers was a mystery. But she never wanted to unravel it.

She just wanted more.

Chapter Twenty-Two

Dex captured Nicki's mouth and drank her in, an elixir sparking every other sense. Probably not a smart move, but his brain no longer functioned. Running into Nicki today had not been a considered possibility. Yet she was never far from his thoughts. She came to him at night in dreams too real to ignore. At the most inappropriate times during the day, he'd remember long legs in leather pants, a short skirt inching up sexy thighs, strong but delicate fingers grasping his tie to pull him closer. Their lips devouring each other like they couldn't survive without that connection. He pulled her closer, molding her tall body to his. His libido roused with a familiar jolt.

"Come back to my place," he growled, so demanding in his need.

"I'd like nothing better." Her smile parted the curtains that had been drawn around his soul. "I'll race you," she teased and started running in the direction of Rittenhouse Square.

He was more than happy to run there, for he had plans once they arrived.

Out of breath and panting when they got through the door, Nicki laughed. "This is not a well thought out detour on my part. These clothes are sweaty, I have nothing to change into, and I need a shower."

"You're in luck, Ms. Reading. I have a washer and

dryer in the kitchen and a shower—if you share it with me." He raked her body with his gaze. "I will gladly help remove those sweaty clothes."

She unzipped her jacket and moved closer to him. "I do believe I could use some help." Her smile was deliciously lewd.

Dex slid her jacket over her shoulders, his fingers gliding over damp skin. The jacket fell to the floor. Then he reached for the hem of her tank top, drawing it slowly up her torso, over her sports bra, and over her head, depositing it on top of her jacket.

He knelt in front of her long legs and untied her sneakers. "You may not want to be too close when those come off." She pulled her foot back.

He looked up into her face. "There is nothing that can stop me from getting you naked." He held her calf and removed one sneaker and sock, then the other. Then he hooked his fingers into the waistband of her running pants and eased them down her legs and over her feet. He drank in her strong legs and flat belly as he stood. One last impediment.

"Put your arms over your head."

"Bossy, aren't you?" Smoldering eyes burned into his as he pulled her bra over her head.

A blonde braid fell over her chest, and he touched the end, fingering the fine strands before removing the elastic band and unweaving it.

"So much better," he breathed, allowing the reality that Nicki was here to overtake him.

"What about you?" She arched her eyebrow.

With that he pulled his sweatshirt and T-shirt over his head and tossed them on the growing pile. He bent over and untied his shoes, then kicked them off. And in one continuous motion, did away with his sweatpants, shorts, and socks.

"You are very efficient, Dex. I like that in a man."

He narrowed his eyes at her. "I don't expect to be compared to any other man from your past."

He grabbed her hand and pulled her toward the bathroom, where he turned on the shower with one hand, keeping her in his clutches with the other. While waiting for the water to warm, he stole a quick kiss.

"This is one lucky day," he said, escorting her into the shower.

"Because you're going to get some?" Nicki asked, laying her head back under the spray to soak her hair.

"There is that," he teased. "I was thinking more about our meeting in the park."

Nicki opened her sparkling blue eyes, a mixture of playfulness and seriousness shining through.

He palmed the soap and began washing her neck, her shoulders, her arms. Her breasts. Then he leaned over and seized her mouth, pressing his chest to hers, backing her against the tile wall. He grabbed her wrists and pulled them over her head, imprisoning her with his body, with his mouth.

She moved against him, sliding her slippery breasts across his chest. So erotic. So enticing. He pressed his erection against her abdomen, before positioning it between her legs, rubbing against her clitoris. Her head dipped back and luscious lips parted as her breathing became ragged.

Assaulting her neck with his mouth, he kissed and nipped the delicate skin, moving to her ear lobe and circling the rim with his tongue before doing the same to her inner ear. She shivered, then moaned, writhing against him. He'd fantasized about this for the past few months, never believing he'd actually be here—with her.

He released her wrists and pulled her away from the wall and under the stream of water as he soaped her back then her rear, squeezing it as he washed. Kneeling before her, he massaged her thighs with his soapy hands, moving down to her calves, then her feet. She watched him with hooded lids and parted lips, clearly enjoying his work as much as he was.

He stood, then turned her, her back to his front. Pulling her against him, he smoothed his hand over her taut belly, then down between her legs. He slipped his finger into her opening and massaged her inner walls. A gasp escaped her mouth as she turned her head into his neck and ran her tongue over his jaw, her breath coming in rasps as he increased the pressure and intensity. Within moments her whole body stiffened and she clenched around his finger, crying out his name. Her arms came up and around his neck, and she held onto him as the spasms subsided.

He whispered into her ear, "I love when you come for me like that."

She turned to face him, a dreamy, erotic look on her face. Taking the soap from his hand, she murmured, "My turn."

Yes, this was one lucky day.

****

They played in Dex's bed for hours, going from hot and demanding to sensual and languid. Nicki never wanted to move past today. It was perfect. The here and now worked for her. Visions of the future led to trouble.

"How's Bobby?" asked Dex as Nicki dressed in

her now clean and dry running outfit.

Nicki swallowed. "Good."

Dex pulled her down to sit on the bed next to him. "Did he have the bone marrow transplant?"

"Yes. It went well. And he's doing great. Back to school. Getting stronger every day."

"Have you been seeing him?" Dex's voice was blanketed in sympathy, and she leaned into his welcoming embrace.

"Yes. He knows I'm his birth mom."

"How did it go?"

Nicki breathed in, then let it out slowly. "As well as can be expected. He kept a good face on when we told him. And I've been trying to spend some time alone with him. Not so much to talk about the past, but to let him know I care. I can only apologize so many times. I told him I was too young and knew I wouldn't have been a good mom to him. That I wanted him to have a better life. I don't know if any of it sank in or whether he thinks it's an excuse. Denise said she's been taking him to counseling to deal with all his issues."

"At least he's seeing you, right?"

"He doesn't slam the door in my face, if that's what you mean. When I show up, I try not to be too intrusive. If he doesn't have friends over or if he's not involved with some video game, I talk to him. Ask him about school, his interests. He's not always in the mood to talk, so I don't push it."

"Do you call him other times?"

"Yes. I email with him too. Or text. To let him know I'm thinking of him. I try to come up with things he'd like to hear about. Like exclusive information on a few of the bands we represent. He thinks it's cool that I know some of the guys in the groups he's really into."

"Oh, yeah? What guys?" Dex's voice held a smile.

Nicki elbowed him. "No one who compares to you." She held his gaze with hers, to assure he knew how she felt.

"If you're not careful, we'll end up back between the sheets," he murmured as he nuzzled her neck. "And you said you were hungry. Let's get out of here before the temptation is too great."

In alliance with her, Dex put on his running clothes too, and they stepped out into the cool November night. "Where to?" he asked.

"Somewhere casual." She tugged on his sweatshirt as they got into the elevator.

As soon as the door closed, he pulled her into his arms and gave her an earth-shattering kiss. Maybe she wasn't as hungry for food as she'd thought. Someone had the nerve to get on at the next floor, and they had to behave. Too bad.

They settled at a nearby pub and ordered burgers and fries. Everything seemed so easy with Dex. Their conversation poured out with no lag in topic or information. The pain of the last seven months melted away as if it had never been. Especially when he held her hand or kissed her temple. How could they be so in sync within minutes of getting back together?

But were they back together? Or was this a temporary pause in their storm?

Nicki chose to believe they were so right for each other they were destined to make it work. They would now give each other enough time to reconnect and move forward without jumping too far ahead of themselves.

"What's going on at Snow Leopard?" he asked, bringing Nicki back to the present.

"As VP in charge of marketing, I have a lot more responsibility."

"What exactly does that mean?" His smile didn't quite reach his eyes.

"I oversee all the marketing campaigns for our artists in the United States. Before I had my own list of artists. Now, I supervise the regional managers. My traveling schedule is more hectic since I meet with the managers as well as the artists and their people every few months. I also orchestrate launch parties in major cities."

"I remember the party you ran in New York City turning heads in your company."

Pride swarmed through her. "Yes. That certainly helped."

"But no move to New York?"

"They asked. But I could do the job from here and I like living in Philly. The CEO was fine with it."

She didn't get into the back and forth she'd had with her boss about how beneficial it would be to her career to move to the Big Apple. At the time, she'd been on her campaign to run into Dex at the gym, which would make him see the light.

"It sounds like you're not around much."

"I'm around enough." She grinned coyly, appreciating the disappointment in his statement. "How about you? What have you been up to?"

Dex sat back in his chair and stretched his legs out. "I'm involved in a hotly contested divorce case. Hired as the expert for the husband in evaluating his business for equitable distribution."

"What kind of business?"

"A vodka bar in Atlantic City."

"Do you get to sample the spirits?"

"He's offered, but it's not conducive to working with numbers. They start to blur." He was always so serious when talking about his job, so Nicki assumed he was not joking.

"Why are they getting divorced?"

"He persuaded his wife to have sex with a stranger who was at the bar. He hid in their bedroom closet and watched. Then he accused her of liking it too much." Dex shook his head. "What an idiot."

"He wants the divorce after she did what he wanted?"

"Yup. Go figure."

"I hope you don't have any similar fantasies."

"Not a chance. If I'm ever lucky enough to get married..." He stopped as if catching himself from going to a bad place. "Never mind."

A shadow crossed over Dex's eyes, making them darker, sadder.

Nicki didn't know whether to acknowledge the elephant in the room or ignore it. But they had to talk about it at some point. Perhaps she should give him the choice of whether that point should be now.

She put her hand over his and rubbed it, searching for the right words to say.

Dex motioned to the waitress for their check. "It's been a long day. I'll get you a cab."

So she was being dismissed. Her heart dropped and cracked.

They left the pub in silence, and Dex hailed a cab as he said he would. To her chagrin, one arrived within seconds.

He placed his hands on both sides of her face and kissed her mouth. "Thanks for today. It was incredible."

What was he thanking her for? She didn't know how to respond. She thought they'd spend the night together and all day tomorrow. But one normal conversation thread led to the word "married" and he shut down.

"Good night," he said as he opened the taxi door.

She got in, putting more distance between them. No further conversation would be had. Confusion marred her brain.

What the hell?

****

Nicki's night was punctuated by dreams. In one, she was flying, her arms catching the updrafts, the high incredible but a little scary. In another, she was heading to her final exam in economics but hadn't gone to any classes and hadn't studied. A failure waiting to happen. When her eyes popped open at three thirty, they refused to shut again. She finally picked up her e-reader. By six, she could no longer keep her eyes open. At least it was Sunday and she had no plans. She fell back asleep, but the incessant buzzing of her cell phone interrupted her unconsciousness.

She squinted at it to see who was disturbing her but couldn't make out the name.

"Hello," she croaked.

"Hi, Nicki. It's Dex." She nearly sprang from the bed.

But no words came out. She waited for him to break the silence.

"I'm sorry about last night. Can we talk?"

She nodded. "Sure." Did he mean now, with her brain all foggy?

"I'm a block away from your apartment. I'll bring coffee and whatever else you want."

She attempted to clear the cobwebs from her mind. "Give me a half hour. I need to wake up."

"You got it. See you soon."

She crawled out of bed and headed to the bathroom, her legs unsteady. She was exhausted from her fitful night's sleep due to the roller-coaster of emotions she'd experienced yesterday. She turned the nozzle to hot and stepped into the tub, a vision of yesterday's shower with Dex, erotic and sensual, replaying in her head. Imposed on that was her solitary cab ride home.

Which Dex would show up today?

His tone on the phone gave no clue. He apologized and he probably would again. But what was going to accompany those words? A new resolve to move forward with Nicki or an admission he couldn't because of his guilt over leaving Kylie? Her dreams came back to her as she stood under the steamy mist. She had no clue what they meant but in the good dream, the flying dream, she was flying solo. In the final exam dream, she was about to fail.

Neither was a good premonition.

She turned off the shower and squeezed the water from her hair before wrapping it in a towel. She didn't have long to wait before finding out whether she'd survive hearing what was in Dex's head.

****

Dex picked up coffee for Nicki, juice for him, and bagels, but he wouldn't be able to eat. He walked up and down Nicki's block, waiting for a half hour to pass. He wasn't sure how to begin or what to say. All he knew was he had to see her, talk to her.

In exactly thirty minutes, he was at her door. Anxiety built as she unlocked several locks before opening it. His breath caught in his throat at the sight of her, an angel in dark, skinny jeans and an over-sized, white sweater, her hair not fully dry. Wary eyes met his and her usual smile was missing. He caused that.

"Hi, Nicki." He held up the bag with the bagels in one hand and carried the beverages in a caddy in the other.

"Morning." Her voice rasped.

He headed to the kitchen and put the bag down on the table. He handed her coffee and she sipped it, watching him over the rim of her cup.

"About last night," he started. "I'm sorry I packed you off in a cab. It wasn't my intention. We were having a nice conversation at the pub. Picking up where we had left off." He glanced at her to see if she was angry, but she didn't appear to be. "When I started to talk about being lucky enough to get married in the future, I had a guilt attack. I know I deserve this remorse and much, much worse. I asked Kylie to marry me, promised her a future, and then I took it away."

The self-loathing over having done that to a woman he cared about seeped through him. In retrospect, she was his rebound relationship. One that synced perfectly with his life plan and masked the pain of his breakup with Nicki. Unrealistically, he'd assumed it was meant to be. Yet when he ran into Nicki at the gym and she told him she loved him, the awful truth that he rushed into a relationship with Kylie, hoping to erase his passion for Nicki, had hit him hard. And he had no choice but to break it off with the woman who had given him a life raft.

"Every time I think of what I did to Kylie, I end up in a dark place."

He turned toward Nicki to gauge her reaction. She must hate him about as much as Kylie did right now.

But her face didn't show it. She looked thoughtful, pensive.

"I can understand that. I don't know Kylie, and I feel awful for her. You jumped into a relationship with her with both feet. I was so angry with you for falling in love with someone else, when I couldn't think straight without you."

Nicki sat down at the table and opened the bagel bag, then closed it without taking one. "I'm not hungry. Are you?"

"No." His stomach was in knots, and food would only exacerbate the discomfort. He pulled out the chair across from her and sat.

"What did you come here to tell me? That you can't see me because you feel guilty?" Nicki put it out there in a calm, rational manner, but the strain on her face anticipated the possibility of a wrong answer.

"I came here to talk. To let you know how I feel. To find out how you feel. About me." He needed Nicki to know what a terrible person he was—if he could do that to Kylie, he was capable of hurting Nicki too. As if they hadn't already hurt each other tenfold. But he also wanted her to believe in him. In his love for her.

Nicki nodded. "Talking is good." She paused as if searching for the right words to say. Her gaze sought his, and he could see the trepidation she held. "I love you, Dex. I want this to work out for us. But I know we both have issues. Why don't we take it slow? See each other when we can. We're both busy at work. I'm travelling a lot, and you're making a name for yourself as an expert witness. There are other things going on in our lives too. I need to spend time with Bobby. You love spending time with your niece, nephew, and Kenan. Perhaps we can keep our other worlds separate for a period of time. And focus on us. See where it leads."

Her words were so rational but so safe. Did he want that? She wasn't going where he wanted her to go. Where he needed her to go. He didn't want safe where Nicki was concerned. Their relationship in the past had been defined by passion and risk. Which upped the ante on excitement but led to a steep fall. He needed to spell out what he wanted going forward. But since he had freaked her out last night, he doubted she'd open herself up to him now.

Of course, if he had Nicki back in his life, he could deal with slow and steady if they were both heading in the same direction. She said she had changed her mind about having kids, but there was no doubt she was in her element as VP of a very successful music label. Running high-impact marketing campaigns for various artists, travelling around the country to meet with them and "their people," orchestrating launch parties all over the United States did not seem conducive to having a family. Would she turn and run again when the issue arose?

Or would he change? The one thing he did learn by being with Kylie was that having the same goals for the future did not make him happy. Thoughts of Nicki interrupted his so-called perfect relationship. With all his soul-searching over the past months, he came to the realization that love trumped his idealistic goals. He would rather be ecstatically happy and in love with Nicki than be in a marriage of shared goals but no passion.

She studied his face. He and Nicki weren't talking marriage. They were talking about getting back together. So why dissect his ideas and opinions about children right now? She had suggested they take it slow.

He needed to buy into that plan.

Chapter Twenty-Three

Nicki's shopping cart was loaded with toys, making it hard to maneuver through the aisles of the toy store filled with parents frantically searching for the one must-have item that had been sold out for weeks. The Christmas holidays were upon them.

Dex dropped a remote-controlled airplane onto the pile. "Colin will love this. Help me pick out a doll or something for Chloe."

Nicki smirked. "Have you forgotten I'm not exactly the doll type? I broke the leg off your niece's doll, and she cried like I'd murdered her cat."

Laughter escaped his throat and his green eyes twinkled. "No, I haven't forgotten. But if I'm not mistaken, you've been playing with Jennifer and her dolls. You told me she won't leave you alone from the second you walk through the door."

Nicki shouldn't have shared that piece of information with Dex. Now he assumed she was an authority on the subject. Oh, what the hell. "Chloe would probably like some furniture for her doll house. Let's go look."

They perused the aisle containing dozens of choices of pink and yellow plastic furniture and came to a consensus on the perfect present for Chloe.

This routine Christmas gift shopping foreshadowed holidays to come as a couple. It was so natural. So seamless. But what did it mean? They were back to dating and seeing each other on the weekends. Sometimes more. Yet Nicki cautiously tested the waters of their newfound relationship and tiptoed lightly. She didn't know the rules. Dex may not have either.

"Denise is having a holiday party next Saturday. I'm sure you have better things to do, but you're invited if you'd like to come." She held her breath waiting for his response.

"Is that a real invitation, or are you trying to convince me to find a better offer?"

Nicki lifted a shoulder. "I can't imagine you'd want to spend your day, and possibly your night, with I don't know how many squealing kids and adults trying to control them."

He arched his eyebrow and cornered her with a scrutinizing look. "Then why are you going?"

"Denise and Ben are my friends." She swallowed and lowered her lids. "And Bobby is my son. I think I should go." She glanced up at him. "I want to go."

"Would you like me to go with you, or would you rather go by yourself?" His caring voice surrounded her in comfort, and although they were standing in the middle of a crowded toy store, Nicki could have been on a deserted island with Dex. They faced each other and he held her hands, communicating with not only words but his soothing aura.

"I'd like it if you came with me."

He brushed his knuckles over her cheek. "Was that so hard?"

She gazed into emerald depths. "I was trying to put myself in your place and assumed you wouldn't want to go."

"I would love to meet Bobby as well as your friends. They're all a part of your life. If you and I are going to move forward in this relationship, you're going to have to let me in. All the way."

"Michael will be there too. Bobby's father."

"Is that a problem for you?"

"No." She threaded her fingers through his. "Sometimes I wish it could be just us. You and me."

He hugged her to him as shoppers angled around them. His scent was like an aphrodisiac, and every time she was close enough to breathe in his essence, she wanted him. Alone. And preferably in bed.

Feeling lighter and happier than their task called for—all because of the special man beside her—Nicki glided down the aisles as she and Dex collaborated on the appropriate gifts for each of the children hovering on the edges of their lives.

Last year at this time, Nicki didn't know a Bratz doll from a Barbie. Nor did she care. And while this past year had been a roller coaster of emotions, surprisingly, happiness was the emotion that shone through when she thought about Bobby and Denise's two other kids. Bobby hadn't shut her out, and she learned how to interact with little people despite the walls she built to shut them out in the past.

Now she loved going to Denise's and playing house or building blocks or mastering video games. She found it easy to talk to and interact with kids, once she took off her heels and got down to their level. It was all about letting go of the guilt—and perhaps the assumption that she would be an awful mother—that had taken root when she gave Bobby up for adoption. Denise had helped her with that. Not only with her words, but by throwing Nicki into the role of caretaker for her children without warning—which she managed to do often.

As she and Dex perused the next aisle, she could see them doing this year after year, delirious in their love for each other and happy to be fulfilling the dreams and wishes of the children in their lives. Other people's children.

And maybe, one day, theirs.

****

They arrived at Denise and Ben's the next Saturday laden with colorfully wrapped packages for Jennifer, Johnny, and Bobby as well as Denise and Ben. They were also told to bring a gift valued at ten dollars for some game Denise had planned.

The atmosphere in the house was already jubilant, and the younger children were so wound up and excited they bounced off walls as they ran through the house.

"I'm so glad you were able to come," gushed Denise, depositing a kiss on Nicki's cheek.

"Thanks for inviting us. This is Dex." Nicki couldn't contain the smile breaking free as she introduced the man who held her heart.

Dex gave Denise a warm hug. "I've heard so much about you. And the other Sworn Sisters. It's great to finally meet you."

"I've heard wonderful things about you too." Denise's shining, smiling eyes slid over to Nicki, confirming she now understood Nicki's wild crush on the man. "Come on in and grab a drink. Nicki will introduce you to the others if I get sidetracked from my hostess duties."

Jennifer came bouncing over in a red velvet dress

with a black satin bow. Her hair was pulled up in a bun on top of her head, and four little jingle bells hung from strips of ribbon. "Aunt Nicki! You came."

Nicki knelt to her level and gave her a hug and kiss. "You look so beautiful, Jen." She held out the sides of her full-skirted dress. "Like a perfect doll."

"I have on the socks and shoes you gave me." Jennifer pointed her toe to show off black, patent leather mary-janes with white, ruffled socks.

"They were made for this outfit."

Nicki looked up at Dex who had a huge smile on his face. "I agree. Although I don't know much about girl's fashion, you look good enough to be in a magazine."

"This is my friend, Dex," explained Nicki.

Johnny came crashing over, nearly knocking Nicki to the floor. "Hi, Aunt Nicki."

Nicki grabbed him as he charged past her. "Give me a hug, you little monkey." She tickled him as she held him close, and his jubilant laughter embraced her heart.

She quickly introduced Dex before he was off and running.

Dex's warm hand slid around her upper arm to help her up, and he pulled her close to whisper in her ear. "Looks like you have two fans, Aunt Nicki. You're a natural with them."

His breath tickled her ear, sending delicious sensations over her skin, and all thoughts of Jennifer and Johnny disappeared in an instant. She was about to steal a kiss when Sam's voice entered her consciousness.

"This is a family party, you two. No making out."

Nicki turned toward her friend. "You caught us."

As she hugged Sam and wished her a Merry Christmas, her eyes met Michael's. The awkwardness that could have surfaced due to their past was long gone given their interactions over the last few months. And the best part was that now, Sam and Michael were a couple. She moved from Sam to Michael, and hugged him as well, before introducing Dex to these two other important people in her life.

Although Dex had not been a presence during the most traumatic months of learning that Bobby was her child and had leukemia, she had shared that personal and heartbreaking news with him. And he understood with unwavering compassion when she put Bobby ahead of him.

"Where is our little man?" Nicki looked to Michael.

"He's in the basement with some friends playing video games."

"Of course." Turning to Dex, she took his hand, warm and comforting. "Are you ready to meet Bobby?"

"Absolutely."

****

"What happened to Nicki today?" Smiling, Dex glanced over at her in the passenger seat as he drove back to Philadelphia.

"What do you mean?" Her furrowed forehead confirmed she had no idea what he was talking about.

"The kids flocked to you like you were Mother Goose. Even Bobby put down his video controller when you entered the room and came over to greet you."

The edges of her lips inched up in a secret smile. "They're great kids, aren't they?"

He took her hand and brought it to his lips. "They are. Thanks for inviting me to meet them."

"When you think about the circumstances—with Bobby and me and Michael and Sam and Denise and Ben—and put us all in a room together, you'd think the situation was ripe for a reality TV show. Yet there's no drama." Nicki stared straight ahead, but Dex could tell her mind was far from the traffic on Interstate 95.

"How are you feeling about everything now?"

She nodded. "Good. The time I've spent with Denise and her family over the past few months has eased away the angst. It's odd to think that if Bobby didn't have leukemia, I wouldn't have known he was my son. And no one would have known Michael was his father. The intersecting lives we all lead, without knowing it most of the time, is truly amazing."

"Michael seems like a nice guy," he ventured, hoping not to stir up old feelings of whatever nature.

"He's a great guy. And he and Sam seem happy together. Everyone is so different now than when we were eighteen. A lifetime ago." She sighed. "Of course, I'm different too. After I gave the baby up for adoption, I eventually came around to accepting my decision, but I failed to get to a good place; a place where the guilt subsided. Then when the adoption records were obtained and I came out of my tailspin, I was able to see that Bobby had a wonderful, adoring family and I could be part of his life. Michael indirectly helped me get through it. He stepped up to the plate when he had to. He came to see me, knowing I didn't want to see him." She exhaled as if remembering that painful day. "At first, neither of us wanted to tell Bobby we were his birth parents. But Denise did a great job of convincing us otherwise. And because Michael was a match for the bone marrow transplant, Bobby's doing great now."

"Why didn't you want Bobby to know the truth?"

"I was so conflicted. I didn't know if it would damage him more by knowing one of his mother's best friends abandoned him. I agonized over it for a few days, then I went to see Denise. That was all I needed to do. She's a rock. And a great friend."

"You've been a great friend to her as well. Helping out with her kids when she took Bobby to the doctor's, reaching out to Bobby, even when he didn't want to talk to you." Nicki's efforts helped Denise and her family tremendously.

"Thanks for saying that." She gave him a lopsided smile. "We're all in a good place." She turned to him. "I hope I'm not sounding too Pollyanna."

He laced his fingers with hers, needing the connection. "I'm good with Pollyanna."

Nicki settled back into her seat, looking content, relaxed. It was a far cry from her demeanor on the trip back to Philly from his sister's house ten months earlier. That day she couldn't wait to get away from his niece and nephew. They had cut the visit short, making the car ride home tense and silent.

Yet today, they'd stayed at Denise's house for six hours. Although a long time, it went by quickly with good friends, good food, games, and presents. Laughter rang throughout the house the entire day. And Nicki moved freely from adults to children and back again with the utmost ease. Whether with Dex or mingling with others, she had a smile that lit up the room.

"I like this new Nicki," he teased, kissing her hand.

"Oh, really? You like the Nicki who plays with

dolls and video games better than the Nicki who plays with syrup and neckties?"

"Now there's a loaded question. I misspoke. I like both Nicki's. And I'd like to encounter spicy Nicki the second we get back to your apartment."

"Can you wait that long?" Her voice dropped to a purr, and her hand drifted up and down his thigh.

He caught her wrist. "You don't want us to get into an accident, do you?"

She withdrew her hand and sat back. "You are no fun."

"I will be in twenty minutes." Needing to get his mind off their evening to come, he brought the conversation back to Denise's party. "With all the excitement, I didn't see what you got from Bobby."

"He gave me a Christmas tree ornament. It's an angel and there's writing in the middle of the halo that says, 'Thank You, Love Bobby.' " Nicki's voice broke and Dex took her hand and massaged his thumb over her palm.

"That's very special."

"I'm sure Denise had a lot to do with it, but I couldn't help notice Bobby's anxious look as I opened his present. As if he were afraid I wouldn't like it."

"I'm sorry I missed it, but special moments like that should be between the two of you."

Nicki nodded. "It was good for those few seconds. Then Jennifer and Johnny jumped into the fray to give me their gifts. Jennifer made me an ornament out of Styrofoam, glitter, and little metallic snowmen, and Johnny gave me a train ornament. Now I'm going to have to put up a Christmas tree."

"Is that something you generally don't do?"

"Never."

"Why not? Do you have something against Christmas?"

"It didn't seem practical. It's a lot of work, I live by myself, and am rarely home. Besides, I'm not one to invite people over for the holidays. I go to other people's houses." She laughed at herself. "Not very hospitable of me not to reciprocate, but oh well." She shrugged.

"What about this year?"

She turned toward Dex, and he glanced at her, seeing eyes full of emotion, maybe love. Or was that wishful thinking?

"This year is a must. I have three beautiful ornaments I have to display. Although that's all I have."

"They're selling trees three blocks up from your apartment. Since Christmas is next weekend, we should buy one tonight." He'd have to postpone their night of debauchery until a little later than anticipated.

"Sounds like a great plan." Nicki squeezed his hand in thanks as they drove through Saturday night traffic to buy her a Christmas tree.

****

"Why don't you park in your garage, and we'll walk back to my place. I could use the exercise and cool air after the craziness of today."

Dex complied, and it wasn't long before they were walking hand in hand down Walnut Street toward their destination.

Although Nicki had loved watching and listening to the squealing and laughter as the kids tore brightly colored wrapping paper from gifts brought by friends and family for their pre-Christmas celebration, the buzzing in her ears didn't die down until they'd been driving for a good ten minutes.

"It was a bit chaotic," Dex agreed. "I'm a little more used to it than you. I deal with my sister's kids every year at this time."

"When are you going to celebrate with them?" Nicki wondered if after her last disastrous appearance there, she'd ever be invited back.

"I go on Christmas Day for dinner."

Nicki ventured a glance at Dex to see if an invitation was following, but he seemed content to walk in silence.

He must have felt her gaze, or maybe the tenseness entering her body.

"What?" He tugged on her arm, then brought her to a stop.

She lowered her lids, refusing to let him see her disappointment over his failure to invite her. Although she couldn't blame him.

He lifted her chin with his fingers, forcing her to look him in the eye. "Would you like to come with me?"

His question seemed so much more than a mere invitation to his sister's house. The intimate tenor of his voice, the serious set of his jaw, the impossible-to-break connection with his eyes had Nicki leaning toward Dex begging for a kiss and more.

He met her mouth with his, hot and greedy, sparking carnal need and lust.

He dragged his mouth from hers toward her ear and whispered, "You didn't answer my question."

Nicki's breath came in short gasps as his words tickled her lobe and sent wild sensations down her neck and beyond. "Yes, Dex. Yes."

Her verbal response answered the question on the table; her physical response promised a lust-fueled night in bed as she found his mouth with hers and tangled with his tongue.

Dex moaned against her lips before pulling away. "You are sidetracking us from our mission."

"Me?" Nicki laughed, grabbing his hand and putting on her fast-paced city walk. "I did not start that, Mr. Hanover."

"Apparently you did. All you have to do is look at me with those iridescent eyes, and I'm gone."

"Good to know." She smirked, storing that bit of information away for the future.

They arrived at the appointed corner filled with Christmas trees for sale. "For such a small spot, they sure do give you a choice," Nicki remarked, sticking her nose into the branches of a blue spruce. "Which ones smell the best?" she asked a gangly young man sporting a wool hat, plaid jacket, and ragged gloves.

He pointed down the aisle. "Those balsam firs have a nice scent."

Nicki inspected the trees. Once deciding to have a tree, she needed it to be full size. With no holes between branches or odd shape. She stood back, then moved around one particular tree, analyzing every angle.

"You put the bad side against the wall," offered Dex. "Trees are never perfect."

"Someone with experience, I see." Nicki tilted her head, assessing a different tree. "This one is better. What do you think?"

Dex's mouth tipped up on one side. "For someone

with three ornaments, I'm not sure you have to be so picky."

"That's the reason it has to be perfect. I don't have anything to cover the bad spots." She turned to the sales guy. "How much is this one?"

"One hundred ten."

"A hundred ten dollars?" Impossible. It was a cut down tree that would last a few weeks.

"You got it, lady. Do you want it or not?" The impatience in his voice shone through.

"Do you have any less expensive?"

He pointed to a few straggly trees half the size. "Those are fifty."

Dex came over and slid his hand around her waist. "You're pissing off the salesman, who is about to move on to the next customer, and you're preventing me from ravaging your body. Do you think you can make a decision? Now?" He nuzzled her ear.

"Yes," she murmured, enjoying the electric tingles shooting through every nerve. She motioned to the scruffy seller. "I'll take that one."

"Do you want it delivered for another fifty, or are you taking it with you?"

Nicki looked at Dex. "We can manage. Right?"

"Sure. It's only three blocks."

Nicki begrudgingly paid for her tree, then hooked her arm around the limbs at the top, waiting for Dex to grab onto the heavier part of the trunk toward the back. The first block wasn't too bad, but by the third, they had to stop and take breaks every few yards. Luckily, she lived in an elevator building, or they'd be lugging this behemoth up six flights.

Struggling into her apartment, they leaned the tree

in a corner of the living room, Nicki grunting with the effort. "Now I know why I didn't do this before."

"Some people buy smaller trees, Nick." Dex brushed his hands against his coat, removing pine needles before unbuttoning it.

"I suppose I should have. But I got carried away in the moment." She beamed at her purchase. "We need to buy a stand and some lights."

Dex moved behind her, removed her coat, and kissed the side of her head. "Not tonight. I have other plans for you right now. We'll have all day tomorrow to deal with this tree."

Nicki turned in his arms and ran her hands around solid shoulders. She brushed her lips against his, barely touching as she teased his mouth, her tongue roaming over the seam, tasting him. Delicious.

She increased the pressure, little by little until Dex's breathing became ragged. Pressing her body against his length, she covered his mouth with hers and demanded more. Everything.

And he was oh so willing to oblige.

Skilled hands roamed up her arms and down her back until they rested on her hips, pulling her into him. His erection pressed at the perfect spot, and she shamelessly rubbed against him, manipulating the erotic sensation cascading through her core. Arching her back so the tips of her breasts collided with muscled chest, Nicki ached with pure, raw need. Grabbing the hem of his sweater, she pulled it over his head and tossed it on the couch, the heat from his skin burning through her own barrier. Tearing her cashmere sweater off in one hasty movement, she laid her palms flat against his chest, feeling its rise and fall with each breath, then ran her tongue over his nipple, eliciting a surprised gasp.

Dex lifted her head with caressing hands and crushed his mouth over hers as if needing to consume her, and her him. Deft fingers pulled her bra down, releasing her breasts to cool air, before his hot mouth claimed one tight peak, then the other. Sweet, sweet torture.

"I need to feel all of you," she moaned as her hands glided over hot skin and toned muscles.

He gazed at her through hooded lids. "I'd like that."

He guided her to the bedroom where they discarded the rest of their clothing and met on cool cotton sheets. Dex hovered over Nicki, kissing her hungrily, trailing his hand down her abdomen and between her legs. Strong fingers kneaded the soft flesh of her inner thighs, and her sex clenched with each erotic caress. But she wanted more. Needed more.

Her hips rose, pushing her mound into the palm of his hand, begging for the ultimate contact. Dex moved over her, nudging her legs apart with his, fitting himself between them before plunging in. Raw need and a deep ache pushed her to meet his every thrust, reaching for the pinnacle. And it came, crashing and thundering around her in euphoric waves.

He met her in seconds, and she clung to him in carnal bliss until she was totally spent.

Chapter Twenty-Four

"I'm exhausted," declared Nicki as they left Dex's firm's after-holiday party. It was mid-January, and his company scheduled their event to avoid conflicts with every other holiday celebration on their employees' plates.

Dex slid his arm around her waist and kissed the side of her head as they walked to the parking garage. "I've never heard those words come out of your mouth. You have more energy than the northeastern grid. Although we have been on this crazy treadmill for a month now. I hope you're not coming down with the flu."

"Don't say that. I have two work trips planned this month." Just contemplating the hours it would take to get through airport security, flying, and endless meetings in airless conference rooms weighed down every cell in her body. "Maybe it's eggnog withdrawal or melancholy over the end of another year."

Dex stopped walking and turned her face toward him. "You do look pale. And you've been dragging now for a week. Do you think you might be pregnant?"

All motion stopped within her, as if those words froze her blood as well as her brain.

"Nicki?" Dex's voice seemed far away, yet he was standing right in front of her.

She shook her head, hoping to dislodge whatever

foreign plague had momentarily taken over. "No. I can't be. I'm on the pill."

Yet his question brought to the forefront the suspicion she'd had but thrust far back into her consciousness, refusing to let it surface.

She couldn't tell if it was disappointment flitting across his face, but he rapidly recovered and guided her to the car. "Let's get you home and to bed. A good night's sleep will help. I'll try to keep my hands to myself." He chuckled. "And since tomorrow is Sunday, you can stay in bed all day if you want."

Despite eight hours behind her in a dead sleep, she felt no better the next morning. She credited Dex's words about being pregnant with her odd mood this morning. She couldn't be. But maybe she could. Unable to focus on the simplest of tasks, like making coffee, she allowed her mind to spin with the possibility.

"I'm going to the gym," Dex announced. "Are you coming?"

"No. You go ahead. I'm going to relax today."

Nicki waited for him to leave before she jumped into her yoga pants and sweatshirt and dashed to the closest pharmacy.

Her heartbeat tripled, then quadrupled as she held the pregnancy test in her hand, reading the directions in the privacy of her bathroom. She bit the bullet and waited the few minutes it would take to present the news that could change her life. And in those few minutes, a myriad of emotions ran through her, but the domineering one was excitement.

"How are you feeling?" asked Dex as he blew through the door with a bag from the bakery containing chicken salad and fresh rolls.

The aroma of fresh-baked bread usually made her mouth water, but at this moment she couldn't process sight, smells, and hearing. "I don't have the flu," she managed.

"Good." Dex pulled the container of chicken salad out of the bag as Nicki studied his face, but all she saw was mild relief. "If you had the flu, I'd be next. Ready for lunch?" He sliced the rolls and set them on a plate in the middle of the kitchen table. "Come sit."

She needed to tell him now. She sat, working through the right words to break the news. It shouldn't be that hard. She'd known since their breakup last March that Dex wanted to be a father. Was her procrastination based on her sentiments? Should she ponder this news for a few days until she wrapped her brain around it?

But there was no way she could keep this secret for one more minute. The second Dex sat, he began talking, oblivious to her odd behavior. "This was a special Christmas. Maybe you're sad it's over. But we do have something to look forward to."

He was referring to the weekend getaway to New Orleans she had booked for next month as his Christmas present. It was also meant to celebrate their one-year anniversary, with eight months off in the middle for stupidity.

"Maybe we have something more to look forward to." She zeroed in on his eyes.

His brow furrowed.

"I *am* pregnant." The words tumbled out. "I just took a test."

She studied his eyes, his face, his body.

He swallowed hard, then a smile took over his lips

274

and moved straight to his eyes. "Oh my God, Nicki. This is the best Christmas gift you could ever give me."

He came around the table and pulled her from her chair, hugging her tight.

Nicki released her breath. Although he loved kids and would be a great father, they hadn't discussed having a family of their own right now, and maybe now was not the ideal time. Dex was being sought by other accounting firms through head hunters, and Nicki was taking on more and more responsibilities at work.

He sobered as he zeroed in on Nicki's face. "What about you? How do you feel about this news?"

She nodded. "Good." She ventured a smile. "I know I was against having a child ten months ago, but once I learned about Bobby and got involved in his life, along with Jennifer and Johnny's, I started to believe I could do this." Bobby was happy, and the guilt over giving him up, though still a presence, lessened due to their relationship.

Dex beamed. "I know you can, Nick. You're fabulous with all three of Denise's children, and you've come around with my niece and nephew."

She arched her brow. "Do you think so, or are you trying to pump me up?"

True, she loved spending time with Denise's kids, but she hadn't made it all the way across that bridge with Dex's sister's kids. Although things were much better there than the first time she'd met them.

"I mean it." Dex's eyes turned serious, and if she could read into them what she felt in her heart, she'd see love.

"Thank you," she whispered, the emotion of what passed between them pure and simple. Tears sprang to her eyes.

"What's wrong?" He cupped her cheek in his hand.

She nuzzled into it and smiled. "Nothing. I love you."

Dex held her gaze, as if to verify her words. She didn't blame him. He'd wanted so much more from her for so long. Could he trust she was now willing to give it? But she knew she arrived. And not just because she was pregnant.

"I've loved you for a long time, Nicki." He reached for his coat on the back of the kitchen chair and dug into the inside pocket. "I've been carrying this around for a while. Waiting for the right moment. Not sure when it might come. I've been close. But I didn't want to spook you." He held a royal blue velvet box.

Nicki's heart thudded in her chest. This couldn't be.

He opened the box, and nestled in satin was a solitaire round diamond set in platinum. She drew her hands to her face and covered her eyes, then peeked through. "Is that what I think it is?"

Dex removed the ring from its pillow and took Nicki's left hand. "I'm supposed to be on my knee, aren't I?" He dropped to the floor and looked up at her. "Nicki Reading, will you marry me and make me the happiest man alive?"

Tears flooded her eyes and she couldn't control the torrent. She nodded vigorously, searching for her voice. "Yes. Yes. Yes."

Her hand shook as he took it and placed the ring on her third finger. "It fits perfectly." He admired the jewel on her hand.

"How did you know my size?"

"I borrowed a ring out of your jewelry box and had the jeweler measure it."

"How long have you had this?" Nicki stared at the beautiful diamond in awe.

"Since mid-December."

All lethargy had gone by the wayside, and Nicki's glow emanated from her pores. "Do you want a long engagement?"

"Hell no. After the fantastic news you delivered today, I'd marry you tomorrow."

"I hope you don't mind, but I'd like to have a wedding. It doesn't have to be big and it can be soon. As soon as we can plan it. I'm sure you want your family to be there, and I want my girlfriends with me."

"Of course. You should have what you want."

Nicki had no close relatives to invite. Neither of her parents had siblings. But she did have her closest friends from high school—the Sworn Sisters—who were her family. Denise, Sam, and Alyssa would be her bridesmaids and Bobby could also have a role. "I want to do it before I look too pregnant. Maybe in three months. How about the end of April?" Excitement burst from every word. They had gotten engaged two minutes ago, and she was already planning a wedding. She needed to slow down.

Dex took her hand and kissed it. "Whatever you want. I'm all yours."

Those last three words showered her with a calmness and contentment she'd never dreamed she'd achieve. At least not because of a man.

This was the best day of her life.

****

The next two months had Nicki working at warp

speed. Her job took over her days, including a few weekends when she had to travel to California and Texas. She didn't have time for morning sickness and told her body that. It listened for the most part.

Dex left the wedding planning to her, knowing she didn't actually want his input. He was the perfect groom, not questioning her choices or the expense.

"What hideous color are you going to put us in?" asked Alyssa, the designated bridesmaid to accompany Nicki on their quest for bridesmaids' gowns.

"How about chartreuse?" Nicki held back a smile.

"Not my color. I'd prefer black."

"You are not wearing black to a spring wedding that takes place outside in the gardens. How about violet or blush? Something light and breezy."

Since there wasn't much time, they couldn't shop at a bridal boutique. Those establishments wanted six months to order. So they ended up at King of Prussia Mall knowing they'd find something appropriate in one of the upscale department stores.

"How about this?" Alyssa held up an over-the-top beaded navy-blue gown.

"This is not a black-tie Gala. We are looking for light and airy, remember?"

"But I never go anywhere to get dressed up. I wear scrubs every day. Humor me."

Perhaps Alyssa wasn't the correct bridesmaid to choose for this task, but Denise was too busy with the kids and Sam was getting her new law practice off the ground in Red Bank. Besides, Sam had her own wedding to plan with Michael.

"*Ooohhh*. Look at this red dress." Alyssa held up a satin, poufy-skirted dress that would look great on a teen going to the prom.

"No. How about if I look. You're here to try on."

Nicki skimmed through the rack and found several gowns that might work. She wasn't in the mood for this, although she couldn't pinpoint why. Yet the time had come to tackle the job, since Sam kept at her to get it done or they'd all be naked.

"Are the three of us wearing the same gown?" Alyssa, fingered the fabric of one of Nicki's choices.

"No. Just the same color. I like this light pink." Nicki held a gown up for inspection.

"That color washes me out."

Nicki was not going to be waylaid by Alyssa's whining, especially since she wasn't far behind in the grumbling category. Finding a bridesmaid's gown was not her idea of a fun day of shopping. Nicki liked edgier things and preferred boutiques with one-of-a-kind designs.

"Perhaps you can spend some time outdoors and get an early tan," proposed Nicki.

"Perhaps," Alyssa capitulated as they headed to the dressing room. "Did you get your gown?"

"Yes. I love it. It's a Chantilly sheath gown with an illusion neckline. White. I hope I don't develop a baby bump in the next few weeks. If I gain too much weight between now and then, I won't fit into it."

"*Humpf.* That's not going to be a problem. You look like you lost weight since becoming pregnant."

"I know. The obstetrician is not happy with me. She told me to eat more. I'm not gaining enough—at least not in her eyes."

"I'd love to hear that. Any woman would. Except, of course, a pregnant woman. You need to take care of yourself and that baby."

"Yes, Nurse Beckman. I know. But I've been constantly on the go and don't always have time to eat right. Things will settle down, at least a little, after the wedding. Then I'll focus on better nutrition."

Nicki had been surprisingly happy when she first found out she was pregnant, and over the moon to be marrying Dex, but in certain moments of every day she questioned her sanity. Could she do this?

She zeroed in on the assignment at hand, and although they'd blown through at least six dresses, all nixed by Alyssa, the seventh was a charm. Light blue, strapless, and belted with a white satin ribbon around the waist, the filmy gown floated on air as Alyssa walked up and down the dressing room aisle, twirling and swirling to showcase the movement of the dress. Nicki loved it and Alyssa was happy too. Success.

From the other gowns of the same hue, Nicki chose one for Denise and one for Sam, hoping they'd like them. If not, they could return them and choose something else. At least they'd know the right color.

"Is it time for lunch?" asked Alyssa, anticipation sparking her features.

"Sure. I could use a rest."

Once seated in the second-floor restaurant, Alyssa continued her questions about the wedding. "Tell me about the venue."

"It's at The Grounds for Sculpture. Not far from your house. The ceremony will be outdoors in the amphitheater, and the reception will be in the restaurant."

"I haven't been there, though it's so close. I hear it's beautiful."

"It is. The restaurant is surrounded by ponds and gardens based on Monet's property in Giverny, France."

"I've never been there, either." A frown furrowed her forehead. "I've never been anywhere. I'm going to have to change that." Alyssa sipped her water, perhaps contemplating a European vacation, although Nicki knew she wouldn't go. Alyssa was a homebody, never venturing far from Lawrenceville. Wanderlust was not part of her DNA.

After they ordered salads and iced tea, Nicki studied her friend.

"You're in an odd mood, today. What's going on? Are you still seeing Cole?"

Alyssa's sigh was heavy. "Yes. But not as much. I can't tell if he's trying to put some distance between us or if he truly is as busy as he says."

"Maybe it's good you're cooling off. You were so freaked out a few months ago when you were spending a lot of time with him. Perhaps your affair will fizzle out."

Alyssa's eyes widened in shock. "Why would you say such a thing? I don't want that."

"I thought it would be better for you since you seemed so unhappy that you'd fallen in love with him." *Obviously not.*

The waitress came by with their salads, giving Nicki a chance to swing the conversation in a different direction.

"Are you bringing a plus one to the wedding?" Nicki hoped Alyssa would find someone soon to get her away from Cole.

"I contemplated asking Cole, but I know he won't

be able to come."

No kidding. He's married with kids. At least Nicki didn't say it out loud.

"You may not want to hear this, Alyssa, but you should put an end to the affair with Cole. He's ruining whatever you could have with someone else. Someone eligible." She sipped her iced tea, questioning whether she should be saying any of this to her friend. Ignoring her concern, she continued. "You're so blinded by Cole, you can no longer appreciate that there are other guys out there who you could have a real relationship with. In the end, you know this affair is going to end and you're going to be the one left behind."

Alyssa bit her lip and pushed her salad away. "You're right. I don't want to hear it."

Alyssa stared off into space, and Nicki hoped her words would sink in and help her see the disaster looming.

Avoiding further talk of her dilemma, Alyssa turned the conversation back to Nicki's wedding. "You seem to have everything under control for your big day. I remember planning my wedding. The wedding that never happened." Surprisingly, Alyssa's tone was missing the usual bitterness spewing from her mouth when she talked of her broken engagement from David. "It was so difficult trying to get the church and venue available on the same date."

"We're all set." Nicki preened, proud of herself for pulling it all together in two months' time. "Given my job in marketing and event planning for our label's artists, organizing our wedding was a piece of cake. Our guest list grew to thirty, but it's still a small celebration. After choosing the venue, food, music, and flowers, I sent the invitations out. I can't believe it's only six weeks away." She smiled at the thought of marrying Dex, the man of her dreams.

Then a stray fear crept in. While ready to make this huge commitment to Dex, she still wasn't quite sure she was prepared for the child that would come soon after.

****

"How do you do all this wedding planning and still get work done?" Dex sat next to Nicki at her kitchen table helping with the seating arrangements.

"I've learned I don't need to agonize over decisions. I met with the florist once. When she asked if I wanted to consider other options or look at different websites for ideas, I told her I didn't have time. I made a choice and that was the end of the discussion."

Dex nodded. "I love a decisive woman. But of course, I knew that about you already."

"The most difficult thing so far was getting Alyssa to choose a gown. She's so picky and her taste is a little over the top. I had to reign her in or she'd be wearing gold lame with a tiara."

"Does she know this is your wedding?"

"That didn't seem to be an important fact." Nicki smiled at their interesting day of sparring while Alyssa tried on dress after dress. Then she sobered. "I wish Alyssa would find someone to date that's worth her time."

"Why? What's going on?"

Nicki hadn't divulged Alyssa's affair with Cole. She chewed her lip, considering how much to share without denigrating her friend's reputation. "Ever since she and David broke off their engagement, she hasn't gotten involved with anyone eligible because she doesn't trust men. She dated David for nine years before they got engaged and spent another whole year as his fiancée. In reality, she was more excited about the wedding than in marrying him. And David felt pressured into putting a ring on her finger since they had been dating so long. Alyssa wanted the big, fancy wedding, which was probably another issue. His means of escape was to cheat on her so she'd find out and break up. Which she did. But that really affected her in moving forward. So instead of dating someone who would be right for her, she fell into an affair with a married guy—a doctor who works with her. They've been having an affair for a year already. And now, she's in love with him." Nicki had predicted this disaster, but Alyssa refused to listen. "Not a good place to be since he'll never leave his wife according to Alyssa."

"That's surprising."

"That she's having an affair or that he's not going to leave his wife?"

"They never leave their wives. Doesn't she know that?" Dex stood and stretched his legs. "Your Sworn Sisters seem so normal, so nice."

"Alyssa's nice." Her innate defense of her friend surfaced with a vengeance.

"Not to her paramour's wife. And they probably have kids, right?"

Nicki nodded, pushing the seating chart aside. She opened her mouth to respond but couldn't come up with a rationalizing statement. For she too believed Alyssa was going down a dark, dangerous road. But having mad, passionate sex in the utility closet at the hospital was obviously more important to Alyssa than worrying about whose lives she and Cole were blowing up.

Dex must have sensed Nicki's discomfort with this conversation, and he changed the subject. "What else needs to be done?"

"You're in charge of the honeymoon. What have you decided?"

"I thought you might feel too queasy cruising on the ocean, so I booked us a river cruise. On the Danube."

Nicki bounced up and squealed. "That's perfect. I've never been to eastern Europe." She hugged him from behind before Dex slipped his arm around her waist and pulled her onto his lap.

He massaged her still-flat stomach. "Garfield or Gwendolyn will enjoy it too."

"Those names are atrocious." Nicki laughed. "We'll have to work on an acceptable list when we have time. But right now, I want to go over the menu with you."

She started to rise, but Dex pulled her back down. "Later." He kissed the side of her neck.

His tongue ignited the neurons close to her surface, and Nicki turned in his arms, claiming his mouth with a languid kiss. His hand cupped her breast and a moan escaped, for the sensation shot straight to her core. Needing more contact, Nickie straddled Dex, grinding her sex against his hard length while arching her back, begging for his hands to continue their sensuous assault.

Taut nipples pushed against the satin of her bra, pleading for release. Dex unbuttoned her silk blouse and fingered the smooth edge of her undergarment, heightening the tension building within.

Dex stood with Nicki in his arms, and she wrapped

her legs around his waist, refusing to break the erotic contact she craved. "I'm moving this to the bedroom." He took control, holding her tight.

"You won't hear any complaints from me." Lifting her head, she gazed into the eyes that melted her at every turn. "I love you, Dex. I never want anything to interfere with this—with what we have." Tears stung the back of her eyes. Emotions were so close to the surface these days.

Dex stroked her cheek. "I love you too. There is nothing that could come between us. Ever."

And Nicki believed him.

Chapter Twenty-Five

"You ladies are amazing." Nicki stepped into the black stretch limousine parked in front of her apartment building on Friday evening, dressed in a navy, one-shouldered gown with a slit to the top of her thigh. "Thank you so much for planning this."

Her friends were also dressed for a special night, and Nicki couldn't control her smile.

This was her watered-down bachelorette party. Denise, Sam, and Alyssa wouldn't take no for an answer and decided on Henri's, a new, trendy restaurant for dinner, and dancing at Equinox, *sans* alcohol. In solidarity, her friends agreed to stay sober along with Nicki and the baby. What amazing friends!

"Two weeks to go." Denise's enthusiasm was boundless. Not only did she seem thrilled that Nicki had finally found her match, but Bobby's leukemia was in remission after the successful bone marrow transplant, and joy bubbled from every pore.

"Sam has seven weeks, right?" Alyssa confirmed they had another wedding around the corner.

"Yes, but my wedding is a little more low-key than Nicki's. On the beach in front of Michael's house. I hope it doesn't rain."

"Rain means good luck," said Denise, who always looked for the silver lining.

Sam scowled. "I'd prefer good luck and a nice day.

I want it all."

"Can't say I blame you," added Nicki. "I'm hoping the same thing. If it rains, we can't have the ceremony at the amphitheater."

"What happens then?" Alyssa smoothed her long brown tresses. "If it's humid, I'll have to wear my hair up."

"It's not all about you," laughed Sam, elbowing her friend.

The women continued talking wedding plans, both Nicki's and Sam's until they got to the restaurant. Nicki had been dying to go here for months but never remembered to call weeks before her desired date for a reservation. It was elegant, classy, and five-star, perfect for a celebration with her best friends and bridesmaids.

Halfway through dinner, Nicki felt a cramp. Then another. The food was rich, and she admonished herself to push the sauce to the side, but the cramps turned more and more painful. Mild alarm ran through her brain at the possibility they might not be related to rich food.

"Excuse me." She made a hasty beeline to the ladies' room.

Chills coursed over her skin and nausea swarmed her gut. Could she have eaten something that didn't agree with her? She turned on the faucet and ran cold water over her hands, then grabbed a paper towel, wet it, and pressed it to her forehead.

Denise entered at that moment. "What's wrong, Nicki?"

"I don't know. I feel sick."

Denise's face paled. "Are you bleeding?"

The pain in Nicki's stomach stabbed again. "I…I

don't know."

She blindly entered the stall, tears blurring her vision. She hadn't thought about that. But there it was. Blood on her panties.

A gasp escaped on a sob as she pressed her forehead to the door.

"Nicki?"

"Yes, there's blood."

"Let's get you to the hospital."

"No! I'll go home and call my doctor. She has a service who will get in touch with her." She emerged from the stall and saw her ravaged face in the mirror.

Denise looked as shell-shocked as Nicki felt. Then she wrapped her arms around Nicki and hugged her. "Maybe it's not as bad as you think. Maybe it's a sign you have to slow down."

"I hope so." Nicki walked out of the ladies' room in a fog, with Denise hovering nearby.

"What is it?" Alyssa stood and went over to Nicki, studying her face. "Here sit down for a minute. I'll call an ambulance." She grabbed for her purse.

"No. No. Please don't. I'm going to go home and call my doctor."

"You should go to the hospital. You shouldn't waste any time when you're pregnant." The nurse in Alyssa kicked in. "Call your doctor from here. I'm sure he or she will tell you to get to the hospital immediately."

All three women talked at the same time, agreeing to a plan which ignored Nicki's request. The phone call was made and as Alyssa predicted, Nicki was told to go to the Emergency Room.

Having a limo at their disposal, they piled in, their

plan of dancing after dinner forgotten.

"Where's Dex tonight?" asked Denise. "I'll call him to tell him to meet us at the hospital."

"No," Nicki demanded a little too loudly. "I don't want to alarm him if it's nothing. Let's go. I'll get checked out, and when I get the all clear, I'll go home and rest."

While plausible, this was more than a false alarm. Nicki could sense it in her bones.

And in her heart.

****

It seemed like hours later when Alyssa appeared at her bedside. "Oh, Nicki. I'm so sorry." Alyssa's teary eyes and downturned lips reconfirmed Nicki's worst nightmare.

Nicki felt numb, and although her head pounded, the tears had stopped. "This isn't happening." Her voice was calm, sedated. "When I wake up, I'm going to remember we had a great time at dinner, then went dancing." Her lids were heavy and she fought them from closing.

"You can sleep, Nicki. I'll stay right here with you until Dex comes. He's on his way."

"*Ooohhh*. What did he say?" Nicki's heart nearly stopped beating.

"He's so worried about you. He said he'll be right here."

Dread, hurt, and pain squeezed her lungs as panic set in. One of the monitors connected to her body started beeping rapidly, and a nurse appeared out of nowhere. She checked Nicki's vitals and asked how she was feeling.

Alyssa answered for her. "Her fiancé is on his way.

I think she's worried about how he'll take the news."

Tears flooded Nicki's eyes again, and she could barely see through the watery haze. The nurse gave her a look filled with sympathy, so Nicki turned her head toward the wall. She didn't want sympathy. She wanted her baby back. Her throat constricted and the pain surged from there straight to her heart.

"Nicki." Dex stood in the doorway, his face pale, his eyes glassy with tears. He rushed to her side. "I was so worried you might be in danger." He looked toward the nurse. "Will she be okay?"

The nurse nodded. "Physically she's fine, although she just had a spike in her blood pressure. She needs to rest."

Dex cupped his hand against her cheek and zeroed in on her eyes. "I'm not a religious guy, but I prayed the whole way here, begging that you'd be all right."

"I'll let the two of you talk." The nurse slipped out of the room.

"Me too." Alyssa came to the other side of the bed and gave Nicki a kiss on the cheek. "Now that you're in good hands, Denise, Sam, and I are going to leave. I'll call you tomorrow."

Nicki grabbed Alyssa's hand. "Thanks for being here with me tonight. Tell the others too." Her voice came out in a whisper.

Alyssa nodded, her shoulders slumped as she exited the curtained room.

Nicki closed her eyes, not wanting to look at the pain on Dex's face. "I'm sorry," she murmured, not knowing what else to say.

Dex raised her fingers to his lips and kissed them. "There is nothing for you to be sorry about. This wasn't your fault, Nicki. There was something wrong with our baby, and he or she just couldn't make it. Don't believe for a moment it's your fault." Emotion clogged his words.

He sat on the edge of the bed and gently pulled her into his arms, stroking her back, her head, her arms. "I'm so glad you're okay. I was so scared." He kissed her temple. "Now that I know you're fine, I can breathe again."

A sob escaped Nicki's throat at his touching words.

"It's okay, Nicki. It will be okay." He kept saying the same thing over and over as he held her close, cocooning her against his body.

Eventually, she fell asleep, the one state that kept this traumatic experience at bay. But when she opened her eyes, the whole awful, depressing event came flooding back. Dex sat in the chair by her bed, holding her hand, his head falling to one side, his lids closed. She pulled her hand from his and he jumped to life.

"Are you okay?" he asked, almost by rote.

Not by a long shot. "I keep reliving the last time I was in a hospital, leaving without my baby." She shook her head, so wanting to dispel those images, those thoughts. "When I finally came around to thinking I could do this again, although I had promised my baby I wouldn't have another in his place, it didn't cross my mind that God wouldn't let me go back on my promise." Her soul held overwhelming regret.

"That's not what's happening, Nicki. There was a medical problem. I'm not questioning your faith, but I don't see it like that." He smoothed her hair back. "Did the doctor say you could have children in the future?"

Nicki's body stiffened. "Yes," she almost hissed.

So maybe Dex wasn't as concerned about her personally as he seemed. Maybe his concern stemmed from his goal to have a child. If not now, then at least in the future.

She turned her head away from him.

"Nicki, please don't shut me out." His words caressed her as his fingers interlaced with hers.

She sighed. "The doctor said we should wait for a few months. But she didn't see anything that would prevent me from becoming pregnant again." Although Nicki did.

She wasn't about to tell Dex right now that getting pregnant was not in her future. She was never going to go through this again, and no matter what Dex said, she was convinced this was a sign to remind her of her promise to Bobby.

Dex broke into her thoughts. "Were you still at the restaurant when this happened?"

"Yes. I thought maybe I ate something that wasn't agreeing with me. I felt nauseous, so I went to the ladies' room. There was blood." A sob escaped.

"I'm so glad you were with your friends."

She nodded. "They refused to listen to me when I said I didn't want to go to the hospital. Nurse Alyssa took charge." Nicki stared at the bed covers, not wanting to see the same agony in Dex's eyes as hers. "I want to get out of here. Can you check with the nurse and find out if I can leave?"

"Sure." His brow furrowed. "Are you well enough to get out of bed?"

"I'll feel much better if I can rest in my bed at home."

Dex stood and left in search of the nurse.

Nicki looked around the room at the monitors, the white walls, the plastic chair. She felt so lost, so alone. How could her sheer happiness from a few hours ago be replaced with this complete and utter loss? She rubbed her hand over her abdomen, and new tears coursed down her face. She mopped at them with the sheet, begging herself to hold it together so she could escape this place.

Dex appeared back with the nurse. "I need to check your pressure and your other vitals." She recorded Nicki's heartrate, blood pressure, and temperature. "Everything looks fine. Make an appointment with your doctor on Monday."

Nicki nodded, barely registering her words. She'd agree to whatever promise it would take to get released.

When they arrived at Nicki's apartment, Dex treated her with kid gloves, leading her to the couch to sit. It was already seven in the morning, and a gray dawn peered through the windows. She curled her legs beneath her and pulled a pillow into her stomach, needing to feel something, anything there.

"Can I get you tea, coffee, juice?"

"No," she croaked with effort. She could sense Dex studying her as if she were a science project specimen.

He reached over and rubbed her shoulders, but she stiffened under his ministrations. "It's all so raw," he said. "You need to…we need to mourn our loss. It will get better with time." He kissed the side of her head, which usually would have made her snuggle closer, but her body inched away from his. "Maybe you should get some sleep."

She did want to close her eyes, not so much from exhaustion, but to close out the world. To close out

Dex. To close out the devastating loss.

He stood and drew her up and toward her bedroom. Dex pulled down the covers and she slid in, her eyes closing before her head hit the pillow.

****

"We have to call off the wedding." Nicki stood in the doorway leading to the living room, her hair tangled and her eyes dull.

It was getting dark outside as it neared six p.m. on Saturday night. Dex had napped fitfully on the couch here and there, not wanting to disturb Nicki, who needed the rest. For the past few hours, he'd tried to work on his laptop, but concentration was nowhere to be found.

He stood and went to her, hugging her. Words collided in his brain in response, but he didn't want to appear insensitive or rash. In his mind, there was no reason to postpone their wedding. He loved Nicki with his whole heart, and the lost pregnancy didn't affect that love. But he had to be mindful of her emotions. Perhaps a celebration would seem too crass after their loss.

"Let's take a few days. We don't have to make a decision right now."

"The wedding is two weeks away. We'll lose all our deposits, but we might be able to stop the food and flowers from being ordered. We need to tell our friends, your family, so they can cancel whatever plans they've made."

Nicki's voice approached panic, and Dex saw his dream shattering into a million pieces. He needed to soothe her, but his own pain rose to the surface. He wanted—needed—to convince her to stay on track. To marry him in two weeks. To go away with him and spend twelve glorious days travelling the Danube. But how could he put his dream before her needs?

"What if we cancel the public wedding and you and I elope? We'll set up something at City Hall here in Philadelphia and go on our honeymoon as planned. It will give you a chance to rest and recuperate. We can have a celebration in a few months if you'd like." Hope burned bright at his suggestion, and he saw a flicker of spirit in Nicki's eyes.

Then she lowered her lids. "No. We can't. I need time to think this through."

The fire dimmed and sputtered out. "Think what through? We love each other, Nick. We want to be together. There's no reason to wait." His heartbeat thrummed and echoed in his ears as her words sent off warning bells.

She moved away from him. "I'm sorry, Dex. I can't talk about this now. I'm tired and upset and…" She dragged her hands through her hair. "I don't know what I am."

He had to back off. "Okay. I understand. I don't mean to push. Why don't we order in something to eat? Then you should go back to bed. We can talk more later. Or tomorrow."

"I don't want to talk about this later." Her eyes bored into his. Was that anger? She swallowed. "You should go. I'll be fine. I need to be alone."

She was pushing him away. Should he let her? They'd lost their baby, not just hers. They should be mourning this together. Helping each other.

Nicki went to the door and opened it. There was no mistaking her intent. "I'll call you later in the week."

"Later in the week?" Confusion and hurt bombarded his brain.

"I'll cancel things."

Her words reverberated in his head as he walked to the door. He always kissed her when he left, but her features were hard and his heart had just been stomped on.

"Good bye," he said, not at all sure precisely what that meant.

Chapter Twenty-Six

"I'm glad you called, Nicki." Sam placed a pitcher of iced tea on the glass table out on the deck overlooking the ocean.

It was a mild day for April, and Sam had the perfect location for talk and tears, having moved into Michael's Crescent Beach house a few months ago.

"I had to get out of Philly. Thanks for cancelling your appointments at work and babysitting me." Nicki looked out over the railing, mesmerized by the waves rising up to an enormous height before curling and crashing into the churning sea. White foam raced across the sand as the tide inched up the beach. Last night's storm encouraged the angry waves despite the sun peeking through cumulus clouds. Nicki understood the dichotomy perfectly.

"I'm not babysitting you," broke in Sam. "I'm here to listen, talk, or be still. Whatever you want."

Nicki attempted a smile. It had been one week since she'd lost her baby. She was stronger physically, but emotionally she was a basket case.

"It's been a tough week being alone with my thoughts."

"Where's Dex?" Sam's voice gentled with the question.

"I don't want to talk to him. I can't."

"He's your fiancé. The father of your child."

"There is no longer a child, and the wedding has been called off, so he's no longer my fiancé." Nicki's words came out harsh and angry, the exact way she felt.

"You postponed the wedding," Sam said in her reasonable tone.

"No. I cancelled the wedding."

"What do you mean you cancelled the wedding?" Alyssa came through the sliding glass door, and Denise was not far behind her.

Surprise caught Nicki off guard. "What are you doing here?"

"Is that any way to greet your best friends and bridesmaids?" Alyssa hugged her from behind. "We're here for moral support. Sam called us early this morning to tell us you were coming. I was able to switch days with one of the other nurses, and Denise got a babysitter. So instead of questioning us, you should thank us."

Nicki couldn't help the laugh that escaped. She stood and gave each of them a proper hug.

She turned to Sam. "You didn't need to call in the troops."

"Oh, yes I did," confirmed Sam. "I figured I needed all the help I could get. Now start from the beginning. What did you say to poor Dex?"

Alyssa and Denise sat at the round table along with Nicki and Sam, and six eyes zeroed in on her.

"I know I'm a monster. But I can't talk to him. He stayed with me all day Saturday while I slept, but I sent him home when I woke up. I haven't spoken to him since."

"That was six days ago," reported Denise, as if Nicki didn't know. "Has he tried to contact you?"

"He calls every day. He texts. I haven't called him back, but I texted to say I'm alive."

"Why haven't you spoken to him, seen him?" Sam's brow furrowed.

"There's nothing I can say to make this better. I copied him on my emails to vendors as well as our guests."

"How could you ignore Dex? I'm sure he's hurting too." Sam's eyes shone with tears.

But Nicki was through crying. She had cried for the past seven days, and all the water in her system had dried up. Now she was empty, numb. And sullen. And depressed. And miserable. Perhaps coming to Crescent Beach hadn't been a good idea.

"I don't want to hurt him anymore. We need a clean break. It will never work out between us. He wants children. I thought I could do it. But now I can't. I won't go through this again."

Denise took hold of her hand. "Just because you had one miscarriage doesn't mean you'll have another one. You're still young and healthy and able to have children. You can't let this affect the rest of your life."

"I'm clearly not meant to have children. I gave Bobby up for adoption almost fifteen years ago. I swore then I wouldn't have another child. The pain was too great, the guilt tremendous. But with Dex, I loved him so much..." Her voice broke, and she inhaled. "I believed I could put the past behind. For us. It took me some time to get there, but I finally did. And look what happened." She grimaced at the physical pain these words elicited. "It's not in the stars. And Dex wants kids so badly. He deserves to have children. I can't ruin his dream, and that's what I'll do if we get married.

Because I'm not going to change my mind."

Sam filled everyone's glass with more tea. "It's still new, too raw. You shouldn't make a major decision seven days after a traumatic event. Give yourself some time to heal. To consider the future."

"I've made up my mind. I need to tell Dex it's over." She twisted her engagement ring, knowing she shouldn't be wearing it any longer.

Alyssa set her glass down with a thud. "Of course you shouldn't get married if you're not one hundred percent sure. I almost made that mistake."

Sam snorted. "Alyssa, you and David were different. You were going to marry because you thought it was time after ten years together. All your sisters were married and starting to have kids. You were ready to do the same. Apparently, David wasn't. But that's your story, not Nicki's and Dex's."

"You're right." Alyssa lowered her lids, obviously feeling chastised. "I shouldn't compare the two. I have no sense when it comes to relationships."

"Are you still seeing Cole?" asked Nicki.

"The affair is on life support." Alyssa stared out toward the ocean.

"You know that's the best thing for both of you. And his family. You need to end it, move on, and stop pining over him."

"I'm not pining," sulked Alyssa. But Nicki, as well as the others, knew otherwise. "And who uses that word anyway?" she huffed.

Denise took up the gauntlet, but not with Alyssa. Unfortunately, she circled back to Nicki. "You love Dex. You shouldn't let anything get in the way. Love doesn't come around very often. You know that. How could you walk away?"

Nicki's voice rasped. "Because I do love him, I can't ruin his life. He should have the family he deserves. The family he doesn't want to live without."

"You changed your mind before," pushed Denise. "You'll do it again. Give yourself the time you need. But don't drive Dex away while you're doing it."

Sam jumped in. "You've been so happy. Happier than I've seen you in years. You can't toss all that away."

"It's not just me. When I tell Dex I won't get pregnant again, he'll do the walking. He did it before. I'm not going to let him do it to me again. It's better for me this way. I'm in control."

The words sounded good, but Nicki's hold on that control was seriously precarious.

****

Nicki did it by email. What a coward, but she couldn't look Dex in the eyes. Her trite statement that it was all for the best was short and to the point. She couldn't bring herself to wish him well or keep a window open to an eventual face to face. She'd fall apart the moment she saw him and would promise him anything. Her head hurt, her eyes hurt, her heart hurt. It was hard to breathe.

But she made the decision. She wouldn't get pregnant again. Although their baby had only been four months along, she'd established an incredible bond. To go through another nine months, waiting, watching, worrying whether something bad would happen again was not in her chemistry.

Having taken two weeks off to mourn her loss, Nicki jumped into work with a vengeance. She crisscrossed the country to meet with the musicians, put in time on nights and weekends to perfect marketing plans for the launch of new albums, and micro-managed everyone under her, much to their chagrin.

When she wasn't working, she ran miles through the streets and parks, careful to stay away from places she might bump into Dex. Even though she accomplished her goal, his face was imprinted on her brain. The anguish, pain, and hurt she'd inflicted when she asked him to leave her apartment was staggering. The breakup email excruciating.

She hadn't seen him since.

The only thing that would cure her was total abstinence. She convinced herself it was in Dex's best interest as well.

Unfortunately, he didn't understand her message or refused to, because there he was, standing in her doorway at work.

Her heart flipped and her stomach somersaulted. "Dex." Her voice sounded raw, raspy.

"You remember who I am?" His jaw clenched, making him look sexier than usual in a dangerous sort of way.

Nicki swallowed and motioned to the chair across her desk. "Work isn't the best place for a discussion."

"I agree. But you gave me no choice. You refused to answer my calls, my texts, my emails. I started to believe you'd lost your phone." He closed the door and sat where directed. "I knew you wouldn't answer your buzzer at home."

His face was drawn, his eyes shadowed. Like hers. Although nothing could interfere with Dex's gorgeousness.

Nicki focused on a contract on her desk. Anything to keep from gazing into Dex's eyes, her downfall. His secret weapon.

"I said what I had to say in my email to you. I didn't think it would be good for either of us to drag this out."

"You don't get to make all the decisions, Nicki. I lost a baby too. I hurt too. But walking away is not the answer. We should be helping each other get through this. Talk about it. Talk about our future. Give us hope."

"I thought I was clear in my email. There is no future. No hope. I can't…I won't have another child." Her voice caught on the words and repressed the sob craving to escape.

"You were clear. I get it. About a baby. What I don't get is why you wouldn't give me a chance to let you know I can live with your decision. To let you know that I love you so much I'm willing to change my expectations if it means having you in my life."

"But…"

He held up his hand to silence her. "It's my turn to talk. You cannot presume to know what I can live with and what I can't live without. You're stubborn and opinionated and inflexible. Even with those very negative traits, I'm still willing to marry you. All I ask is that you work on loosening your hold on those traits." Dex stood, his temperament as black as when he arrived. "Let me know if you can manage that."

Nicki gawked at his retreating back, her mouth unable to close. Did he say he wanted to marry her even if she wouldn't have his baby? Or was her brain too frozen to understand his words?

Dex left as quickly as he'd arrived, leaving Nicki to replay their conversation, hoping to make more sense of it. He'd called her out on being stubborn, opinionated, and inflexible. Yet he was willing to marry her. Why the hell would he want to? Maybe he felt some obligation because he'd already asked her. Or was it a conditional statement? In order to fulfill his promise, she had to change. To become substantially less stubborn, opinionated, and inflexible.

The latter probably wasn't going to happen. And she wasn't going to marry Dex because he felt some moral compulsion to do so. She knew what was best for both of them, and she would stand by that notion, even if it killed her.

Chapter Twenty-Seven

The day of Sam's wedding arrived. Nicki laid in bed, knowing she needed to pack and get on the road. But she couldn't move. She missed calls from Denise and Alyssa, knowing full well they were concerned about her state of mind and no doubt were there to give her a pep talk.

Nicki buried her head under the pillow and let the tears fall for the thousandth time since the miscarriage. But this time, they were over Dex. She missed him desperately. The emptiness in her belly had subsided somewhat, only to be replaced by a gaping hole in her heart.

And her soul.

A little over a month ago, Nicki pictured Sam's wedding as an extension of her own. She'd be ecstatically happy, still shining with the glow of the newly married, fresh off their honeymoon, five months pregnant, and standing next to the man she loved more than life itself. During the ceremony, she'd catch Dex's eyes, and the love they shared would rain over Sam and Michael, a gift to be enjoyed and passed on.

Instead, she'd be standing alone, absent her baby, and absent her man. She must have done something in her life to deserve this fate. But considering her past would get her nowhere.

Nicki threw the pillow against the wall and tossed

the covers aside. She'd refused to attend this wedding alone. Brendan, Snow Leopard's accountant, had been after her to go out to dinner. Inviting him to her best friend's wedding seemed a little over the top for a first date, but what the hell. At least she'd be concentrating on introducing him to her friends and making sure he was having a good time. Enough to take her focus off Dex and feeling sorry for herself.

The time had come to suck it up and put on her big girl panties. No more crying, no more wallowing in self-pity. Decisions had been made, and there was no use agonizing over them any longer.

Nicki was not a mush woman. She was strong and resilient and independent. And she would get through this weekend with a smile on her face, a bounce in her step, and an insignificant other on her arm. As long as no one asked her to take a peek into her heart, she'd be fine.

****

The wedding ceremony was scheduled for six p.m. on the beach. Dex arrived at 5:55 and wondered what kind of mood he'd find Nicki in. Would she be emotional and vulnerable given the setting of her good friend's wedding? Or would she be impenetrable, strengthening her walls to keep him at bay?

They hadn't talked since he'd walked out of her office, giving her the room she needed to make the right decision. A lesser man might be prone to take her silence as answer enough, but Dex refused to give up. She'd likely be surprised to see him here, but after all, he was invited too.

He sat in the last row of chairs set up on the beach, staying out of the fray until he could corner Nicki and talk some sense into her. With any luck, the time he'd given her to contemplate his words would work to his advantage. He knew she loved him. What he didn't know was exactly how stubborn she could be. His insides jumped and ricocheted at the thought of their meeting after the ceremony.

The music started and Alyssa was the first down the aisle. Despite her alleged penchant for over-the-top bridesmaids' gowns, the simple elegance of this one suited her perfectly.

His heart stopped as Nicki came next. Her long, blonde hair was pinned up on the sides and cascaded down her back. A flowy violet gown blew softly in the breeze. She carried a bouquet of baby roses, white and pink, tied with a white satin ribbon. On her wrist was a familiar bracelet.

His stomach knotted at the memory of their day in Key West. A magical day had turned into a magical week, then into a magical relationship. Until it ended.

Of course, no engagement ring circled her finger, but the bracelet gave him hope. Why would she wear that small and inexpensive gift from him to her friend's wedding if she didn't still carry him in her heart?

She floated up to the front and stood next to Alyssa, who gave her a quick squeeze around her waist. That minor gesture wasn't something he would normally notice. But his eyes drank in every movement, every nuance that was Nicki.

He swallowed and tugged at his tight shirt collar and tie.

Next came Denise, who despite the year she'd had—with adopting Bobby, learning of his leukemia, finding his birthparents along with the shocking fact that Nicki was his birth mom and Michael his birth dad—beamed with her eternal optimism. And why shouldn't she? Bobby's illness was in remission, his natural parents were involved in his life, and one of her best friends was getting married.

Michael and his groomsmen stood to the right, Bobby included, as they waited for Sam to walk up the aisle made of sand.

Dragging his eyes away from Nicki, Dex watched a glowing Sam float toward the man she loved. Emotion showed plainly on her face, and Dex felt it in his bones. That look of adoration, amazement, elation, and hope all rolled into one; the look he'd expected he and Nicki to exchange a few weeks ago.

His chest tightened and his breathing quickened as a chill rolled through his body, despite the warmth of the May day. His gaze met Nicki's and he stopped breathing altogether. Everyone else fell away and he pulled at her spirit with all his strength.

Her blue eyes registered something close to shock. Not the emotion he wanted to see. She clearly hadn't expected him to come. Perhaps didn't want him there. She turned away from Dex and focused on Sam and Michael as they said their vows. Their words buzzed around his head, but he couldn't hear them, couldn't concentrate on them. Nicki's alarm confused him.

When the ceremony came to an end, Dex headed straight for the bar. A glass of scotch would settle his crazy insides. The bridal party spent time on the beach, talking, laughing, hugging, adding more angst to his frayed nerves. He kept Nicki in his sight, determined to take charge of the conversation the second she was freed from her duties.

He watched as she headed away from the bridal party and toward the deck. She was coming to find him. He began walking toward her, then froze in place. A tall, blond guy dressed in a light suit met Nicki at the bottom of the steps. She draped her arms around his neck and gave him a kiss on the mouth that lasted a little too long, was a little too passionate. Not a chaste kiss you'd give a friend or acquaintance. That was clear. When she pulled away, her smile dazzled, and she guided him back over the sand to talk to Sam and Michael. She cast a look over her shoulder and caught Dex's stare.

Anger and dread collided in his chest. She wanted him to see her kiss another guy. She wanted him to see her bring another guy into her fold.

If Dex had any fantasy they'd get back together, she'd just shredded it, shot it, hammered it, and driven a stake through it.

As well as through his heart.

****

She couldn't face him, so Nicki did what she had to do to assure he understood her message. Yet kissing Brendan in front of Dex killed her. His eyes were locked on her, and the pain shot straight from his heart into hers.

She hadn't expected the fluttery butterflies winging through her stomach the second she saw him during the ceremony. Handsome as ever, his intense stare sent her heart tumbling. Surprise caught her, since she was sure she'd done everything she could to harden her heart against the magnetic pull of his. But their connection was so strong it didn't work. So she resorted to severing that connection with the only ammunition she had.

She walked in a trance back to the beach for photos with the bridal party. They went on forever. Nicki found herself in another world, not participating in the happy chatter around her. She scanned the crowd over by the bar set up on Michael's deck, searching for Dex, having second thoughts about her cruel message. Nicki couldn't bring herself to ask Sam if she knew Dex was coming. Of course, he'd been invited with her. But what misguided notion would make him come?

"Are you with us, Nicki?" asked Denise, concern on her face.

"Did you know?" Nicki accused without saying the words.

"Know what?" Denise avoided Nicki's eyes and pulled Jennifer and Johnny close. "Say hello to Aunt Nicki. Doesn't she look beautiful?"

Jennifer raised her face for a kiss, and Nicki bent down and hugged her. "You look so pretty. Like your princess doll."

Jennifer beamed and spun in her pink, puffy dress. "I told Mommy I wanted my hair like yours."

Nicki noticed for the first time their hair was styled the same way, and her heart melted. "It does look like mine. We're twins."

Jennifer laughed. "We can't be twins. You're a lot older than me. Like ten years."

Nicki smiled. "More like twenty-nine, but who's counting?" She turned to Johnny and tugged on his arm. "And what a handsome guy you are. I love your suit. Will you dance with me later?"

Johnny giggled when she tickled him. "I'm too little to dance with you, Aunt Nicki."

"I could pick you up. Then we'd be the same

height."

He looked at her with skepticism. "Maybe." Then he ran toward his father who grabbed him and swung him around, eliciting shrieks and laughter.

The hole in Nicki's heart grew bigger. She'd thought she would have that with Dex. Her hand circled her abdomen, confirming no baby grew inside. Tears blurred her vision. She couldn't do it again. And no matter what promises or concessions Dex said he would make to be with her, he'd resent her eventually for not giving him what he wanted so desperately. It was a no-win situation.

She'd agonized over Dex's words for weeks, parsing them and putting them together then taking them apart and putting them together in a different blend. But in the end, she couldn't do that to him.

"Someone should have told me he'd be here." Nicki whispered to Denise.

"No one knew, Nick. But he was invited, and you did respond for both of you weeks ago." Denise gave her friend a sympathetic look.

"When we broke up, he should have had the decency to let it go."

"Maybe he wants to see you. Talk to you. Since you won't return his calls, perhaps this was the one place he could get your attention."

"Well it wasn't a good idea. Besides, I invited someone else."

"What?" Denise's voice raised an octave. "You didn't have anyone with you this afternoon when you showed up."

"I told him to meet me here. I didn't want him standing around while we were getting our hair and make-up done."

"Why did you do that?" Denise looked horrified.

"I was invited with a guest. I didn't want to be at a wedding alone."

"You were not invited with a guest," hissed Denise. "You were invited with Dex."

Heat rose to Nicki's face. Several emotions vied to get out, one of them anger, but she didn't want to unleash on Denise. "I should go find Brendan. He doesn't know anyone here." But she didn't move.

Dex was still on the deck, his eyes boring a hole through her. She vacillated between throwing herself into his arms, apologizing for her bad behavior, and ignoring him by continuing her play-acting with Brendan. Her armor was failing her if she could even contemplate doing the former. She couldn't talk to him. Not here. Not now. Not ever. He had too much control over her heart.

"Go to Dex."

Nicki's head snapped up at Denise's last suggestion. She was like a pit bull not allowing this to go. "There's nothing for me to say to him."

"You know I'm behind you, no matter what you decide. But if I have a vote on the matter, I would suggest the words 'let's try to work through this issue together.' "

Nicki swallowed the tears building in her throat. She wanted to scream, stomp, throw a tantrum at the audacity of Dex showing up at her best friend's wedding, at Denise's insistence she talk to Dex, at the angst building in her core, questioning her sound decision to stay far away from the source of all pain.

Denise gave her a little shove. "Go find him, Nicki.

And good luck."

The war in Nicki's head continued. She'd made her decision. Why couldn't Dex let it be? Why couldn't her heart stop reaching for his, ignoring Nicki's instructions? She swallowed, trying to quell the rolling, queasy storm threatening to take her down. The nerves in her legs twitched as she walked slowly through the sand, taking as much time as possible to cover the distance between her and Dex.

Climbing the stairs, she gripped the railing so tight her fingers ached. With each step, she said his name, as if to pull him from the crowd and appear before her. But when she got to her destination, he was nowhere in sight.

She picked up a glass of champagne from one of the roving waiters and waited by the sliding glass doors. He must have gone inside to talk to some others who populated the living room. Too much time went by without Dex appearing.

After a toast to the bride and groom, Nicki walked over to Michael and tried for nonchalance. "Have you seen Dex?"

"He left about ten minutes ago."

The promise of reconnecting defused like a puff of smoke blown away on the Atlantic breeze. And with it her unexpected hope. The sympathy on Michael's face was almost more than she could handle, and unwanted tears burned the backs of her eyes.

She fought them off and shrugged. "Oh. I guess he had another commitment."

Which she knew wasn't true. Dex had watched her performance with Brendan, and it did what it was meant to do. Show him she'd replaced him. There was no room for a reconciliation.

Nicki hated herself for doing what she'd done. But it had been necessary. Now Dex would hold no hope they'd get back together.

And neither would she.

****

Nicki slogged through the rest of the evening as if wading through muddy water. Her happiness at her friends' commitment to each other was diluted by misery. After an acceptable amount of time, she suggested that Brendan leave, explaining her need to spend some time with her friends before she too left the party.

As she sat alone at a table in the corner of the deck, Nicki's silent musings were interrupted by a young voice. "You look sad."

Nicki turned and there stood Bobby.

Nicki dug deep for a smile. "No. I'm tired." She couldn't tell him about the spreading depression that had been growing since she'd seen the look on Dex's face after she kissed Brendan. "You look very handsome tonight."

His face reddened over the compliment. "Thanks."

"Would you like to sit down?"

Bobby sat, looking as if he had something on his mind.

"How's the end of the school year going?" That should put him at ease.

His face lit up. "Great. Our baseball team is in the playoffs."

"Congratulations. That's awesome." Bobby's pride streamed through her.

"Would you like to come to our game next

Saturday?" He glanced at Nicki with anticipation evident on his entire face, then quickly added, "If you're not too busy."

"I'd love to, Bobby. What time?"

"Eleven. Then if we win, there's a game at three. You don't have to stay for both."

Her heart expanded, not only with his invitation, but because he was giving her an out if she wanted it. Which she didn't.

Their relationship had grown as each month passed. Nicki gave him the space he needed but didn't let a week go by without connecting with him in some way. Sometimes by phone, sometimes by text, sometimes in person. She took whatever he would give and never pressed for more.

She was lucky to have what he gave, given their history.

"I was wondering…" He paused, clearly uncomfortable with his next statement.

"Go on," Nicki encouraged, reaching out to touch his hand.

"Can I call you Aunt Nicki like Jennifer and Johnny do?" His eyes wouldn't meet hers, and his Adam's apple moved up and down in his throat.

Nicki's breath caught. "Of course. I would love that."

He looked up, his eyes shining and his lips smiling. "*Phew*. Thanks."

A twinge of sadness speared through her just thinking he'd stressed even a moment over his sweet request. All she'd ever wanted was for Bobby to feel comfortable around her whenever their paths crossed.

Just then his phone chirped and he glanced at the

text he received, a hundred-watt smile beaming from his lips.

"Good news?" she asked, not wanting to lose the connection they'd made.

"Great news. Adria asked me to go to the end-of-year dance at school with her."

"I take it you're going to say yes."

Bobby looked at her as if she had two heads. "Hell yeah." His hand flew up to his mouth. "Sorry. Mom doesn't like when I say that."

Nicki grinned, hearing Denise reprimand Bobby to watch his mouth—although she was sure much worse came out when he was amongst his friends at school.

"Tell me about Adria." Nicki sat back in her chair, hoping for more than a one- or two-word answer.

"She's really pretty. Long, dark hair. Kind of like Mom's color. But she has these blue eyes that are different than most other people's. Darker. And really long legs." He glanced at Nicki as if to see if it were okay for him to be talking about a girl's anatomy with her.

"She sounds beautiful."

"She is. And she's a softball player. First base. She made the varsity team for next year, and she's only going to be a sophomore."

"You two have a lot in common. That's good." Perhaps Bobby was already open to forming a relationship with a member of the opposite sex. Something Nicki clearly had a problem doing.

"She's smart too. I always ask her for help in math."

A clever ploy by this young man to get close to the girl he liked, since Bobby was a math whiz, according to Denise.

"Does your mom know you like her?"

"Nah. You know Mom. She's always worrying about me—my health and all. She tries to get me to slow down and not put too many things on my plate. Those are her words. Not that hanging out with Adria would change anything, but… I don't know."

So Bobby was sharing a part of his life with Nicki that he hadn't shared with Denise. Maybe Nicki was going to be the cool aunt who he could tell things to.

"Your mom is pretty cool, you know. And she dated your dad in high school."

"She did?" Bobby's eyes widened. "She didn't tell me."

Nicki supposed Denise and Ben's love story wasn't a big topic of conversation in the household given all they had to deal with. "You should ask her sometime."

"What about you and Dex?"

Heat ran through Nicki at the mention of his name. "What about us?"

"Mom said you broke up, but I saw him here before. Why aren't you getting married?"

From the mouths of babes, the straight questions came. No filter. No guilt about raising a bad subject.

Nicki sighed. "We decided we weren't meant for each other. We wanted different things."

"What kinds of things? Like a house or a car?"

If only it were that simple. "No. Not material things." This was hard to explain to a fourteen-year-old boy. It was much easier to talk to her girlfriends. "He wanted us to have a baby and—"

"Awesome." Bobby's eyes sparked. "If you have a baby, will he be my little brother?"

"Well. Yes, I suppose he would be a half brother. If it was a boy."

"I like Johnny. He's a cool kid. Jennifer too, when she's not bossing me around and making me play with her dolls. I'd like your kid too. I could teach him things."

Nicki had seen how kind and caring he was with Denise's other two children. Today he'd helped them with their food and didn't push them away when they followed him around like little ducklings.

Speaking of the devils, here they were, coming to take Bobby away.

"Duty calls. I'll see you later, Aunt Nicki." He beamed at his new name for her.

So did she.

Chapter Twenty-Eight

An odd blend of melancholy and clarity followed the weekend into the work week. Sam's wedding day had started out with Nicki's attempt to cut Dex out of her life forever, knowing it would be best for him if he had no choice but to move on. But then Bobby had turned her around.

How could a young boy do that in so little time? And with so few words? Not only did he want to include her in his life despite having given him up for adoption, he went further by saying he wanted her to have a baby so he could have another sibling. A half brother or sister.

Not that his wishes on the subject were gospel, but her promise to him when he was born, that she wouldn't replace him with another child, now seemed irrelevant given his view on things. If he could forgive her, then perhaps she should forgive herself.

But how did all this play into her next step? Dex must hate her after her public display of affection with Brendan. And who could blame him? He'd given her his heart and soul and said he'd marry her even if she couldn't have his baby. Instead of opening up her heart to him, she'd built up more barriers. Her *modus operandi* for years.

She needed to turn this around and the sooner the better.

Since no work was being accomplished, she picked up the phone and called Dex at work, having no clue what she would say once he picked up.

"Dex Hanover is no longer with the firm," came the response to her inquiry.

What? But of course, he had been interviewing at other accounting firms prior to their planned wedding. "Do you know how I can reach him?"

"I'm sorry. We have no forwarding information."

She hung up, more than a little unsettled. Yet there'd be no reason for him to advise Nicki of his new employment. She dialed his cell.

"The number you have reached has been disconnected," said the computerized message.

No way. No one changed their cell phone number. Nicki's heart thumped against her ribs. *Calm down*. Just because he changed his number and job didn't mean she couldn't reach him. Although changing his cell phone number was a clear statement to Nicki he never wanted to speak to her again.

Nicki turned to her computer and typed in his name. His affiliation with his old accounting firm still popped up, along with a few articles he had written on forensic accounting. No announcement of his joining a new firm.

The hairs on the back of her neck stood at attention. What if he'd moved out of Philly? She furiously continued her search, desperation and fear swirling in her gut. Then she saw a link to Big Brothers Big Sisters and clicked to open the page. A photo of Dex appeared naming him as the chairperson of the five-kilometer race coming up in two weeks at Fairmount Park. She exhaled, slumping in her chair. At least he'd be here for that.

The wheels started turning.

It took her most of the day to email, call, and text every person she knew who might be willing to run on her team or donate money to the cause. Convincing Denise, Sam, and Alyssa hadn't been hard at all. They would participate as the principals of the Sworn Sisters team.

Getting her music company behind her was easy as well. Every summer they chose a charity to donate to, and Nicki's request sailed through the charitable giving committee. Why this seemed easier to Nicki than showing up at Dex's apartment, she didn't know. Perhaps because she was afraid he'd moved and she couldn't handle that. Besides, this big gesture had to get his attention. And once she had it, she would grovel, beg, and plead her case.

But would he listen?

****

The day of the race had Nicki on pins and needles. At least she had her posse behind her.

Bouncing from foot to foot, Nicki stopped and stretched before going back to bouncing.

"Could you please stop?" asked Alyssa. "You're making me twitchy. It's only a five K race. We don't have to win. All you want to do is see Dex at the end of it."

Nicki gave her a scowl. "And that shouldn't make me as jittery as Ann Boleyn waiting at the guillotine?"

Alyssa caved. "A little overdramatic but I get it. Keep bouncing."

Denise put her hands on Nicki's shoulders. "It's good you're running before you see Dex. It will get rid of some of the anxiety."

"I can only hope. The other possibility is I'll look like a sweaty pig, drained from burning up every ounce of adrenaline I possess. That should make him want to talk to me."

Sam chimed in. "Once he sees how much you collected for his cause, he'll have to ignore your soggy appearance and thank you. Maybe with a kiss."

"That won't be happening." All Nicki could hope for was a cordial pat on the back.

Attempting to take her mind off her unsure future, Nicki turned to Denise. "Where are Ben and the kids?"

She'd seen them a half hour earlier, sporting T-shirts hand-lettered with "Team Sworn Sisters."

"Ben took them toward the finish line so they can cheer us on at the end. Bobby has his camera ready to capture our final moments."

"I shouldn't have gotten him interested in photography." Nicki grimaced, knowing her appearance at the end of the race should not be captured in digital memory. Although she was secretly proud he'd followed up on her suggestion to take a class during the summer, after she'd given him her rarely-used high resolution camera.

The race was starting in five minutes, and the women entered the crowd of runners at their designated spot. Nicki was the only one of them who ran for exercise. Alyssa stood beside her, grumbling about the experience to come, while Sam and Denise sucked it up and congenially fell into place.

"At least it's early and the sun isn't baking us. Yet." Alyssa pulled her baseball cap lower over her eyes.

Denise elbowed her with a smile. "Stop whining. We're helping our best friend take a giant step toward Dex."

"You're right. Sorry. I should have eaten another power bar this morning. I'm hungry."

Nicki stayed focused on her goal. Joining the discussion about what Alyssa should have eaten this morning seemed fruitless.

Finally the starting horn blasted and interrupted the conversation. Just five kilometers stood between her and a meeting with Dex.

It was an amazing sight to see, with hundreds and hundreds of people in a sea of blue T-shirts with the Big Brothers Big Sisters logo on the front and the date and place of the race on the back. Nicki was number 676—a lucky number she hoped.

Running at her normal pace as she got into the zone, Nicki couldn't keep her mind from straying. Had Dex, as chairperson of the event, noticed that Nicki and her friends joined the fray? Would he be impressed with the amount she'd raised, or was it a drop in the bucket compared to other teams? Most importantly, would he be happy to see her, or would a calm coolness set into his eyes—those magnificent, beautiful, green eyes—telling her to stand back?

Unfortunately, she wouldn't know until the race was over.

****

Most of the runners had finished a half hour ago, but stragglers still came in here and there. Nicki spurred them on in her head. The Sworn Sisters stood together, chatting with each other and those they'd brought along with them.

Bobby came up to Denise and Nicki and gave them high-fives, the most demonstrative a fourteen-year-old boy would get according to Denise. His blond hair was spikey and his smile impish. In a few years, maybe less, he'd be a heartbreaker.

Jennifer and Johnny played tag, running into and around the people they knew, having fun on a warm June Saturday. Ben attempted to get their attention by suggesting they get their faces painted as they waited for the awards to be handed out and the event to end.

Denise grabbed Johnny as he passed by. "Hey, buddy. Did you have a little sugar this morning?"

"Daddy got us cotton candy." He beamed, his teeth blue from the sticky treat.

"At least it kept them occupied," Denise said to Nicki. "Maybe I'll get you some to keep you busy until the awards ceremony."

A tapping on the microphone and a male voice sent Nicki's nerves into overdrive. "Welcome to the Big/Little Race for the Kids." Dex's words streamed over the crowd, and clapping and cheers came from all directions. "I want to thank every single one of you for coming out here today to help us raise money for our programs. Without you, and without your sponsors, we wouldn't have the success we're having here in Philadelphia." Another enthusiastic round of applause followed.

"Let's get to our winners."

Dex called out the names of the serious racers who came in first, second, and third, shared their impressive times, and placed medals around their necks. The photographer took pictures as well as anyone with a smart phone in the area.

"Next," continued Dex, "are our most important awards. The recognition of our teams who raised the most money. As I said before, without your dedication and support, our programs to help our kids wouldn't be half the success they've been. In third place, we have Stella's Pacers who raised an amazing five thousand three hundred dollars. Come on up here."

He gave Stella a plaque and stood with her team for photos as Nicki bounced in place, new nerves ricocheting around her body. She now knew for sure her team would be recognized.

"In second place is Team Kendra and Friends who raised six thousand seven hundred thirty dollars."

The Kendra team danced up to the dais pumping their fists, celebrating their positive outcome. Angst sped through Nicki's system while she waited impatiently for more photos to be taken.

"Our first-place team beat all records for this event."

Dex looked over the crowd as if searching for the winners. Nicki held her breath, waiting to be called up.

"The Sworn Sisters raised an unprecedented ten thousand five hundred and fifty dollars. I'm breathless just saying the words."

Nicki hugged Denise, Alyssa, and Sam and drew them up to the dais with her. Her heart hammered an arrhythmic beat and her mouth went dry. She'd been waiting for this moment all morning, hoping her team would have placed in the donation category.

Denise hugged her waist. "You did it, kiddo. I don't know how you raised so much in such a short period of time, but you did it."

Nicki beamed. "Usually, when I set my mind on

something, I can accomplish it. We'll see if I can pull off this next hurdle."

Dex's eyes zeroed in on Nicki as she and her friends neared him. The heat those eyes generated should be lethal. She held onto his gaze, not letting go. When she stood before him, the noise of the crowd fell away. It was just the two of them. What would he say?

His Adam's apple moved up and down in his throat. He moved the microphone away from his mouth and asked her one simple question. "Why?"

She smiled at his confusion. "I wanted to get your attention."

Dex raised his eyebrow. "You have it. What is it you want my attention for?"

"To tell you I shouldn't have pushed you away. I shouldn't have built up barriers to keep you away. You offered me everything you possibly could have when you said you'd marry me even if I couldn't have a child."

He waited for her to continue, the tenseness in his face smoothing, the clench of his jaw softening.

"I'm sorry, Dex. I love you and I want to marry you. And I want to try again to have our child. If something goes wrong"—her voice cracked—"we can adopt."

Dex tossed the microphone to the ground and pulled her close before capturing her mouth with his and giving her a searing kiss.

A woman a few feet away said, "If that's what first place gets, I'm going to raise a lot more money next year."

Nicki threw her head back and laughed, knowing she had the prize for life.

Epilogue

Nicki sat sideways at the edge of their private pool at the upscale Bermuda resort, one leg dangling in the water. She faced the sun, head back, the early rays warming her body after a refreshing swim.

Through slitted lids, she watched Dex free-style through the water, his muscles rippling with each stroke. She could ogle his body twenty-four hours a day, and now he was all hers, to do with what she wanted.

A smile inched over her lips at the thought.

Just then, Dex placed his hands on the coping beside her and lifted himself out of the pool with ease, using his arm strength to rise over Nicki, a waterfall cascading over warmed skin.

A squeal escaped. "Soooo cold."

"I'll warm you." He coaxed her to recline, laying his full body over her, his lips capturing and teasing hers open.

Nicki sighed. She'd never tire of his kisses, despite the discomfort of concrete pressing against her back.

Dex eased his body up marginally, gazing into her eyes. "I love you, Mrs. Hanover."

"I love you too." Her heart squeezed at the emotion, so intense, so beautiful.

"Come join me in the hot tub." He stood easily, then took her hand and pulled her up.

She followed him to the heated jacuzzi on the deck beside the entrance to their bedroom. Easing into the hot water, she moved to sit on his lap, needing his arms around her.

He nuzzled her ear. "I hope you're not regretting having an informal wedding."

"Not at all." The Justice of the Peace at City Hall was perfect. "We should have done that the first time."

He shook his head. "I do believe I offered that."

"You did. And I stupidly thought I needed a formal ceremony for our friends and family to witness. I now see the error of my ways. Doing it quickly and quietly gave me no time to mess things up."

He laughed. "We can still have a party when we get back if you want. Just say the word."

Nicki turned in his lap, straddling him. "I don't need a party. All I need is you."

His green eyes darkened and his jaw tightened. He stroked her cheek. "All I ever needed was you. I was a fool to condition our marriage on having a family. You had asked me, the first time I proposed, if you weren't enough for me. I believed at the time I needed the promise of children to make me whole."

Nicki placed her forehead against his. "And I couldn't give you that promise. At least not then. But we're two different people now, having learned the hard way. Me, that I can let go of the guilt I've been carrying around over giving up Bobby for adoption, and you…"

"That I can live with whatever fate brings to us, as long as you're by my side."

"But of course, we're going to try to have a child."

"Or two. Or three." His smile morphed into a tease.

Nicki pushed his shoulder. "Don't get ahead of yourself. When we see how much our lives will change, we may only want one."

"True." He nipped her lower lip. "What are you going to tell your Sworn Sisters about our elopement?"

Nicki sighed. "They are going to kill us. But they'll get over it. They just want me to be happy, and I can tell you they were pretty pissed at me for breaking our engagement. And for ignoring your calls and texts. I believe they were ready to kick me out of the group and circle around you."

A gleam sparked his eyes. "I knew I liked them. But seriously, we should at least invite them out for dinner to celebrate."

"Since they now like you better, I'm going to let you break the news to them when we get back."

Dex's brow furrowed, looking even more sexy than usual. "That's not fair."

She glided her fingers over his forehead, erasing the lines. "Don't worry, they'll understand."

Nicki pressed her hips into his as she teased his lips with her tongue. A delicious, erotic ooze swarmed through her, accompanied by heat and need. Dex pulled her against him, his hands gliding over her back, fingers inching into the bottom of her bikini, before untying the laces on both sides in one efficient move.

Within seconds her bottom half was naked, her top half following with a deft pull on the string around her neck.

Dex stood with Nicki wrapped around him, her legs encircling his waist, water sluicing off their bodies. He carried her into the bedroom a few feet away and dropped her on the bed amongst tangled cotton sheets before joining her, his wet swim trunks puddling on the floor.

"I like this pre-breakfast workout." His gaze held hers, the shadow of a grin pulling at his lips.

Nicki traced his jaw with her fingers. "A little swimming, a little teasing, a lot of sex. Perfect to burn off those calories I intend to consume. My mouth is watering for bacon with syrup."

Dex's smile grew mischievous. "Your wish is my command. Tomorrow morning, it will be room service with the required items. Including you in an oversized bathrobe. But for now…"

Dex's mouth covered hers, devouring her lips and sweeping his tongue inside. A delicious accompaniment to his wicked intentions.

Her world spun and danced, with Dex at the center of it. Commitment—before, an unwanted state of being—now brought focus and love and life.

Nicki had found her soul.

A word about the author...

I am a divorce lawyer and partner in a central New Jersey law firm where I litigate as well as mediate family law cases. I have a JD from Fordham University School of Law and a Bachelors degree in Psychology from Rutgers University. In addition to practicing law and writing fiction, I enjoy spending time with my husband and two daughters at home or at the Jersey shore.

http://mariaimbalzano.com

Thank you for purchasing
this publication of The Wild Rose Press, Inc.
For other wonderful stories,
please visit our on-line bookstore at
www.thewildrosepress.com.

For questions or more information
contact us at
info@thewildrosepress.com.

The Wild Rose Press, Inc.
www.thewildrosepress.com

To visit with authors of
The Wild Rose Press, Inc.
join our yahoo loop at
http://groups.yahoo.com/group/thewildrosepress/